W9-BJL-095

MURDER
AT
MEDICINE LODGE

ST. MARTIN'S PRESS
NEW YORK

MURDER
AT
MEDICINE LODGE

A TAY-BODAL MYSTERY

MARDI OAKLEY MEDAWAR

Design by Nancy Resnick

Library of Congress Cataloging-in-Publication Data

Medawar, Mardi Oakley.
    Murder at Medicine Lodge / by Mardi Oakley Medawar.—1st ed.
        p.   cm.
    ISBN 0-312-19925-2
    1. Kiowa Indians—Fiction.   I. Title.
    PS3563.E234M87   1999
    813'.54—dc21   98-37611
                                                                        CIP

First Edition: March 1999

10 9 8 7 6 5 4 3 2 1

For the Black Leggings Society
and Gus Palmer, Jr.

In October 1867, Kiowa, Comanche, Arapaho, Apache, and Cheyenne Indians signed peace treaties with the Federal government. Fifteen thousand Indians camped near by during the council, among them the famous chiefs Satanta, Little Raven, and Black Kettle. Five hundred soldiers acted as escort for the U.S. commissioners. Interest in this colorful spectacle was so widespread that Eastern papers sent correspondents, among them Henry M. Stanley, who later was to find Livingstone in Africa. While the treaties did not bring immediate peace they made possible the coming of the railroads and eventual settlement. The site of the council was at the confluence of Medicine River and Elm Creek, a little southwest of Medicine Lodge.

—Medicine Lodge Peace Treaties, historical marker erected by the Kansas Historical Society and State Highway Commission in Medicine Lodge, Kansas.

ONE

The most annoying sound I've ever known is that high, nasally voice of a pouting child. I find it especially grating when heard on an unseasonably hot day when sweat is rivering down my skin and pesky gnats dart determinably for my eyes. As if that weren't enough, because the day was too hot to wear protective leggings, I was riding bare-legged and the blanket covering my saddle was doing nothing at all to ease the chafing of my inner thighs. In the year of 1867, the early autumn was proving itself to be just as brutal as the passing summer, the sun beating down with the force of a striking hammer.

You would have thought that such lamentable traveling conditions would be enough to shut up my wife and son. You would have thought wrong. Under no conditions does a five-year-old boy know how to shut up, and my wife was laboring under the delusion that each of his complaints should be met with logical, and therefore rather lengthy, responses. When I rolled wearied eyes, she sent me a rebuking look that clearly said, This is all your fault.

She was right.

Before beginning the grisly trek from our country just north of the Red River, venturing north to the Osages' country, I had presented my new son with his very own pony. Ordinarily, children of his age rode safe inside protective cages that were strapped onto a travois. Because of my gift of the pony, Favorite Son wasn't where he should have been, but between my wife and I, the joy of him having his very first pony was quickly fading for all of us.

Crying Wind was losing her voice trying to console and reason with a dyspeptic five-year-old and I was trapped, unable to ride up front with the other men. It was unthinkable for a father to abandon his child while that child was learning to ride properly. Longing with every particle of my soul to be with the other men, I wormed in the saddle, trying to find a new patch of skin somewhere on my buttocks that wasn't completely blistered, while Favorite Son mewled and Crying Wind tried to distract him.

"Oh, look there, my little heart," she said, pointing off. "See the redbird?"

Dutifully, Favorite Son and I looked in that direction just in time to see a flash of scarlet as a bird careened against a cloudless pale blue sky. The landscape boasted only tall grasses undulating with each dry hot breeze, like the waves of a fast-moving river. A sigh slipped out of me as I found myself longing for our home country of red buttes, tall trees and incalculable rivers and creeks. And humidity. Wonderful, cloying humidity. I have never been a high prairie person. On the high prairie, the air is so dry a person can watch his skin crack.

I went on this occasion because the entire Nation was gathering in Kansas. To go there, we had to travel through the very heart of Osage country. The Osage were certainly aware of our numerous presence. They were allowing their former enemies to pass safely through. Still, because the giant Osage were known to be somewhat contradictory, our great mass of warriors rode farther ahead, leaving the women and children to travel about a half mile behind.

Women always traveled or walked behind men, but not, as is so widely supposed, because men considered women to be inferior. The first time I heard this statement, I was too appalled to speak. I simply stood before the smug individual, who voiced this as a fact, with mouth agape, looking very much like an astonished carp.

Indian men walked or rode ahead of their families because the Indian men of a long-ago day were gallant. I love that word *gallant*—it is so full-bodied, so completely right for the men I knew back then. And it was because of their gallantry that they placed themselves in harm's way. For if an enemy struck, those men were more than prepared—out of unconditional love—to give up their lives in order to buy the time needed for their wives and children to run away, hide, survive.

That is not to say that women and children traveled wholly on their own. A smattering of warriors were selected to ride with them. During this journey to the place called Medicine Lodge, I was a member of the smattering. I didn't particularly care for this because I wanted to be with my friend Skywalker. Something seemed to be the matter with him and I was worried. But I had sealed my fate by giving my son the pony. So, he was with the noted warriors and I was with the women. A place my other friends, who only meant to tease, said I belonged anyway.

Sadly, that was all too true. While the true warriors of our nation liked me, even respected me for my unusual doctoring skills, they knew I was not a very good warrior. If I were with them and the Osage decided to come out for a fight, my Kiowa brothers would first have to concern themselves about my safety before taking on the Osage. So, as it turned out, my blunder about the pony worked to their advantage—they wouldn't have to worry about hurting my feelings by suggesting that I ride with the women because I'd trapped myself. Although, these same warriors weren't overly concerned about my tender feelings when it came to teasing me about my name, Tay-bodal.

Bluntly put, Tay-bodal means Meat Carrier. It was not my first name but it has been my name for so long now that I can't really remember the first one. This second name was earned during the time when I was just entering my twenties and newly married to my first wife—a good woman who died long before I ever even met my second wife, Crying Wind. In my childhood, it was generally agreed that I was a bit eccentric, so overly fascinated by all things living that I did not properly study the lessons necessary for ordinary life. Hence, when I came of age to join a warrior society, none of the leaders of the societies approached me for membership. Because my people have always been a forgiving lot, I was allowed to go my own way and become a doctor, but not a traditional doctor. The two doctoring societies, the Owl Doctors and the Buffalo Doctors, did not invite me to join their memberships, either. When I married for the first time, I was totally unprepared to support a wife and it was for her sake alone that I tried to fit in where I clearly did not belong and the first step of this fitting in was to join an organized hunt comprised of about a dozen warriors.

I was quite nervous about the whole thing, for generally I hunted with my father—a gentle, quiet man who rarely corrected me while taking great pains to protect me from myself. The seasoned warriors I'd attached myself to, were neither gentle nor quiet and they most certainly did not have any great concerns regarding my welfare. Still, I was determined to bluff it out, prove that I was a man, that I was not too young to have the responsibility of a wife. The way I chose to carry off this great pretext was by acting just as cocky as possible.

It's a long hard fall from cocky. I should have known I was headed for the fall the day I neatly packed my portion of the kill onto the back of my horse, ignoring the other men who were taking the time to salt down their portions. While I was tying tight the travel pack, one of them stopped what he was doing and came over to me, asking what I was doing. I was quite terse with the man, appallingly rude. He backed off and went back to the clump of men. Turning away from the sight of them, I busily kept on with what I had been doing while listening to their muttering and muted laughter. All I thought, as I tied the last cord that would keep my prize from slipping off my horse's flanks, was how glad I was to be going home. During the time spent with those men, I realized that they had a companionship I could not share. Their brotherhood made me feel left out, sorry for myself and resentful. Which is why I had acted no better than an angry child. I wanted to go home and I wanted to go quickly. They weren't being fast enough to suit me and I let them know it.

Everything would have been all right if they hadn't decided to get back at me for my arrogant and sullen attitude. For two days they all pretended that we were lost. I didn't know the area at all and was completely dependent on them. If they were lost, so was I. By the third day, the hunt leader. (I suppose because he was becoming tired of their game) announced that everything was all right, that he knew where we were. Well, that was good news but I would have felt better had it not been for the persistent and increasingly noxious smell of rotting meat. After three days of being wrapped up inside a rawhide blanket and without any preserving salt, my portion had gone off. Realizing now that I had been the brunt of a joke, I stubbornly held on to that portion, torturing all of them with it for as long as I could stand it. When the air around us became so fetid that the others were pleading with me to throw it away, I finally did. So, it was from that time that I have been called Tay-bodal (the Meat Carrier). And for years following that humbling hunt, whenever my new name was said in polite society, the typical question following the mention was, "Isn't he that idiot?"

"Redbirds are sacred to the Osage people," Crying Wind continued. "In their religion, the Osage came from the stars and were redbirds before they became human beings."

I was tempted to add that our council hadn't entirely decided if the Osage were indeed human but they did agree that the Osage had come from somewhere other than this earth. In the days of my childhood, Little Bluff, the greatest chief of the Cauigu (Kiowa), had made peace with the Osage. Being much younger than me, my wife didn't remember the terrible years of war and so she was inclined to be frustratingly broad-minded about those people. My offering a differing comment, while she was working hard to be sweet-voiced and reasonable with our pouting son, would have set her off and she was already mad enough about the pony.

All right, I admit it, giving a five-year-old a pony was stupid. But I hadn't known just how stupid until Crying Wind became stony-faced, unnaturally quiet, and the air between us as heavy as the lull before the onslaught of a tornado. Now, before you begin to think that, as my wife, she should have been diffident to whatever I did simply because I was her husband, think again. The wives ran the households and any husband who acted first and consulted with his wife later could find himself staring into the eyes of doom. It was because I had presented the pony at the last moment before the Nation left our old camp behind, and because our son was so excited by the gift, that she reined in her temper. But throughout the long day of travel I'd felt her anger. Oh yes, I most certainly did.

The distraction of the redbird and its fable lasted no longer than the time it took for that bird to disappear. When it was gone, lost among the tall grasses, Favorite Son began the slow unhinging of his lower jaw on the verge of another gripe when a shot was heard and the entire mass of plodding women and children came to a stop. Being one of the few men riding among them, naturally their heads turned toward me, uncertainty and fear evident on every face. The riding-ahead warriors were over the next rise, lost from our view. Everyone remained completely still, horses not even flicking away flies with their tails as we waited the interminable seconds in a silence so total that it reverberated in our ears.

My eyes were trained on the rise, my entire body tense as we waited. Feeling a pressure on my arm, I glanced down. Favorite Son was leaning against me, welling tears sheening dark eyes. Feeling instantly protective, I was readying my rifle when a fast-riding warrior crested the rise.

"Tay-bodal!" the warrior cried, whipping his horse to faster speed. "Tay-bodal! White Bear needs you."

Women quickly maneuvered their mounts and pack-horses out of the way, as the young warrior known as Big Tree galloped hard. I let him know where I was by standing in the stirrups and waving both arms over my head. When he spotted me, he aimed to the left, barely dodging the living obstacles in his path. As he neared, he drew up hard on the reins, the back hooves of his warhorse skidding precariously beneath the large animal's body. Big Tree was close to me now, barely a foot away, but he shouted as if we were yards from each other as he gestured excitedly in the direction of the distant rise.

"Three Elks has been wounded."

Hearing this, the women gasped sharply and children whimpered.

"We've been attacked?" I cried.

"No," he answered, inside a heaving breath. "There's no time for talk." He turned away from me, bellowing out over the heads of the women. "Get down from your horses. Rest and feed your babies. There is nothing to fear."

As this was Big Tree, a man of considerable merit, the women were prompt to obey. He turned again to me, his mouth working as he swallowed in whole gulps the scalding air. During this space of seconds I was again struck by his extraordinary looks. Big Tree was a young man of slight build, but he was incredibly strong. He puts me in mind of a coiled bedspring, amazingly light yet able to bear considerable weight without breaking. But it was his face that was his most striking feature. From the time of his infancy, people tended to mistake him for a pretty girl. While this greatly appalled him, I secretly envied his unique looks. I have always been an ugly person. Even though in those days I was a man in my prime, my otherwise fit condition did little to alleviate the irregular planes of my features or hide the deep pits left along the sides of my face. The pits were caused by a bout of the smallpox I had been lucky to survive. That brutal illness took not only my dubious handsomeness but lost me my first wife and both of my parents. Deeply hurt by my loss, I shunned any close ties for years following that plague. But that solitude became a type of gift. Without any family connections, I had time to perfect my healing craft and, getting used to my ugliness, I became an ardent admirer of all things and all persons truly beautiful.

Crying Wind was beautiful. So was Big Tree. My wife could be quite vain about her beauty but Big Tree was mortified by his. I think this was on account of the teasing he suffered. He was so pretty, and, being almost dainty, he continually worked to prove his courage and manhood.

Which is why, during his twenties, Big Tree was a To-yop-ke, a war chief. Throughout the whole of his life, he was known to be utterly fearless, wholly dependable. So when he said the situation was not dangerous, the women did not question his word. Instead they climbed down from their horses and set to making a rest camp.

After several more gulps of air, Big Tree spoke again. "White Bear says to bring your medicines. Three Elks is bleeding badly."

My medical supplies were packed up somewhere on the trailing travois. Scrambling down from the saddle I asked, "He's bleeding from what part of his body?" This was a thing I needed to know in order to take along the proper bandaging.

Feeling his hesitation, I peered around the neck of my horse. Crying Wind had not dismounted. She was staring at Big Tree. Looking away from her, finding my peeking eyes, he blushed, his cheeks turning a muddy rust color.

"His . . . um . . ."

Crying Wind craned her head forward, intent on hearing the juicy details. This was a fault of hers that, during the first years of our marriage, I battled to break. A healer's wife could not be a gossip. People came to me with all sorts of peculiar problems and it did their troubles not one iota of good knowing that her big ears were anxious to hear everything. Realizing that she was at it again, Big Tree gave up.

"You'll need a lot of bandages!" he said sharply. "And you must hurry."

The sight that greeted me was almost laughable but, because of Three Elks' undeniable pain, I did not laugh. A difficult

10

thing not to do considering that his naked rear end was lifted skyward while he bent himself double and held on to his ankles. The bleeding wound was in his left buttock and it looked quite deep. Even worse for Three Elks, the bullet was still in there. But the type of bullet was the thing I needed to know. Warriors had all manner of guns, the e-pe-tas (repeaters) being the newest. The trusty flint lock, or trader gun, was still in the majority and the most common bullet used in those guns were round pebbles. Pebbles could be a discomfort if left inside the body but if the wound was treated right, that would be all the harm they would do. But the e-pe-tas used lead bullets and lead caused blood fevers, putrefying wounds, and killed the victim slowly.

Looking away from Three Elks' aloft posterior I demanded, "Exactly how did this happen?"

The question was posed to a scowling White Bear. He turned slightly away, wiping a trickle of sweat from his forehead with the back of his hand. The unrelenting sun radiantly outlined his near-naked body, the aura emphasizing his great height and girth. With his hair partially tied up in a knot just behind his crown, his head seemed to erupt from his shoulders. White Bear did not have much of a neck—what there was of it, blended in with his shoulders in a manner similar to the neck muscle of a great bull.

White Bear was known as Satanta by the whites. Not only did they get his name—Set'tainte—wrong, they also erred in believing that the vacant expression he could sometimes get while enduring the long hours of the peace councils the American government seemed so desperately fond of, meant that mentally he was as blank as a board. They failed to notice the quick, dangerously alert eyes set in that broad expressionless face. If they had, they would have known that there was a lively mind inside that large head. White Bear had the same cunning of one of their own tactically brilliant generals. But the side of himself he readily showed the world, was that of a very large man who loved practical jokes. Yet even in this boisterous display he could be quite lethal. That humor of his was threatening the moment now, as he tried to explain to me just how Three Elks had received his very peculiar wound.

"My favorite nephew"—he said, meaning The Cheyenne Robber—"seems to be the cause of this unfortunate accident."

He glanced back over his shoulder to his nephew, a shockingly magnificent specimen of male animal. The Cheyenne Robber did his best to appear contrite. The attempt failed. The best he was able to manage was a defensive arrogance. If you could have seen him, you would have understood why. Any human being that splendid could not help but be arrogant. In fact, as his friend, there were times when I wanted to be arrogant for him. But he didn't need my services. He already had a swarm of lieutenants willing and able to carry any excesses of his vanity between them.

His haughtiness was not seen as a fault, but his natural due. As with the genesis of the Osage, The Cheyenne Robber looked as though he had appeared by divine hand from the sky and was content, for a time, to dwell among thoroughly undeserving mortals. He stood somewhere over six feet in height and every inch of him was perfectly proportioned. Broad shoulders tapered to a narrow waist and below slim hips were two long legs as well-muscled as any horse's. As you might imagine, he wore everything disgustingly well and on that blazing hot day he looked especially well in a very short breechcloth, a Navaho silver belt slung low on his hips, a pair of knee-length moccasin boots, and hair the color of pitch left to hang down his back to his waist. He was so good-looking that even the half-disgusted expression on his face failed to dull his handsomeness. Mistaking my quiet admiration of him as a wait for an explanation or an apology, he folded his arms across his bare chest and commenced to glare at me from under hooded eyes. As always, when realizing that I had The Cheyenne Robber's full and concentrated attention, I began to feel weak in the knees.

In my defense, I was not the only one thus afflicted by his piercing gaze. Women were known to drop in a dead faint whenever they were singled out by him. To my knowledge, there was only one female who ever proved the exception. A young woman known as White Otter. When he first met her and she failed to swoon or drool on herself, The Cheyenne Robber had to know why not. This needing-to-know began a hot pursuit of her, culminating in their marriage. White Otter did eventually faint at his feet but only because she was pregnant. Now she was the mother of his baby son and her attentions had become so divided that she simply didn't have the strength or the inclination to feed her husband's massive conceit. Not surprisingly, The Cheyenne Robber's temperament was known to be surly of late; his moods so foul that it would not have surprised me in the least to learn that he had shot Three Elks in the butt on purpose, and for no other reason than he was feeling the need to shoot something.

The Cheyenne Robber turned his face away from me,

looking at his older brother Skywalker, who was squatting down, not looking at anyone in particular, his expression pensive. Skywalker was an Owl Doctor; a mystic—if you must qualify him as such—having the ability to blank out every living thing around him while he listened to the voices speaking to him from an unseen world. He wasn't blank now, so he wasn't having one of his "spells" as we called them. If anything, he was very aware and highly irritated. I knew for a solid fact that he didn't approve of our Nation going into Kansas. He'd been more than vocal on the subject, saying that the Kiowas should show their contempt for the peace talks by staying away. But our people heard that the army would be bringing many wagons filled with gifts and that there would be great feasts—presents and food are two things Indian people love.

In the end, Skywalker had been overruled. Our new principal chief, Lone Wolf, was a man of great pride. He couldn't see himself excluded from the talks with the Washington government when the chiefs of the other nations of the Plains Confederacy were certain to be there. This was the first truly important event in the early days of his chieftainship and he was not about to miss it. The vote naturally upset him, but Skywalker wasn't normally a sulker. His less-than-social attitude of late sprang from something else. Something he would not share, not even with me, a man supposed to be his best friend. As a matter of fact, for almost a week now, he hadn't spoken to me at all, causing me to worry about a friendship I'd formerly taken for granted.

Standing to his feet, not looking at me or anyone else, he went for his horse. No one tried to stop him or call him back. If he would persist in being ill-natured, then he wasn't wanted—at least, by the majority. I—decidedly in the minority—wanted him to stay, but after he brushed by me as if he'd never known me, I held my tongue and did nothing more than watch him as he rode off, disappearing over the rise.

Once he was out of sight, with effort I concentrated my attentions on my patient, examining the wound while White Bear and The Cheyenne Robber began to argue. As Three Elks' condition wasn't funny to him anymore, White Bear was now demanding to know precisely how the man had come to be shot.

The thing that happened—or at least, it was The Cheyenne Robber's explanation—was that his horse had stumbled or shied, and as he worked to bring the horse under control, the rifle resting across his lap went off, the bullet finding its way to Three Elks' left haunch. Had this happened in battle, it would have been considered a lucky shot; but as Three Elks was a friend, it was quickly put down to a freakish accident. One that would cost The Cheyenne Robber many expensive gifts, as Three Elks was in considerable pain and, because that bullet was now known to be lead, he would experience a great deal more while it was being dug out.

To lessen (granted a bit late) Three Elks' dire humiliation, those warriors not needed to help with the procedure were told to go back to where the women were, to guard the camp and have a meal. The Cheyenne Robber volunteered to be in that number; and as he was becoming even more grim-natured about the entire incident—and a grim The Cheyenne Robber was distinctively of no help to anyone—White Bear granted permission for him to go. Led by

Lone Wolf, there was the subsequent departure of the host of warriors, leaving me with Big Tree and his brother Dangerous Eagle, Kicking Bird, White Bear, and a warrior known as Raven's Wing to help me with Three Elks. I had wished mightily that White Bear would go, too, but because he did not like being shown up in any way by his archrival Kicking Bird, he stayed.

As did his warped humor.

The trouble with tending the wound was its inconvenient angle. My digging around inside for the bullet caused Three Elks to be understandably squirmy. To keep him still, it took the combined strength of all the men present to try to hold him in place. Unfortunately for all of us, White Bear found himself standing almost directly behind the patient, holding Three Elks' twitchy hips as best he could. I was using the small metal digging tool that Haw-we-sun, a Thai-qahi (white man) and friend of mine who is also a doctor, had given to me. Hawwy was a Blue Jacket (soldier) doctor. He had all sorts of amazing tools. To make friends with me, he allowed me to choose any three of his doctoring tools that I wanted. The digging tool had been my first choice. It was wonderful because it was able to dig and scoop at the same time. At least I thought it was wonderful. During the procedure Three Elks hollered an entirely different opinion. It was over Three Elks' caterwauling that the indignity of his position in the scuffle finally struck White Bear.

"Tay-bodal!" he thundered. "Be a little quicker. If the Cheyennes and Arapahos should suddenly appear, I really wouldn't care to know what they might think we're doing with Three Elks."

Big Tree looked back at White Bear, then he fell over

laughing. He was followed rather rapidly by Dangerous Eagle. The instant Three Elks found himself partially free, he wormed out of White Bear's grasp and began to run, howling with pain and pumping blood from the gaping wound. Which meant, of course, that we had to chase him around. Not an easy task seeing as how we were all running against high grass, bobbing our way through it like panicked rabbits.

Raven's Wing, a very leggy man, was approximately my age, which would have put him a bit over thirty years. But Raven's Wing looked much older. The texture of his skin was like that of an old boot, a condition common to warriors on the war road and having to go without water for long periods in the punishing heat of full summer. Warriors of Raven's Wing's class, the Odegufa (meaning "less wealthy"), wore their leathery skin like badges of honor. It was also a clear indication that they were striving hard to become Ondes, members of our Nation's highest class. Myself, I have always been content to be a Kauaun (roughly translated, "common"). As such, other than the pox pits, my skin was baby-smooth and I liked it. So did Crying Wind. But I digress.

Raven's Wing, a man whose sole desire in life was to be White Bear's first lieutenant and thus was always seeking ways to impress him, put a flying tackle on Three Elks, successfully bringing him down. And while he was down, being held there by the others, I dug that bullet out despite Three Elks screaming and writhing. Then I stitched him up—which produced more yelling (he really was the worst patient I've ever known)—and finally bandaged him. It wasn't a very good bandage but considering the grappling

17

circumstances, a botched bandage had to do because the smell of blood was attracting biting flies. The insects were trying hard to get at the wound and their success would not have done at all. At any rate, as a hurried attempt, it would do until such time as we made a suitable camp. He wasn't yelling anymore, just sort of snuffling and flinging away tears with the flat of his hand, looking at all of us—me most especially—as if we were evil.

When I returned to my wife, she was eagerly waiting for any juicy tidbit concerning my patient, her dark owl-shaped eyes literally glowing with anticipation. Really, this love for rumormongering was her most unflattering trait, and despite the fact that months ago, gossiping tongues set against her had very nearly cost her her life, she still wasn't cured. I was barely dismounted when she was all over me like a heat rash.

"Is it true The Cheyenne Robber shot Three Elks in the back?"

Looking at her with a hard expression, I wordlessly set to the task of hobbling my horse. She ignored the warning look, coming after me, squatting down beside me chattering like a busy squirrel.

"A few days ago, two women saw Three Elks speaking to White Otter." Her tone became more whispery, filled with wonder. "They were alone." I glanced at her and she nodded meaningfully. In a much lower voice she finished, "He even helped her as she tied on the cradle board and—"

"I fail to see anything untoward about his actions," I shouted. "It sounds to me as if he was being nothing more than a helpful brother."

She slapped my arm. "Do you never understand anything? Three Elks touched another man's wife! That's why The Cheyenne Robber shot him."

I turned a pained face toward her. Crying Wind's expression was utterly self-satisfied. I suppose I was remembering too clearly what gossip had almost cost me—cost us. That's the only excuse I have for the complete loss of my temper. I really let her have it, and as each word stung, her lovely face became more stricken.

"How many times do I have to tell you that as a doctor's wife your love for tattling is both unseemly and insulting? And may I remind you that this nature of yours is also unsafe? It wasn't so long ago that you were accused of being a witch by those who should have known better. Yet here you are, eager once again to believe the worst of a simple accident and actually help your tongue-wagging sisters and aunties spread this harmful tale. You should all be thoroughly ashamed of yourselves."

She stood and walked away.

I was not given anything to eat and she did not speak directly to me for the next three days. If it hadn't been for Favorite Son's continual grousing, I would have enjoyed the peace for, not long after arriving at Medicine Lodge, those three days were the only respite I was to know. Most especially after learning that, in the Blue Jacket army, no one liked the bugler.

TWO

■ I think my most favorite thing is the grass-dancing, a ceremony that signals the opening of a camp. Teams of our longest-legged warriors wearing their finest dress, ventured out into the open fields and, to the music of the drums and the singing of many voices, they danced in skillful leg-swinging motions, trampling down the tall grasses. We had safely reached the wide valley of Medicine Lodge and the dance celebrated the end of tedious travel.

In life, it is always the simple things which give us the most pleasure, and this simple thing of opening the camp lifted our spirits as nothing else could. Our voices grew stronger, filling the valley with our presence. We wanted the already-encamped Blue Jackets and various tribes to know that the true People, the Cauigu (Kiowa), had arrived. When our own voices came back to us from the surround of foothills, we knew the other camps had clearly heard.

Next came the rush for the best places for individual family camps. Crying Wind wasted no time or words, for she had already decided on a shady place close to the creek. She was a canny woman but also somewhat lazy. She always set up our home close to a good water source and wood supply. That way she never had to walk very far for either. Taking my faster horse, she galloped off, racing against the other women who had designs on such a location themselves. With my wife's departure I was left with the task of struggling with our temper tantrum–throwing son, as well as moving along our tiny herd, while guiding the horses pulling the travois containing everything we owned. The false summer was holding, the day was hot, and sweat poured from me as I coaxed and cajoled child and horses.

The trouble was that both had understood the grass-dance ceremony, too. My son didn't want to move another inch and the horses wanted to go immediately into pasture. The herd I grappled with consisted of five extra horses, Crying Wind's mare, Favorite Son's pony, and the three drag-horses. Not a great number, really, but enough to give me trouble. Pulling and tugging, I strained all of us forward. I couldn't see the campsite my wife had gone for. The landscape rose a bit and all I had left of my wife's determined direction was a faceful of dust. Impatient and cranky, I yelled at my horses and my son. My son began to bawl and Crying Wind's mare wasn't happy with me on its back. As I was heavier than it was used to, it responded by prancing sideways, nodding its head in a dangerous manner. To add to my worries, the old roan pulling one of the travois just stopped dead-still and began to graze, sending me one-eyed furtive looks.

22

Now, I have never beaten a horse, and for two very good reasons. One, horses are sacred beings and must be treated with complete respect. Two, an angry horse can hurt you. That old horse was telling me in no uncertain terms that if I did not allow it a moment to replenish itself, that it would bolt, tipping the travois and leaving me to pick up our household goods, which it would spread all over the valley. Now, considering the heat, that really would have hurt me.

Heaving a dejected sigh, I dismounted and went to my squawking son, pulling him down from his pony. Then I tried not to laugh. After many days of riding, his little legs stuck out oddly, for they were still too short to bend correctly around the pony's belly. Favorite Son was having a hard time trying to pull his legs together and was being quite specific about the pains in his groin. Patting his head, I thought, Welcome to manhood.

I did not have time to offer manly advice, for just then my wife came stomping over the rise. She stopped at the crest and waved an arm, her manner intolerant of our loitering. That she was on foot meant she had left my horse as a marker in the spot she had selected for our home camp. She then turned her back on us and, with her hands on her hips, she kept a sharp lookout for any unscrupulous woman that might take it into her head to move the marking horse. Housewives could be sneaky, worse than the Lakota, really, and even though some of the women she watched out for were her own sisters and aunties, when it came to prime camping areas, Crying Wind didn't trust any one of them.

Encouraging my son to walk out the pains in his wobbly, bowed-out legs, I began leading the horses up the slight incline toward her. And— I forget. Did I say it was hot?

Well, it was. I cannot stress this too much, for this is a memory of Medicine Lodge that comes to me each and every time I think of the place. An arid heat filling the valley of about twenty miles, shimmering under a sun so blazing-hot that the skin blistered and lungs were seared with each drawn breath. This was the way of the high prairies. There the land is either boiling hot or freezing cold. This was Osage country and, as far as I was concerned, they were welcome to it.

Despite the heat, the snuffles of my son, and the uncooperative attitudes of the horses, I pulled all of us forward, up an incline that felt steeper than it looked. With each step I took, I believed it would be my last, as I was about to expire from heatstroke. My own peril quickly reminded me to spread the word among our people to double up on their daily ration of salt. I was thinking about that, thinking that we Kiowa who preferred more humid climes were at risk in this awful place, when the horses, my little boy, and I, finally made it up that hill.

She was an amazing woman, my wife. I might balk at giving the roan a swift kick to hurry it along, but she felt no such hesitation. As soon as we were close enough to her, Crying Wind took over boy, man, and the horses, and we were quick to obey her scolding words, get out of the way of her slapping hand. With her in charge, we were quickly at the chosen site. The instant we arrived I fell down, lay sprawled on my back while Crying Wind, after sending Favorite Son off to cool himself in the creek, began the work of unpacking. With a groan, I rolled to the side, then eased myself into a sitting position. Crying Wind sent me that look. The look all married men know. The look that told me we were still having a fight, that she was still carrying a grudge. Well, I thought, fine. If she wants to fight, we'll have a really good fight. I peeled myself off the ground and proceeded to do something guaranteed to irritate the very breath out of her.

Another myth about Indian men is that we are feckless, content to sit around while our poor women are made to do all of the work. What a load of— Indian men are not shiftless and we are not helpless. We can make a camp as good as any woman, and during the many years I lived alone, I took care of myself wonderfully well. It was only since my marriage that, according to Crying Wind, I couldn't do anything right. Normally I would just take myself off, stay out of her way until she had our home exactly the way she wanted it. But on that day, just to prove to her that she could not growl at me like a badger, bossing me the way she had our horses, I was just as helpful as I knew how to be.

And, *oooh*, did that make her mad!

Marriage is like a dance, the constant circling of partners seeking a workable coexistence. I've known a lot of men who felt that once a comfortable life was made with a woman, that the excitement of marriage was over. I never felt that way. But then again, I was married to Crying Wind and they weren't. Even though I adored her—would have given my life for her—when she set to snarling and snapping at me, I would lose all patience and give her just as good as I got.

This was how a handful of warriors found us, me helping to raise the lodge poles, and Crying Wind and I quarreling and saying a number of unflattering things. Only when I turned my head, saw the three of them standing there, smirks twitching their lips, did I feel any remorse about the way I was intentionally baiting my wife.

"White Bear wants to see you," Raven's Wing said.

To my mortal embarrassment Crying Wind tipped back her head and shouted, "Thank you, Father above!"

I was mad at her for a long time because of the way those men laughed.

I was led to a place where an impressive number of men had already gathered, all of them listening to White Bear.

"We will go to the Blue Jacket camp, let them see our greatness. A little fear in their hearts before the peace talks begin is a good thing."

"What about Lone Wolf?" someone asked.

White Bear's expression became sour, his eyes fixing on the one asking the question. Any reminder that Lone Wolf was the rightfully elected principal chief irked White Bear. His was the firm conviction that if the election had had only two candidates—meaning himself and Lone Wolf—and had not been split by a third candidate, Kicking Bird—that he would have won the majority of votes. But Kicking Bird had been a candidate, and the contesting between the two old rivals had been ugly. The thing White Bear would never admit was that he and Kicking Bird both had been guilty of name-slurring. By staying well out of their bickering, Lone Wolf had managed to win the election without ever having to say a campaigning word. But, true to form, White Bear blamed Kicking Bird, and in turn Kicking Bird blamed White Bear.

"Lone Wolf has nothing to do with this," White Bear

declared. "He may be the chief over all of us, but he runs no one. It is every man's born-to right to say where he will go and where he will not go."

White Bear's statement produced a round of men softly grunting, "Hau," meaning yes. Then White Bear angled his head and looked in my direction.

"Tay-bodal, you will ride beside me."

"Me?" I cried. "Why should I go? The sight of me will impress no one."

Normally this form of sniveling made White Bear smile. Unless the conceit belonged to him or his favorite nephew, The Cheyenne Robber, White Bear loathed braggarts. But this time he was having nothing to do with suitably humble pronouncements. Moving through the crowd of men like the bear for which he was named, he came to stand before me, looming like a bulky shadow. As he spoke, his pointy finger jabbed my bare chest.

"You have lived among the Blue Jackets," he said through clenched teeth. "You can advise me. So you will ride on one side of me and Skywalker on the other." With a broad wave of his arms he bellowed, "That's all I have to say."

Still looking for a means of escape, I stammered, "I—I walked here. I have no horse."

"Then you will use one of my horses," he scoffed. "The worst of mine are better than the best of yours." He then looked me up and down, saying almost to himself, "And something must be done about your appearance."

When a beefy arm slung itself around my shoulders, I knew I was thoroughly trapped. And afraid.

For, you see, the days I had lived among the Blue Jackets

could be counted on the fingers of one hand and for over half those days I had been gravely ill, recovering from wounds suffered in an attempt on my life. The Blue Jacket doctor, Haw-we-sun, had saved my life, but while I was his patient, I had also been his prisoner. I had not, as White Bear chose to believe, roamed freely among the soldiers during my short time in their encampment in the Wichita Mountains, a place we Kiowa called Medicine Bluffs. For the first five years of its life, before it became known as Fort Sill, this most famous fort was nothing more than rows of tents and three log buildings. One building belonged to the commander, the second was for the supply store. The smallest building was Haw-we-sun's little doctoring house. The whole time I was there, I had barely ventured farther than the porch of Hawwy's little house, and so I had no idea just how White Bear believed I could advise him.

I felt overdressed for the occasion, wearing clothing borrowed from Skywalker, and riding a powerful warhorse belonging to White Bear. To make the disguise complete, I even carried a borrowed lance that was marked with the designs of the Jaifegau (Crazy Horses Society), the projectile point aimed at the sky while the rounded end was balanced on the toes of my right foot. I tried my best to look the part of a fiercesome warrior, but felt the fraud.

The other warriors were told to keep watch over me, make certain I made no mistakes. Meanwhile I did my utmost to mimic their every move. There was a certain expression warriors showed outsiders, an expression I've heard described as stoic. Actually, what they were going for was *surly*, but *stoic* has its merits.

At any rate, the men who convinced the world that they had only this one severe side to them were actually lively pranksters. All other emotions were intentionally hidden, resulting in a terrible misjudgment—that warriors did not laugh, did not cry. The greatest injury of this opinion is that it robs these men of their humanness. And so I tell you this truth: Those men laughed, they cried, they loved, and when they weren't involved in a fight to the death, they were happy rascals.

But on this day I am telling you about, they were being stoic and keeping sharp eyes on me so that I would not bungle.

The Blue Jackets' camp was sprawling and, as was their wont, organized into well-defined rows of two-man tents. To the back were the large tents belonging to the officers and dignitaries from Washington. There were about ten of those.

What immediately caught my eye were the two officers' tents set apart. I was looking at these tents when White Bear and Skywalker dismounted, their hands busily being shaken by the three greeting generals of the Blue Jacket army. I remained sitting stiffly on my loaned horse, trying very hard to remain blank-faced as I considered those curiously placed tents. During my brief stay among the Blue Jackets, I hadn't learned a lot, but I had learned enough to know that those two out-of-place tents went directly against their fervent sense of order.

While I studied them, the answer to the tent stuck off farther to the left became known, as an Indian woman dressed in white woman's clothing emerged. Seeing her, one of the generals smiled, extended his arm, indicating that she was welcome to join us. She proceeded forward, holding herself in a curious fashion, ample breasts hoisted up almost to her neck, rear end jutting out, the hem of the long skirt of her dress dragging on the ground. I could not see her feet, so I wasn't certain if she was walking, for I had never seen a woman walk with such a tottering sway. She was such an extraordinary sight that she held every warrior's complete attention. Realizing this, she deliberately slowed her approach, seemed to enjoy the effect her peculiar appearance caused. As she passed the mounted gawking Kiowa, I was instantly taken by her hat.

I love hats, but that isn't why I fixed on hers. My long-dead father used to sell feathers and inadvertently he had passed his love for feathers of supreme quality on to me. The feather sticking from the back of that woman's hat was the most marvelous red feather I'd ever seen. It was long enough to arch and hang far over the back brim of her hat. I learned later that this was a dyed ostrich feather. I have never seen an ostrich—not even a picture of one—but the memory of that single feather leaves me to believe that an ostrich is a formidable bird, one that must be as large as a buffalo. It would taken an even more formidable woman to dare to pluck a feather from it, and for this reason I have always held the Arapaho woman known as Mrs. Margaret Adams in my highest regard.

But I do try to forget that when she turned her back to us we were all further appalled that she'd chosen to accentuate her already high, round backside with a large, blindingly white bow. The sight of all that elevated whiteness put me in mind of a white-tailed doe coming into breeding season.

30

Evidently Dangerous Eagle was having the very same thought. As I was closest to him, I was the only one to hear the soft humming sound he made as he struggled not to laugh out loud.

The generals were at once deferential toward Mrs. Adams, placing her between themselves and White Bear. She made a grand show of speaking to White Bear, who wasn't listening. Then, too, she spoke only Arapaho. White Bear could not understand one word the woman rattled off, and he was already concentrating on her uplifted breasts, tilting his head in order to study them from various angles. It was with superhuman effort that the rest of us maintained deadpan appearances, never mind that tears of mirth were beginning to shine in our eyes. Even the gloomy-of-late Skywalker was affected, having to turn away, run a hand over a tightly clamped mouth. When he was more composed, he turned again to the three generals who, seeing that White Bear's gaze had become quite fixated with Mrs. Adams' offered-up bosoms, were glowing with embarrassment. On the command of one of them, a white man came quickly forward, this man able to speak Comanche.

White Bear spoke pretty good Comanche but he was better at ordering Comanches to speak to him in Kiowa—a thing our Comanche allies complained about, saying our language is too hard, that it is the most difficult language of all the Nations. I'm afraid that this is true. Most of our words are identical, the meanings altered by the way the words are pronounced. For example, said one way, "A-ho" means *thank you*. Said another, "A-ho" also means, *Kill him*. As you might well imagine, when using this particular phrase it is imperative the speaker's pronunciation be exactly right.

31

And therein lies the problem. Every Nation has its own distinctive sound. Ours is a loud popping of the lips when saying words that begin with your letter *p*. Then, too, there is the overstressing the hard *s*. When doing this, a considerate speaker leans back slightly to avoid spitting in another's face. These little quirks require a lifetime to master, and even our own children have a tendency to mangle the language. My own son was at that time only just nearing six and the way he spoke was hilarious. I think his difficulty would be described as a lisp. The truth is, my son did not have a lisp. Until he was eight, he simply couldn't pop his *p*'s.

As White Bear and the Comanche-speaking man made halting stabs at understanding each other, Skywalker stood quietly by his side. My attention was pulled away by movement to the extreme right. A small guard of soldiers had been present when we rode in, but due to our unexpected number, more soldiers were quickly arriving. As they came to a stop and formed two straight lines, an officer quietly walked before them, making certain that they stood just right, with shoulders almost touching. He was also concerned that they hold their rifles fixed tightly across their chests. The greatest number of these soldiers were the black-white men known to us as Buffalo Soldiers, on account of their short curly hair.

One soldier in their company was noticed by all of us, not because his was a white face set among the black, but because of a shiny thing hanging down from his belt. This shiny thing caught White Bear's attention. Dismissing both the Comanche-speaking man and Mrs. Adams' displayed breasts, White Bear turned to stare at the newly arrived soldiers. His hand toying with his chin, he muttered a ques-

32

tion. The Comanche-speaking man answered in a voice loud enough for all of us to hear.

"Buug-lah."

White Bear first looked to Skywalker, then, turning at the waist he looked back at me. I shrugged, indicating that I had no idea what a Buug-lah might be. Disgust creasing his broad face, White Bear turned back to the Comanche-speaking man.

After a bit of a conference with the generals, the Comanche-speaker beckoned the man called Buug-lah to step forward. That man came to stand before the generals, smartly saluting his chiefs. In those passing seconds, White Bear's hand went for the shiny thing the man wore on his belt. When this soldier felt the touch, he absently slapped away White Bear's hand.

The action instantly incensed White Bear's honor guard. Big Tree was the first to raise his lance and let go a murderous holler. Mrs. Adams gasped and the Comanche-speaking white man visibly paled. The Blue Jackets followed suit as more warriors raised their lances and hollered. I was doing my best to do that too when, not liking it at all that a soldier had struck him, White Bear grabbed Buug-lah by the throat. Using only the strength of one arm, he lifted the soldier from the ground, his hand squeezing the neck so hard that the man was going blue in the face. The warriors *kawed* louder, shaking their lances at the sky as both Skywalker and the Comanche-speaking man dove against White Bear, forcing him to let go of the offending soldier. The generals stepped clear, retreating a safe distance, and Mrs. Adams, lifting her skirts, fled. The soldiers in the recently formed line lifted their rifles awaiting the order from the officer poised with a raised saber.

There I was in what could have easily become a war—a thing both my wife and I worked very hard for me to avoid. Her first husband had been a notable warrior. So notable that he'd made her a widow with an infant child. She said she wasn't bitter, but I believe the thing that convinced her that marrying me was a good idea, was the nasty rumor that I was a sincere craven.

But anyway, at some point in the scuffle, Raven's Wing jumped from his horse and joined the fray. By the time I'd sufficiently recovered from fright, Skywalker and Raven's Wing had hold of White Bear and the soldier was lying like a broken doll on the ground. The warriors were *kiiy*ing and whooping, sending White Bear their very vocal support, and I heard my own voice blending with theirs but I was watching the officer with the sword. He was shouting sounds that reminded me of counting and his sword was beginning to rise. Even at a distance I could see beads of sweat breaking out on the faces of the soldiers sighting down their rifles. Seeing the muzzle of one rifle trained on me, I mentally kissed my beautiful wife good-bye.

"For God's sake, don't shoot!"

Haw-we-sun was running fast, long legs pumping. A half-step behind him was Billy. It was Hawwy who had yelled at the officer with the sword and Billy was yelling in Kiowa to the warriors. I have never, before or since, felt such relief. On White Bear's one-word command, all of the warriors fell silent. In that tense second, one of the generals also yelled, and the soldiers lowered their rifles and assumed their former stance while the officer, his expression livid, shakily resheathed his saber. White Bear threw off Sky-walker and Raven's Wing, then, speaking in a querulous tone, he pointed to the soldier still lying at his feet.

Billy talked fast against Haw-we-sun's ear as Hawwy spoke to the generals. Grim-faced, a general turned away, his hands clasped behind his back. Haw-we-sun helped the prone soldier to his feet, dusting the man off. A young officer quickly came forward and led the dazed soldier away.

THREE

Of course, I should have known Haw-we-sun would be at Medicine Lodge; not because, as a Blue Jacket doctor, he was in any way crucial to the upcoming peace negotiations—but because of Cherish, the Kiowa girl he wanted to marry. I was opposed to the marriage. Quite frankly, for a long time into the courtship, I was astonished the army, too, was not objecting to it. Everything became clear when Hawwy mentioned that his superiors knew that Cherish was sister to The Cheyenne Robber, and the niece of White Bear. When one of their minor officers asked permission to marry such an important Kiowa girl, his seniors made haste to encourage the match for they saw this young couple as yet another means of securing peace.

As for how our own people felt about the marriage—

well, as in the case of her older brother The Cheyenne Robber, you'd have to know Cherish to understand. Like her brother, she was a breathtaking sight, which is why Haw-we-sun fell immediately in love with her. But she was also terribly vain and ill-tempered. While at first it galled White Bear all the way to the bottom of his feet that a white man was offering for her, he quickly saw the advantage, winching up the bride-price to an unprecedented amount. Since Hawwy spoke very little Kiowa, he thought he was only agreeing to pay White Bear in mules. What he didn't know—because this term in the agreement had very carefully not been explained to him—was that he'd also agreed to pay with e-pe-tas (repeaters). The half-caste Kiowa known as Billy had used the money Haw-we-sun gave him, supposedly for mules, to pay a pair of white brothers who were longtime traders in the territory, for the guns. Then Billy slipped the guns to White Bear. On the whole I felt badly for Hawwy; but not so badly that, in the frightful moments a soldier was aiming at me, I regretted any reason that had brought Hawwy to Medicine Lodge.

The scene shifted again with the arrival of the Arapahos. Mrs. Adams grandly came forward again, all former embarrassment (of her inabilities to communicate with White Bear, and then running off with a shriek during a tense moment) eased, the instant she began speaking with her kinsmen. It was also clear that the generals were now angry with White Bear, pointedly ignoring him as they greeted and shook hands with the seemingly more docile Araphaos.

Skywalker turned, gave a hand sign, and the rest of us dismounted, taking refuge in the shade of cottonwoods. Skywalker kept Billy close to him, as he knew Billy to be a man able to understand many languages. Because he wore a large black hat pulled low on his forehead, hiding prominent cheekbones and crescent-shaped eyes from the whites, Billy was simply someone in the army's employ, a young frontiersman of very little account. Not one of the generals suspected his mixed blood or noticed that, while they paid homage to the Arapahos, Billy was muttering into Skywalker's ear. In turn, Skywalker muttered into White Bear's. White Bear's expression turned dangerously stony and I could feel my heart beginning to thump again. Incensed that they were now being ignored because the generals were too busy fawning over the Arapaho chiefs, Skywalker and White Bear turned on their heels and went for their horses. On that cue we mounted up and followed White Bear as he left the Blue Jackets' camp, intentionally riding too close to the standing people so that the hooves of our horses would throw back dust in their faces.

So began the first day of our being at Medicine Lodge, Kansas.

Back at our camp, I promptly returned the borrowed horse, clothing, and weaponry. Angry by the way things had gone with the Blue Jackets, White Bear was in one of his difficult moods. When he got like that, only Skywalker could handle him. Grateful that I was not needed or especially wanted, I slumped off. During the walk for home, I planned how to make it up with my wife, praying she would be open to a sincere apology.

She was.

But probably only because I looked so tired and awful. When I think of my marriage with her, I think of a unique partnership that went beyond the usual bonds of our marriage, even beyond the depths of our love. I could always count on her—count on her to put away her anger when she knew how much I needed her. On that day she took one look at me and yelped, "Oh my goodness." Then took me by the hand, led me to the creek. Naked, we both sat in the shallows, Crying Wind directly behind me, bathing me like a baby. Each time she moved I felt the sway of her breasts against my back and the touch of her bent knees against my arms. While she soaped my hair and skin, washing away sweat and dust, I lavishly apologized, taking the blame for every fault of mankind since the beginning of the world.

My groveling was duly rewarded.

The next-best thing my wife did was make wonderful beans. She had a special container she used whenever we traveled. In that container she kept beans soaking so that when we made camp those beans would be tender enough to cook. Then into the pot with the beans would go onions, meat, and spicy herbs. They were delicious. I never could get enough of them, especially when she served them with fried cornmeal cakes that were crispy on the outside but doughy soft in the middle. That was the meal she made for me just after the bath, putting an agreeable end to our former hostilities and a rather unique day.

But then, that was life with Crying Wind. She was tempestuous but gentle, levelheaded but silly. She brought everything into my life: joy, confusion, laughter, passion. The only thing I had to offer in return was my entire heart. I will be forever grateful she felt this small token was enough.

As I've said before, Skywalker was my best friend, but he was also an Onde, a member of our Nation's highest caste. He was also a To-yop-ke, a war chief, as well as an Owl Doctor. It was unusual for such a man, a prince of our Nation, to be friends with a man such as myself—a man of the Kauaun class, a commoner—but that was Skywalker. He was known to be eccentric and I was viewed as just another of his eccentricities. Normally we were together every day, but during the next days at Medicine Lodge, I didn't see him at all. So I visited Hawwy.

I suppose he was handsome, but not in any way that I was used to. He was a well-built man and his hair was very curly and black, almost like a Buffalo Soldier's. One solid eyebrow made a thick line from one side of his forehead to the other. He had a large jaw, a generous mouth, and dark eyes. I suppose all of this is "handsome"—I really don't know. But he did attract a lot of female attention.

I was touched that he was so pleased to see me, and felt guilty. I was still spying for White Bear, and visiting Hawwy was a good way for me to do that. But I'm not a good spy, as I have no ability to pay close attention to anything other than the perfecting of my healing craft. The upshot is, my intentions to spy on the Blue Jackets were almost immediately forgotten when I settled on a camp stool next to Hawwy. I watched only him as he tended to patients.

Soldiers with all manner of ailments came every morning to stand in a line outside Hawwy's tent. In no time at all, I was enthralled with his black bag containing all manner of exotic metal instruments and tiny bottles of medicines. Watching him, I learned how to extract a back tooth using a pulling instrument that, at first glance, appeared to be too large to fit inside a human mouth.

But when it came to treating a black soldier with a festering wound, I quickly intervened. The gash was deep and the man was in great pain. Two of his fellows had supported his weight throughout the time he'd waited his turn in the line. Hawwy was going to pour some of that white smelly-water on it and I knew from past experience just how much that stuff hurt. My form of treatment brought no discomfort, not even a twinge. I cleaned out green pus, seared the damaged flesh with punk wood, and then protected the wound with melted tallow and wrapped it with a clean bandage. When that black-white man looked at me, like a twinkling star in a dark heaven, gratitude shone from his inky eyes. He said his name was William, and he shook my hand.

Hawwy and I passed the next three days just that way, treating patients from the Blue Jackets' camp, and many Indian patients who came in from the outlying camps. Hawwy and I were kept so busy that the rapidly developing tensions between the Nations and the Blue Jackets sailed by us unnoticed.

The one thing I did notice was the man Buug-lah. As he had been the primary reason for almost getting me killed, I noticed him quite a lot. While he wore the stripes of a common soldier on the sleeves of his jacket, he carried himself in a proud way—very like the young officer he was continually with; the same officer who had led him off after Hawwy had picked him up off the ground. Buug-lah talked to that officer like they were the best of friends, but the officer appeared more pensive than amicable.

As on the first occasion of my notice, I was sitting in the shade of the medical tent's awning when the two passed. Feeling my stare, the one known to us as Buug-lah turned his head and looked directly at me. The man had the coldest blue eyes I have ever seen. Our mutual scrutiny lasted no more than seconds, but judging by the slow curving of his lips, I suffered his contempt. Finely shaped nostrils flared slightly, then he returned his attention to his companion. They stopped not far from the medical tent and, after a brief discussion—the young officer appearing quite disturbed by whatever was said—the men parted company, each going his separate way. I didn't think much about the officer, for my gaze followed Buug-lah. Watching him go, I realized he reminded me of someone.

Raven's Wing, the very fellow who had assisted me by subduing The Cheyenne Robber's accidental gunshot victim, was politically ambitious; his burning goal was to become White Bear's right-hand man. His efforts were frustrated by the fact that The Cheyenne Robber, White Bear's favorite nephew, already held this noble office. I have never cared for ambitious men. I know them to be very shallow: friendships formed on who the other person is, rather than on the kindness or generosity of that other person. That's why Raven's Wing wanted to be good friends with White Bear, because White Bear had power and influence—the mere mention of his name causing heads to nod, men to say, "Yes, I know of him." To be White Bear's most trusted man meant that Raven's Wing would bask in White Bear's reflected glory.

It seemed to me that was what Buug-lah was doing too—walking around the camp with that pinched-face young officer and talking in a loud way to draw attention to himself. It was almost as if he was half shouting, "Look at me! My friend is important. I am important too." Mulling on this, in an offhanded way, I asked Hawwy about the young officer and the one called Buug-lah.

Shrugging deeply, he replied, "We are from different companies."

Pressing the issue, I leaned forward, asking in measured words, "Is it usual for a man with stripes on his coat to be friendly with a soldier-chief?"

Hawwy took a long time considering, his full lips twisting to the side. "No."

"Why not?"

Using the ever-present Billy to speak for him, Hawwy launched into a lengthy explanation of the army ranking system. I quickly came to realize that the Blue Jacket ranking system was very close to our own. With one notable difference. In the Kiowa system, through proven deeds of bravery and generosity, a man could jump rank (which is exactly how Big Tree had come from nothing but became an Onde). Hawwy said that officers went to special schools.

"And there are no other conditions?"

Hawwy thought again. Finally he said, "There is one."

"What?"

"A man can buy a commission. But," he added hastily, "that would take a great deal of money."

Putting an end to the discussion, he began treating the next patient, looking inside that man's mouth, having him say, "*Ahhhh.*"

I was so long in the Blue Jackets' camp, and so involved with Hawwy's form of doctoring, that if it hadn't been for

44

my wife—a born-into Onde, therefore one of the few women eligible to serve the great men of the council—I wouldn't have known anything that was going on in my own home camp. It was one of those times when her gossipy nature worked to my advantage.

"Lone Wolf and White Bear argue constantly," she said as we shared the evening meal. "The wagons of gifts the Blue Jackets promised still have not been seen by the scouts. Lone Wolf said we must be patient. White Bear said the Blue Jackets have lied, that no wagons are coming. Kicking Bird said they will come, that White Bear is a fool to say otherwise because no sane people would make up such a lie. Then, of course, White Bear took offense at being called a fool, and the yelling could be heard all over the encampment."

"What did Skywalker say?"

She drew an angry breath through her nose. "Oh, him? Nothing. Not one word."

Shaking my head, I picked at the stewed meat in my bowl.

Thinking that I did not believe her account, and promptly offended, she railed, "You don't know your friend as well as you think you do. I have known him almost the whole of my life and I can tell you Skywalker does not like to be crossed. When he gets like that, he won't talk. Not even when he is asked to."

My head popping up, I yelled, "I know him well enough to know that no matter how angry he might be, he would never attend a council and say nothing."

"Well, all right, then," she fumed. "He did say something, but it wasn't useful because no one understood it."

"Tell me exactly what he said."

A trifle calmer now, Crying Wind pursed her lips. "Well," she drawled, as if trying to remember correctly, "he told my cousin The Bear [White Bear], not to touch the thing on the ground."

"What thing?"

Showing me the palms of her hands, Crying Wind lifted her shoulders in a broad shrug.

The very next day White Bear had far greater concerns than missing wagons or Skywalker's vague message. The officer with the saber, the one who had been so willing—no, *anxious*—to gun down the Kiowa delegation, was named Major Elliot. Newly arrived in Indian Territory, this officer was quite impatient to become known as an Indian Fighter. He also wanted to do something else: kill buffalo. Having become bored with simply being on his guard during the days of the uneasy truce at Medicine Lodge, Major Elliot and a half dozen other officers went on a buffalo-killing spree.

What they failed to realize was just how well sound carries over the prairie. Hearing the distant popping of rifles, White Bear and a team of warriors rode out to investigate and found Elliot happily chasing a herd, killing only the slower-moving cows who were trying to protect their spindly-legged calves. White Bear went after Elliot and, catching the man, beat him to a bloodied pulp. I was present in the Blue Jacket camp when White Bear rode in, hauling Major Elliot, tied belly-down across the saddle of his horse.

Hawwy and I were sitting on the little stools, examining a series of saws as he tried to make me understand why the army's notion of first aid was to remove the limbs of wounded men. Frankly, I never understood that at all. A person needs arms and legs, and cutting them off simply because an arm or a leg is wounded is a terrible waste. Haw-wy and I were arguing about this when White Bear brought in the captured soldiers.

White Bear could be daunting in the best of conditions, but when he was in a rage, he was terrifying. His shouting voice was like the sound of thunder as he untied Elliot, the man sliding from the saddle like an unconscious snake, hitting the ground head-first. The other warriors badly manhandled the remaining officers, pulling them from their horses, forcing them to kneel then roughly shoving their heads into a bow. The Cheyenne Robber, just as infuriated as his uncle, stood over Elliot's spread-out body while White Bear roared the nature of Elliot's and the other officers' crimes. Once again Mrs. Adams chose to retreat. The Comanche-speaking man seemed to be doing well enough without her services anyway, so no one tried to stop her flapping flight.

White Bear was not speaking Comanche, but the interpreter was able to repeat him word for word and without a flaw. I looked at that man more closely and saw something no one else was paying any attention to. Directly behind the Comanche-speaking man stood Billy. With a hand shielding his mouth, he interpreted for White Bear, and Philip McCusker, the paid interpreter, merely repeated everything Billy said.

"I caught this filth murdering my buffalo. He was not killing for food, he was killing for sport. I beat him until he cried, 'enough!' I have brought him to you for further punishment. I give you this promise, if he isn't punished, it will go hard for all of you."

General Gettis was not a man who liked to be pushed. This was evident in the way he stood very tall, puffed out his chest, tightened his jaw. But this anger was not for his misbehaving officers. Following the line of his significant stare, his conspicuous wrath was focused on White Bear. The general issued orders in a snarling tone, and Major Elliot and the other officers were duly arrested, taken to that second tent. Now I felt I knew its use, but still did not understand its location. Nudging Hawwy, I asked in a low tone, "Why has a punishment tent been set so close to the Arapaho woman's?"

Coming out of a shocked stupor, Hawwy yelped, "What?"

After I repeated the question Hawwy answered in his painfully awkward Kiowa. "Not punish tent. Buug-lah tent."

I considered this briefly, then pressed another question. "Buug-lah doesn't mind sharing his tent with punished men?"

Hawwy looked to the side then down at me. Hawwy was very tall. That single black eyebrow of his, furrowed at the bridge of his nose. "Buug-lah, he run 'way."

"Why?"

Hawwy looked frustrated as he tried to make his awkward tongue form Kiowa words. "Stole horse. My chiefs want hang him."

"Must have been a good horse," I replied.

Hawwy sent me a frown, then shouted, as if I were hard of hearing, "Buug-lah run 'way!"

That is another thing I have never been able to tolerate

48

about the Blue Jackets: their fondness for publicly hanging a man by his neck until he is dead. In the Kiowa view of life, when a man becomes unhappy with his band or his band chief, it is right for him to move on. When a warrior becomes discontent with his chief, he cannot be counted on to fight for him. The Blue Jackets failed to appreciate the sense of this. If one of their men left, they hunted him down, then treated him to a despicable death. They called this "discipline."

Since that the first day of our being in Medicine Lodge, the generals had come to blame White Bear as the cause of every unnerving fracas. The promised wagons bringing food and gifts were nowhere to be seen on the horizon and the number of daily fracases, many of them generated by the Arapahos and Cheyennes, were mounting up. Still they blamed White Bear. Now there was the added insult of his beating up seven of their best officers. Never mind that these seven officers most certainly had it coming; the generals viewed White Bear as a threat to the peace negotiations and were eager to cut him down. But considering his importance in the Kiowa Nation, the generals had no idea how to discredit him in the eyes of the other chiefs of the Nations.

During the course of the next days, White Bear had completely forgotten Skywalker's warning. To be honest, everyone had. Much of the problem with any of Skywalker's warnings was his delivery. Unlike other Owl Doctors who practiced the dramatic along with their seer's craft, Skywalker's tone when prophesying bleak tidings was much too mild. Knowing this better than anyone, White Bear really should have known that the carefully measured words

Skywalker spoke were intensely important. But, being a dramatic fellow himself, White Bear was too often more impressed by the Owl Doctors who shook rattles in his face and carried on in a frenzy. Skywalker never once acted like that. He simply said what he had to say and left it to the hearer to make his own choice. Which is exactly why White Bear, quite alone and riding home from the Cheyenne's camp, forgot what Skywalker had said.

Halfway between the two camps, a bright beam off to the right caught his eye. Curious, White Bear veered his horse in that direction and, when he was close enough to the source of the glow, drew to a stop. Recognizing the thing on the ground as the shiny object that Buug-lah had not allowed him to touch, White Bear jumped down from his horse and picked it up. Being a great believer in the old saying that whatever is found on the prairie is a lucky gift for the finder, White Bear hung the bugle from his breech-belt in the same fashion he'd seen the soldier wearing it. Yet his biggest mistake was believing that the soldiers would offer him many valuable gifts to secure the return of the bugle.

This is the way Indians think. It is not the way Blue Jackets think. Not realizing this, White Bear took himself, and the bugle, to their camp.

FOUR

■ I do not know, before this occurrence, just how aggressively the Blue Jackets had been searching for their missing man. I only know that when White Bear appeared in their camp with that bugle, that they were thrown into a great sense of urgency, two officers demanding to know exactly where White Bear had supposedly found the object. Through the Comanche-speaking man, he told them.

Five miles northwest.

Now this made no sense to them at all, for immediately northwest lay Fort Larned. It defied logic that an absconding soldier would ride in the direction of another fort. Most especially a fort which is as actively patrolled, and in a twenty-five-mile radius, as Fort Larned. Only a supremely stupid deserter would strike off in that direction.

Yet again I was with Hawwy in the Blue Jackets' camp

when White Bear came boldly in, behaving just as arrogantly as he knew how to do. Needless to say, the Blue Jackets' reaction was not what he'd anticipated. Not one officer asked to have it back, nor were any gifts offered for its return. Instead White Bear was ordered out of their camp at riflepoint. As I would not stay where my chief was not welcome, I clambered onto my horse and rode out with him.

Too many think of Lone Wolf as a peace chief, a man anxious to appease Washington. The truth is, Lone Wolf—a tall man with craggy features—was in the main a slow talker, a man who preferred to remain quiet while figuring out the benefits or the disadvantages of any treaty talks. But when pushed, he had a notable temper. When he learned how one of his band chiefs had been treated, he formed a delegation and went to the soldiers' camp, where his temper exploded all over the generals. Undaunted, those same generals continued to insist that White Bear was nothing more than a common thief, and most probably a murderer.

Lone Wolf said "Prove it," and the generals said that was what they intended to do. Lone Wolf countered, "As you have been so far unable to find your own man, we Kiowa will find him for you."

The generals' response was, "The search will be continued solely by the army."

Lone Wolf struck a compromise. Four men from our camp would accompany a new Blue Jacket search party. The generals said this was all right as long as one of our men wasn't White Bear. They also stated that their junior officers should not have chased him out of the camp, but put him under arrest and, now that he was back in their camp, that this was what they intended to do. Lone Wolf said the first

Blue Jacket to touch White Bear would be the first Blue Jacket to die.

Alarmed, the generals had a conference. They still wanted White Bear to be under arrest, but agreed to allow Kiowa warriors to stand guard. Lone Wolf said that was all right with him, but that White Bear would not be under guard by anyone, not even Kiowas, inside the Blue Jacket camp—that the place for White Bear to be under arrest was in his own home. Realizing the principal chief of the Kiowas had been pushed as far as he would budge, the generals grudgingly shook Lone Wolf's hand.

With White Bear's honor at stake, the voting among our warriors for the four likely men to accompany the new search team was loud and furious. Keeping my mouth shut, I stood well back behind the crowd. Not a warrior or a tracker, it never occurred to me that I would ever be chosen. As far as I was concerned, I was simply there to listen. Skywalker had shouted down the warriors and now he was doing all of the talking. He said that no one had listened to him about coming to Medicine Lodge, and now, White Bear obviously hadn't been listening when he'd been told specifically not to touch anything he found on the ground. All of this trouble, he raged, could have been avoided if the people hadn't been greedy for promised gifts the army still had yet to give, and if White Bear had shown the barest trace of good sense.

The Cheyenne Robber took umbrage, jumping in to White Bear's defense. Skywalker was The Cheyenne Robber's adopted brother, but White Bear was his maternal uncle, a blood relative. Brotherhood aside, The Cheyenne Robber's first loyalty was to White Bear. Skywalker knew this, of course, but he was livid that The Cheyenne Robber was going against him. Their argument was rapidly becoming dangerous, as White Bear's lieutenants were entering the brotherly fray on The Cheyenne Robber's side, and the society of Owl Doctors were aligning themselves with Skywalker. The arguing was reaching a fevered pitch and guns were being drawn.

The generals were looking quite worried, knowing that it wouldn't take much for the Indians to stop yelling and begin shooting. The Blue Jacket chiefs were visably relieved when Lone Wolf and Hears The Wolf intervened. Their relief faded almost as rapidly as it had come, when Lone Wolf and Hears The Wolf began to argue.

Frankly, at this point, knowing that real danger had been averted, I stopped listening. Turning my face away, I glanced around the soldiers' camp. So many men, all of them dressed in identical fashion. I was wondering yet again just how they managed to tell one another apart, when Hears The Wolf's words entered my consciousness.

"But he's a logical choice!"

Looking pained, Lone Wolf replied tersely, "We're talking about someone who can't track, can't defend himself, can barely stay on a horse."

Growling behind his teeth, Hears The Wolf stepped closer to Lone Wolf. "I know his faults, but even so, I vote for him."

Lone Wolf's jawline clenched as his narrowing eyes bore into Hears The Wolf's. In carefully chosen words he said, "On account of White Bear, I've been made to look weak. If this problem isn't solved, I will have no voice at the peace talks."

"You have my assurance," Hears The Wolf said, "that this one will work for your benefit. And of all of us, he is the better choice. He has spent time among the Blue Jackets. He knows them."

Now, that really should have been my clue, but it wasn't. While it was true that I had been spending a great deal of time at the Blue Jackets' camp, I had been spending every bit of that time with Hawwy—learning from him and trying just as hard as I knew how, to convince him to trade away some of his wonderful doctoring tools. You might well ask why I wasn't alerted to the possibility that it was me Lone Wolf was referring to with his unflattering remarks. That too is easily explained.

Lone Wolf was not at all like our former chief. Little Bluff had had a talent for bringing out the best in everyone. Recognizing that not all men were destined to be warriors, he encouraged men such as myself to do instead what they did best. Because of Little Bluff, at a very young age, I was recognized as a practical doctor and I brought this title with me into the new era. Had I been born later, still trying to find my way while Lone Wolf was principal chief, I would never have been recognized as anything more than a failure, because in his mind if you weren't a valuable warrior you might as well just go ahead and die—a judgment he had been very quick to give.

Almost immediately following his political victory, Lone Wolf had surrounded himself with only the best of the best. He then went on to publicly criticize any man unable to meet his stern standards. So on this day, when he was blowing off on the worthlessness of this latest unfortunate, it is wholly understandable that I had no idea he meant me.

The real indicator that I had been the subject of his recent ridicule was when Raven's Wing grabbed hold of my arm and marched me to the front, placing me in the direct path of Lone Wolf's jaundiced eye.

The few words he spoke to me were bitten off and threatening. "Healer, once again you have come to my attention."

I looked to Skywalker for assistance and found not a whit. It felt to me that I had been desperately seeking support from a complete stranger. He maintained this attitude as the four of us—Skywalker, Hears The Wolf, The Cheyenne Robber, and me—joined forces with the newly chosen men from among the Blue Jackets.

There were two officers and four enlisted men. Hawwy was the senior officer. The junior was Lieutenant Watts, simply called Danny by his superior officers. We called him Danny, too, and he seemed to like that. He was a slightly built young man; so slight that he didn't appear to weigh much more than my wife. This was the same young man I had seen so often with Buug-lah, and he looked just as pinch-faced as ever. He had bright blond hair, red-rimmed blue eyes, and a perpetually runny nose. Danny did not have an illness. At least not one I was able to cure. He could not stand dust, and the dusty, dry thin air of the high prairie was making his life a misery. I tried to help him, offering him a piece of bitterroot, but Lieutenant Danny only smiled and sniffled a "no, thank you."

One of the four black soldiers was someone I already knew—William. His leg wasn't bothering him, I was pleased to note, for he walked quite easily toward his horse. I felt very proud of my skills. William was a nice-looking young man and something of a bashful person. Recognizing me, he sent an awkward half-smile. Then he glanced back to the young lieutenant, an anxious expression creasing his face.

The second black soldier was named Little Jonas. This name was supposedly a joke, because Little Jonas was as big and brooding as a thunderhead. He looked at all of us from narrowed, hooded eyes. His glare was so hard that it left all of us with the distinct impression that he would happily rip our hearts out without the slightest hesitation. Worriedly I began to wonder just how effectively a gentle man like Hawwy, or a lightweight like Snotty Nose (Lieutenant Danny), could control their hostile giant.

The remaining two enlisted men were white, both of them wearing many stripes on their sleeves: Sergeant Hicks having six stripes, Sergeant Cullen having four. Sergeant Hicks was a stocky man with rough, weathered skin and, when he removed his broad black hat to wipe sweat from his brow, I was shocked to see that he had very little hair, the top of his bare skull quite shiny. He walked beside Hawwy as the latter tried to address a sullen Skywalker. During this less-than-productive exchange, I glanced from Sergeant Hicks to the other Striped Sleeve, Sergeant Cullen.

Now, there was a sight. The man was literally swollen with hostility, a to-the-bone meanness that manifested itself as he stood next to his horse, holding the reins too tightly, purposely hurting the animal that was trying to throw its head back, fighting the brutal hold. When the horse did a dancing step to the side, Sergeant Cullen kicked the horse in the ribs. The sound of that horse's scream caught everyone's attention, Hawwy and Sergeant Hicks quickly turning away from us. Sergeant Hicks yelled something, then Cullen, his upper lip curling back in a snarl, mounted up.

Thoroughly embarrassed—first by getting nowhere in the attempt at being civil with Skywalker, then by the brutal display of the soldier—Hawwy was practically babbling. Skywalker rounded off Hawwy's humiliation with a dismissive wave, turned his horse's head, and led the four of us away from the odd assortment of Blue Jackets.

We were two miles out and traveling northwest when Billy came riding out of a clump of scrub trees. As Hawwy had been the only means of communication between our two groups, and his abilities were somewhat sketchy, he was very glad to see the young frontiersman. With Billy now by his side, I could see an almost visible, burdensome weight lifting from Hawwy's shoulders. In all ruthless honesty, Hawwy was about as much a soldier as I was a warrior. He had been chosen for this expedition for precisely the same reasons I had—because the generals, on account of his impending marriage to Cherish and his friendship with me, believed he knew more about the Kiowa than he actually did. But unlike Hawwy, I had no rank whatsoever, so I was not afflicted with the responsibility of leadership. With the arrival of Billy, Hawwy eagerly shifted this responsibility, and with the shift came a lessening of tensions, for Skywalker quite readily spoke to Billy whereas he pointedly had had nothing to say to Hawwy.

The Cheyenne Robber and Hears The Wolf were two of the finest trackers in the Nation but they had a hard task. You must understand that there were thousands and thousands of horses in that valley. The ground was a mess, all churned up and, because of the arid heat, terribly dusty.

The Cheyenne Robber and Hears The Wolf rode at the front. Skywalker—who for reasons I didn't understand, did not want to talk to me any more than he wanted to talk to Hawwy—chose to ride beside Billy. Hawwy, Lieutenant Danny, and I rode behind them. Behind us were the two sergeants, and behind them rode the two black men.

Gradually the ground smoothed out and tracks were found. For a long time it wasn't clear if we were following one horse or two, but when the ground became devoid of other traffic, it became apparent that we were following two horses wearing metal shoes.

Right away The Cheyenne Robber said that a soldier was chasing another soldier, but Lieutenant Danny said no. He said that he had counted a large number of mules belonging to the Indians. Mules with army markings. Well, that put The Cheyenne Robber's hair up. He fired back that any mules belonging to the Nations had been given in trade and that no Indian would accept a mule needing to wear iron shoes. Besides, he knew a mule print from a horse print whereas Snotty Nose didn't look as if he knew anything except how to blow his nose so he should just shut up. Lieutenant Danny finished blowing his nose and then shut right up.

In this spirit of mounting hostility, we continued following the tracks. Ten miles more, when buzzards were seen lazily circling the sky, we pushed our horses into a gallop.

The sight of the man known as Buug-lah and his equally dead horse was horrific. Swarms of flies fed on both bodies. The black soldier, William, walked off to the side and commenced to wretch loudly. Lieutenant Danny panicked, pulled his sidearm, turning the pistol on Hears The Wolf.

The Cheyenne Robber, coming up behind him, used his locked-together hands like a battle-ax, knocking the young man on the side of his head and to the ground. Hawwy and Billy froze. Amazingly, so did Little Jonas and the two sergeants. Hears The Wolf quickly disarmed Billy and the Blue Jackets, then was forced to wait as, throughout all of this excitement, William kept right on vomiting. Finally able to take away this last soldier's sidearm, Hears The Wolf ordered the Blue Jackets to stand together.

As they moved to comply, Hears The Wolf tried to think what to do next. But the man was floundering. As White Bear was known to be in possession of the dead man's property, he would be blamed for his murder. To save his friend, Hears The Wolf could not allow the soldiers to ride back to their camp to report what we'd found. On the other hand, he was bound by his word to Lone Wolf that he would make certain that while he kept the soldiers honest, he would also keep them safe. Having sworn this so faithfully and in public, Hears The Wolf didn't feel completely free to kill them, but then neither could he just let them go.

Loath though as I am to admit this, in those crucial moments, I wasn't of much help. Life had taken on a dreamlike quality, a dream where the colors are too vibrant, the edges too hard. So there I was, trapped in this dreamstreaky state, standing next to Hawwy with my hands in the air too. I came crashing back into the actual moment when, with a cry issuing from his throat, Skywalker laid a hand on my vest jacket and yanked me away from Hawwy, physically reminding me just which side in this dilemma I was supposed to be on. With hard words and another rough shove, he propelled me toward the corpse.

Buug-lah lay on the ground, as dead as a doorknocker. From the look of him, someone had done him in with a sharp, heavy instrument, most probably a metal ax, splitting his once smug face in half. The body was in the advanced stages of decomposition. Even at twenty yards the stench was quite robust. I didn't want to get any nearer than that, but Skywalker was still physically insistent. As he forced me forward, I shoved bits of sage up my nose and tied a protective leather cloth across my face. Skywalker needed no such protection, for he did not have the ability to smell things. Not even really bad things, like a rotting corpse.

More than a year prior to Medicine Lodge, Skywalker had had an accident—a head-first fall from a running horse. The result of the fall left him with terrible headaches and the loss of his senses of smell and taste. The headaches, as terrible as they were, were treatable, but restoring these two vital senses went far beyond my capabilities. He liked to pretend that the loss didn't bother him, but as his doctor, as his friend, I knew the truth.

Before the accident he hadn't paid any attention to the fact that he could smell and taste. He can hardly be criticized for this, as all human beings walk around taking for granted the things they should actually be marveling, failing to appreciate even for a second just how wondrously we are made. The ability to smell, the ability to taste, are two things we simply expect to do. Privately, Skywalker's loss devastated him. Nothing he ate gave him enjoyment and he was frustrated that he could no longer enjoy simple things like the sweet perfume of pine trees after a spring rain or the aroma of a hearty stew on a cold winter's day. Yet there was a dangerous side to his loss.

The senses of smell and taste are primary warning devices. A bad taste instinctively tells a person to spit out whatever they happen to be chewing, that the bad taste means something is poisonous to the body. The sense of smell detects the acrid odor of smoke, a sense vital to those living in a country of grass where fires are known to flash start. Nothing can stop a prairie fire once it flares to life. Man and animals can only get out of its way, and they must do this long before the fire is seen, Skywalker's inability to smell such danger left him subtly dependent on others. Skywalker abhorred being dependent. Even subtly.

Then again, during that autumn when we were at Medicine Lodge, there were a lot of things Skywalker despised. By his surly manner, it was becoming more and more apparent that I was one of those things. Something was going on between us, something I didn't understand, and until he felt ready to share the problem, I was treated not like a friend, but as someone he didn't care to know. When he spoke to me, he snapped, he ordered.

Ordinarily this attitude would have hurt me deeply. On that day, it simply made me mad, for there I was, gagging on account of that putrefying body while he spoke in a demeaning manner, thoroughly unfazed by Buug-lah's whiffy remains. While we were thus engaged, The Cheyenne Robber was putting his tracking skills to good use, looking for any type of sign.

Skywalker looked back at him while I annoyingly brushed flies away from my eyes. "What do you see?"

The Cheyenne Robber circled the area, confusion marring his features. "I can't find anything in this grass." Then he yelped. "Wait! Here's something."

"What is it?"

The Cheyenne Robber stood to his full height, shook his head. "It looks like a deep cut."

Skywalker rose and went to join his brother. Studying the mark, they remained unnaturally quiet. "It's the heel of a boot," Skywalker said. Squatting down, he placed his hand just above the mark.

"Anything?" The Cheyenne Robber quizzed.

Skywalker's hand became a fist. "Nothing. Too much time has passed. No images are coming to me." Raising his head he declared, "It would seem our one hope is Tay-bodal."

Nervously I cleared my throat. "I—I need help. I ask for Hawwy."

His eyes narrowing, Skywalker simply stared at me. I hated it when he got like that. His silences always made me feel defensive. Feeling a degree of malice in that stare, I felt extremely defensive.

"Hawwy is a doctor too," I said, hating the nervous edge in my tone.

Skywalker still said not a word. His mouth slowly compressing into a tight line. All right, I thought, if he wants to be mad at me, then he should be that in a better time and place. Steeling my nerve, I said more forcibly, "Hawwy is a fair person. We are lucky to have him. And as we do have him, we should use him."

"Tay-bodal's right," Hears The Wolf said.

Skywalker turned his silent tactic on Hears The Wolf. I was glad to see that he responded to it no better than I, but as Hears The Wolf was Lone Wolf's chosen leader of this little expedition, he didn't have time to worry about Skywalker's apparent displeasure. Lifting his chin in Hawwy's direction, he shouted, "Hawwy wants to help. Look at his face!"

Skywalker's gaze traveled sluggishly toward Ha-we-sun. His hands still raised even with his head, Hawwy was looking at the body on the ground with a concentrated expression. Skywalker stood and went over to where Hawwy was, stood right in front of him but spoke to Billy, keeping his voice low and even.

"I know you understand the problem of our finding that man dead. Tay-bodal says he needs Hawwy's help. I think you should take time to explain to him just how important his complete cooperation will be."

Even though his face was partially obscured by the wide brim of his hat, I saw Billy flinch. After a moment's deliberation, he nodded, then turned and addressed Hawwy.

Hears The Wolf and The Cheyenne Robber tied up the remaining Blue Jackets, having to grapple first with Sergeant Cullen. During the scuffle William had edged closer to Lieutenant Danny's side. William's face was streaked with tears that, in the strong sunlight, shone like silver lines on his dark face.

When Hears The Wolf and The Cheyenne Robber started after Little Jonas, they were expecting a huge fight, but the man, staring off at William, was oddly compliant. He made not one defensive gesture. Because he was so indulgent, Hears The Wolf and The Cheyenne Robber took their time deciding just which scrub tree wasn't likely to be uprooted by Little Jonas's use of brute force. Once the five Blue Jackets were settled and secure, Billy nodded to Hawwy. At last able to move without fear of being shot, Hawwy tied a cloth over his face and came to me.

He hunkered right down, his dark brown eyes above the mask, eager as he said excitedly, "This not man. Clothes no fit."

He meant, of course, that this couldn't possibly be Buug-lah because the clothing looked too small. Hearing this, Sky-walker ran to join us, coming to stand just behind Hawwy. Looking up at Skywalker, seeing the eagerness in his expression, I wanted to hit Haw-we-sun. His saying that was just like throwing mud clods into a perfectly clear waterhole. How was I suppose to convince the others that his help was necessary if he went on making idiot statements like that? All right, the dead man's face was split in half and I was having a hard time keeping the black cloud of flies stirred so that they wouldn't resettle and cover up the wound. But even in these appalling conditions I could tell that this man was once Buug-lah, for, having watched him for days and simply out of curiosity, I clearly remembered the dead man's face. Hawwy hadn't known him at all before coming to Medicine Lodge and to my knowledge, had only looked at him twice. But only once, on the day he picked him up and brushed him off, had he shown the living man any interest. Now he was basing his iffy identification on the way the body was clothed, giving no thought at all to the ruined facial structure.

Despite the malodorous air, I heaved a wearied sigh.

A decomposing human is an awful sight. Worse than any species of dead animal. With all things formerly living, death has distinct stages but these stages are more apparent in humans. There are other stages for bodies left to molder in deep water, but as the body I am telling you about was on dry land, I will be brief, horrifying your mind only with those details.

In the first twelve hours, the body cools enough to feel cold to the touch. During about half of those twelve hours, blood settles in whatever position the body is left to lay. If it's on the back then blood will seep in that direction, but the blood will not collect in the places of contact. For example, if the body is on a hard surface, like the ground as in the case of Buug-lah, then the shoulder blades, the buttocks, the back of the calves, and the heels will be flat and white while the remainder of the body will look a vivid red.

Also in the first twelve hours the body becomes rigid, beginning in the jaw and neck, finally making the body as stiff as wood. Oddly enough, after another twelve hours the body goes limp again and the blood which was like a jellied mass, will turn liquid again, weeping from cavities like the ears, eyes, and so on—anyplace excess blood can escape. It is not unusual to find bloodred tears on a dead man's face, or to see blood trickling out of the mouth. This display will not tell you how the man died; it merely gives an idea of how long the man has been dead.

When a body is two to three days old, the lower abdomen becomes puffy and the leached skin around the abdomen will seem to have been painted with the colors purple and green. Two days more—making four total days since death—the veins are huge, grossly distended. Also, the purple and green colors are no longer confined to the trunk, but have spread like a blotchy disease toward the neck and limbs. In this stage, the body has become fully bloated, which explains why the dead man's clothing looked too tight, prompting Hawwy's idiotic guess that the body was some other poor soul done up in Buug-lah's ill-fitting clothing.

Take all of this and apply it ten times over to a corpse left out in the grueling sun, totally exposed to the sun's relentless blaze. The skin not covered was blackened, causing the victim to appear as if he had been tortured with fire before being killed. This hadn't happened, but not even Hears The Wolf was ready to believe that one—another reason he'd immediately captured the Blue Jackets.

Actually, his doing that was a good thing, for if the soldiers had gotten away and reported even half of what they had seen, Medicine Lodge would have become the site of an unprecedented massacre. At Medicine Lodge we had almost as many generals as there were soldiers, plus important Washington men, and newspaper reporters. The loss to the white culture would have been staggering. I can only guess that the ensuing rage against the Kiowa Nation would then have been met with the aim of our total extermination. So, as things worked out, it was to everyone's benefit that Hears The Wolf had moved so quickly to capture those soldiers and tie them up good and tight.

But Hawwy had another concern. He was still on about the too-tight clothing, and like one of the hardheaded mules he had handed over to secure his marriage with Cherish, he would not be persuaded from that opinion.

From what I had learned about Haw-we-sun, he had been in the war between the Blue Jackets and the Gray Jackets. As a doctor, he had seen hundreds of dead and dying soldiers. The problem was, he had never seen them in the advanced stages of death. The common soldiers were promptly buried, whereas the bodies of the officers had been ingeniously preserved to allow shipment back to their homes for burial. And even then, as Hawwy had explained, the caskets had been sealed. No one, not the doctors and most certainly not the grief-stricken families, ever saw the dead in a moldering state. He did assure me, however, that he had dealt with dead people in a place he called Medical College. In this place, they cut open corpses in order to examine the internal organs. Isn't that gruesome?

As Hawwy was so determined to take a wife from among the true humans, he needed a good talking-to, needed to be told that bragging about cutting up the dead was an improper thing to do. But, as I didn't have time to broaden his education in that moment, I simply stayed with my argument that the dead man before us was most certainly Buuglah. That Hawwy shouldn't be in such a hurry to base his opinions on the evidence of straining buttons or the sausagelike appearance of arms and legs trapped inside that uniform.

I attempted to tell him all of this between shallow breaths. Too shallow. The fetid air barely reached my lungs. My head was swimming and deep in the pit of my stomach, nausea roiled. I needed clean air or I was going to pass out. Besides, with Hawwy's limited language skills he couldn't, or wouldn't, understand a word I managed to say. So I addressed Skywalker, who was now crouched beside Hawwy and looking up at the sky.

"Could we please discuss this at a distance? I'm not feeling very well."

Skywalker's puckered lips moved to the side of his face as he kept right on studying the sky. "No."

"Why?" I shouted.

In a flat tone he answered, "Because it's going to rain."

68

FIVE

Cold air moves down from the north with amazing speed, engulfing the vast prairie lying open and helpless. Overnight, snow as deep as a man is tall can shroud every mile of the plains. On the other hand, this same wallowing, near-treeless expanse is subject to blasts of warm air from the south. When the warm winds come, the snow melts, turning the prairie into a bog. If, however, there is no offering from the south, then the snow has been known to stay put for a span of days, sometimes weeks. When Indian people became tired of living with all that snow, they turned their faces to the south and prayed for the north wind's enemy, the south wind, to come out and fight.

The winds from the north and south have fought an ageless war, a war so old that during the days when my grandfather was a boy, he heard the ancient wise men of his youth talking about the north and the south winds battling it out over the prairie. The fighting can be so severe that it wakes up the Great Hind Leg, the swirling cloud known to whites as a tornado. To the Kiowa, it is known as Hind Leg of the Great Horse because when the first horse was found by my people, they didn't know what it was. Not recognizing its value, they threw it away. This angered the Creator because He had sent the horse as a gift. Having that gift shunned was an insult, so, from the hind leg of that horse, He made the tornado, and sent it to tear up the villages of His ungrateful children. That taught them a big lesson and soon after that, whenever they found a horse, they kept it.

When they discovered just how useful the animal was, they began to steal more, eventually learning how to breed them. But still the damage against the Creator's pride was not appeased and since those days, the hind leg of the first horse has continued to rampage the earth. Sometimes it isn't just the hind leg that appears. During one really bad storm I once saw all four legs running and great shafts of lightning spitting out from the huge black body. It was a thrilling sight, I watched that storm for as long as I could before having to run away.

Now, some young men never run away. To prove their courage they chased the storm, throwing lances at the hind leg. Older, wiser men, offered up shredded tobacco to the whirling cloud, apologized for the ignorance of their fathers, and for the arrogance of the young men too anxious to be called heroes for chasing the danger away from the people.

One young man I knew a long time ago, payed dearly for this arrogance. That was during the time three bands of us were in the Texas Panhandle. That's a bad place to be during a tornado. Too much sand. That young man didn't care about that, either. He had wanted more than anything, even more than his life, to be a hero and have great songs sung about his courage. With four other warriors who were also in a hurry to prove themselves, he mounted up, waved his lance around, and said, "From this day, Little Bluff himself will say my name with great respect."

He was disappointed by the general lack of interest in his defiant pronouncement, for while he was declaring it, the entire camp was scurrying in all directions, more intent on finding shelter than standing around listening to a young man puffing himself up. The last words anyone heard him say were, "I'll show all of you." Then he kicked his horse and rode out after the storm.

For a while, he and his friends were doing a fine job of chasing the leg away, but then, it turned. The young man was farther out in front, so while the other four were able to pull up, turn around and flee, the unfortunate man couldn't. That leg was on him before he could do anything. The others bore witness that that young man and his horse were sucked up inside that leg—a leg made black by all that terrible brown sand.

He was found a day later, his dead and broken body completely scoured. Everybody cried and carried on about him being dead, but as a doctor, I felt that his being killed was the best thing that could have happened. His being alive would have been too awful to contemplate, for he had no eyelids, ears, nose, or lips. It was as if his entire face had been rubbed off. There was a little bit of hair left on his head, but basically his skull was worn as smooth as a creek bedrock.

That young man is still talked about, but his courage is rarely mentioned. He is an example used to impress children that the prairie is a dangerous place—that being caught off guard, even for a moment, will kill or cripple. As I tell you about all this, it comes to mind that Skywalker was a good example of this, too. He'd been caught off guard, and the result was the fall from his bolting horse, leaving him with terrible headaches and the loss of two vital senses. Having survived this lesson, he took great care never to be caught off guard again.

So when Skywalker said, in that matter-of-fact tone of his, that rain was coming, I didn't doubt him for an instant. I didn't even bother to glance up at the sky. Instead I barked for Hawwy to help me dig in the softened earth around the body and sift that dirt through his fingers. He had no idea why he was doing it, he just jumped to respond to the urgency in my tone, busily digging and sifting the way I was doing.

And all we came away with was gritty dirt.

We couldn't bury the body because I wasn't finished with it.

Skywalker was covering it up with an expendable blanket just as fat drops of rain began to pelt the dry earth. The drops quickly became a deluge. Hears The Wolf yelled orders for us to move to safer ground, away from the few trees. Of course, this meant untying the soldiers. We were all prepared for trouble from either Little Jonas or Sergeant Cullen, but when lightning struck close by, that big black man and that mean white man were instantly too afraid to cause trouble.

Hears The Wolf let the horses go and they ran away like their tails were on fire. Throwing blankets over ourselves, we made our bodies just as flat as we could against the ground. The rains fell faster, pummeling us, winds tearing at our feeble protection, trying to take the blankets away. To prevent this, we rolled ourselves up in our blankets, the way some worms are able to roll themselves up before making the magical change to butterfly.

I can tell you this: It's very unnerving to be under only a blanket while lightning is striking all around and thunder is booming so loudly you can't even hear yourself scream. Mercifully, the storm lasted only about a half an hour, rain-laden clouds taking their own time wafting toward the encampments at Medicine Lodge. But for those of us caught out in it, the brief time seemed like a week, each lightning strike bringing with it the certainty of immediate death. When it was finally over, we sat up, threw the blankets off of our heads. Then we just looked at one another, duly surprised that we were all still alive.

Hawwy called Lieutenant Danny's condition "shock." I've always called it Mind Going, for in times of great stress, the mind goes blank, and if it stays gone for a good length of time, the body shuts down and the victim dies. As the last thing we needed was one more dead Blue Jacket, we hastily made a fire, fueling it with whatever was handy, which after the storm wasn't very much. Grubbing around among the soaked scrub trees, The Cheyenne Robber found a few partially dry dead branches and a limited supply of as-good-as-dry buffalo chips, and Little Jonas helped him bring these things back to us. Billy concerned himself with searching through our soggy food bags that had been hurriedly removed along with the saddles from the horses.

William hovered over the young lieutenant, speaking to Hawwy in concerned whispers while Hawwy crouched before Lieutenant Danny, using his hands to rub the young man's arms and legs to keep the blood flowing in his extremities. I was trying to salvage what I could from my medical supply bag when I looked up and saw Sergeant Cullen sitting all by his petulant self, staring with menace at Sergeant Hicks who was tagging after Hears The Wolf and making every effort to be helpful. The thing that amazed me was that Sergeant Hicks was helping Hears The Wolf place all of the Blue Jackets' rifles and pistols in a blanket, and roll the blanket up. Then he helped carry the stash of guns over to what would be the Indian side of the make-do camp.

It wasn't a good camp, but as dusk was rapidly approaching, it was as good as it would ever get. The scant fire lasted only long enough to boil up a pot of coffee. It took the combined efforts of Hawwy and I to force hot coffee into Lieutenant Danny. William was still hovering, and he talked to me throughout the effort, asking the same thing over and over, his garbled words, sounding like, "He gawn di?" I found out later that what he actually asked was, "Is he going to die?"

Really, the language barrier during that time was an appalling nuisance, which decided me to just go ahead and learn the language. Over the course of the next years Hawwy patiently taught me—only for me to discover that he'd imparted his northern dialect, a thing vastly different from what is spoken throughout the Territory. That's the baffling

74

thing about English, really, the too-many different ways to say the same word. It took me a long time to understand why I was being singled out by the Indian Agents whenever I dared to speak during a conference—why they kept at me about which school in New England I had attended. But I think the worst embarrassment came on a day I was trading in a store in Anadarko and a backwoodsman I had never seen before, leaning against a counter as he listened to me speaking to the store clerk, asked in a very loud voice, "You sum kinda book-learnin' Injun?"

Thank you very much, Haw-we-sun.

Of course, I also learned to pronounce Hawwy's proper name, Harrison. That I don't, simply means I choose not to. Calling him anything else would make him seem a stranger. I can be very stubborn about strangers. Almost as stubborn as Hawwy was being about that body not being Buug-lah's.

When the fire went out, it was dark and cold and we were tired and shivering, but Hawwy wouldn't be quiet, insisting on arguing with me about the body and running on about "science."

Finally The Cheyenne Robber had enough of his soon-to-be brother-in-law's incessant jabbering, and threw a soggy shoe at him, hitting Hawwy in the face with it. Then he yelled, "Shut up, Haw-we-sun, or I will hurt you!" And The Cheyenne Robber flopped back on his damp blanket. I was grinning like a fool as Hawwy peeled the shoe from his face then obediently lay down.

From somewhere in the darkness, I heard Skywalker chuckle. That was the first laugh I'd heard out of him in weeks. A pleased smile was on my face as I drifted off into sleep.

* * *

It seemed as if only moments had passed and then the bright rays of dawn were waking us up. Our shivering bodies had managed to warm up inside the sodden blankets and none of us was overly eager to abandon that warmth. Hears The Wolf ventured first, his knees cracking noisily as he maneuvered to stand. Once he was steady on his feet, he wandered off to relieve his bladder. Not far away from me, Skywalker yawned loudly, stretched his arms toward the brightening heaven. Settling again, he tipped his head back and our eyes met.

"You have a hard day ahead," he said, his voice low, tone solemn. He looked away from me and to the side, finding himself almost face-to-face with Billy, who lay quietly, the lids of his unopened eyes fluttering ever so slightly. Skywalker reached a hand out and shoved him fully awake. "For all of today, you will stay with me." That being decided, Skywalker left his bed, and Billy, with a groan, followed suit.

Because of the haste in making up this new search party, what provisions we'd managed to pack were sparse. Without the means to make a fire, we couldn't even boil up coffee to dull the edges of the awful gnawing in our bellies. In a brooding silence we ate hard strips of jerked meat. While working at my portion I felt Little Jonas's covetous eyes fixing on me. He was a big man and that single strip of jerky was hardly enough to satisfy him. I sensed he might be on the verge of coming after mine, for I was the smallest Indian and he could take my meager breakfast away without half trying. So I did the one thing I hoped would discourage him completely. Pretending I was softening it up, I licked the entire strip. I heard him growl as he looked away, resetting his sights on Lieutenant Danny. Before he could launch his bulk in that direction, Hears The Wolf, understanding what Little Jonas was about to do, thumped him.

The one man in that camp Little Jonas seemed to fear was Hears The Wolf. Following the thump, Little Jonas settled down, contenting himself with his own portion. When we were finished eating, we shook out our blankets, hung them over the tops of bushes so that they would dry. The Blue Jackets, even Cullen, seemed eager to be helpful. Well, they didn't have much of a choice, actually. It was either be helpful or be tied up again. None of them were especially anxious to spend the day tied to a scrub tree. So, on foot, everyone except Hawwy and I, set off to search for the horses.

Hawwy and I went back to that body.

The most vital evidence, the thing I was forced to patiently explain to Hawwy, concerns maggots. As a doctor, I used maggots all the time. They are amazing creatures, and a wondrous tool if you know how to judge their age and use them properly. In cases where I had a patient with a festering wound, I grew my own maggots to treat that wound. It's simple, really. I put out a piece of meat and then waited for flies to come and lay their eggs. Now, the timing must be just right, and that timing is dependent on the weather. If it's cold, the process takes much longer, but as hot as the weather had been, a maggot's progression toward adulthood was very short.

The eggs would have hatched within the span of one day and by the next morning, tiny little white squirmy specks would already be plump enough to be visible without needing to squint in order to see them. After three days the maggots would be nice and large—that's the stage when I take the maggots and apply them to the festering wound of my patient. I could count on the maggots to feed on the bad part of the wound for five days, leaving behind good clean skin. If the wound was very large and required more maggots, I had to get more, for the first maggots would have turned hard.

The hard maggots were still alive, they had just advanced into the final level of their worm existence. At that final stage, they need to burrow into the ground and sleep there until they are ready to emerge as fully grown flies. That was why I told Hawwy to help me sift the earth. Our not finding any hard maggots told me exactly how old the body was.

Maybe it was because of our near starvation that Hawwy turned such an amazing shade of green and bolted off to wretch his stomach completely empty. Or possibly it was because, after I cut away the moldering jacket and he was treated to the sight of all of those white wriggling maggots greedily feeding on what had once been a human being, his portion of breakfast simply refused to stay down. Whatever the cause, Hawwy puked until he was empty and when he came to me, he was so weak he could barely utter a word. A thing I was most grateful for because, even though he was still in the learning phase of mastering Kiowa, his lack of vocabulary did not deter him from being a chatterbox.

The next thing I wanted to do was have a look at the dead horse. There wasn't much to look at, actually. Animals prefer the taste of other animals, leaving human remains as a last alternative. Having so much good horse meat to feed on, Buug-lah had remained relatively untouched, whereas the horse had been stripped to bare bones. But never mind— I found the evidence I had been looking for. I tucked that away inside a little bag hanging from my breech-belt, and when I stood, Hawwy stood up with me.

"What we do?" he asked.

"Now," I said with a heavy sigh, "we bury this body."

After the thirst-quenching rain, the prairie grasses responded, bouncing back to stand tall, a last fit of growth before the first frost of winter. The dead man was almost concealed inside the breeze-soughing high grass. Hawwy and I followed the path we had made walking over to where the rib bones of the horse were visible. It was a good long walk. Irritatingly rejuvenated by the fresher air and needed exercise, Hawwy bounced alongside me like a long-legged puppy, firing a series of questions. What questions I chose to answer, were answered with a disagreeable grunt.

The one thing I loved about Blue Jackets was their ingenuity. Everything they had could be folded down to the size of nothing. The very instant Hawwy unfolded that shovel, I knew I had to have it. Had to, because my wife would be thrilled out of her mind if I gave it to her. As there was a lot to be appreciated in the intensity of Crying Wind's gratitude whenever she was thrilled out of her mind, I sincerely wanted to give her that shovel.

The rainstorm had succeeded in dampening the first inch or so of the soil but beneath that lay hard-packed clay and rock. Hawwy shoveled first and when he became exhausted, I took over. By that time he had already cleared the worst of it, making a good-sized hole for the body to fit inside. I relieved him of the shovel and, enthralled with the thing as well as with the heady anticipation of Crying Wind's delight in such a wondrous gift, I dug like a badger. It was only when I realized that a few inches more would have me bobbing up inside the Comanches' country, that I quit.

Hawwy did not want to touch the body again. I wasn't especially anxious to touch it again, either. So, using a rope which we looped around the booted ankles, we dragged it to the hole. I paused, to take one last look at the fatal wound to the dead man's face, and then we rolled it into the grave and covered it up.

So long, Buug-lah.

I was pulled from this brief farewell by Hawwy stamping down the earth we had backfilled. Letting go a tormented cry, I stopped him.

"You have the grass wrong way up!"

Kneeling, I hastily turned the clods of grass the right way, resettling them in the natural position, restoring order. While I was doing this, Hawwy was on the move again—doing what, I didn't much care to know. But when I sat down for a much-needed rest, his activity gradually intrigued me.

That was the first time I ever saw a Cross.

He made it out of two shovels. One, his own—the very one I lusted after. The second, a shovel he stole out of someone else's saddlebag. He tied them together and, using the blade of one shovel, slammed the Cross into the ground just above Buug-lah's deeply-buried head. When I asked him why he marked the grave, and said that this wasn't right because the dead did not like their resting places known because they didn't want to be pestered, he said that white people didn't feel that way; that later on, when other whites came through this country and saw the Cross, they would pause to offer prayers for the dead man. While he offered his own prayers, I remained suitably quiet, knowing that once this bad business was settled, and before we left Medicine Lodge, that I, too, would come here to pray for Buuglah.

And then I would take those shovels.

SIX

The others eventually returned to find Hawwy and I sitting in the inadequate camp, completely exhausted from having spent a very warm day inspecting a fly-blown decomposing corpse, then digging a deep hole to bury it in. We had cleaned ourselves as best we could, using precious water from canteens and strong soap Hawwy provided. I made a tiny fire using grasses and the cedar chips I always carried with me in order to purify myself from any contact with an unclean thing. Hawwy hadn't objected, nor had he moved a muscle when, cupping my hands over the meager fire, I lifted up the smoke toward him and purified him, too. After that, we collapsed.

The others had been out for the entire day. The sun was low on the western horizon when they came back. Not only had they managed to find the horses, they'd also killed and butchered out a deer. They came back happy, bringing with them a load of wood to ensure a good fire.

Finally our camp had everything it needed—dry beds, a bright fire, hot coffee, and fresh meat. As dusk settled, the twilight sky was a breathtaking sight of color. The display reminded me to give thanks to the Creator for the simple gifts of food, fire, and companionship. These things were making everyone feel better. The only sour note was Skywalker. He was being very friendly to everyone but me and Hawwy. With us, he acted as if we didn't exist. Frankly, after so many weeks of his mood, I was beginning to lose my patience.

I poured myself another cup of coffee and then, whether Skywalker was agreeable to my nearness or not, I sat myself down next to him. I sipped the coffee while he purposely kept his face turned away from me, listening as Billy dutifully translated the comical exchange taking place between Little Jonas and The Cheyenne Robber. It would seem that during the activity of the search for the horses and then the hunt, a bond had grown between those two. I found it odd that Little Jonas could so easily turn away from his black brother and attach himself to The Cheyenne Robber. But he had, and now he and The Cheyenne Robber were sitting close together and laughing. Watching them over the rim of my cup I was taken by the deeply melodious sound of Little Jonas's voice, tinged with mirth as he spoke through Billy.

"You Indians look alike. It's hard for us to tell you apart."

The Cheyenne Robber considered this for about a hot second, then cried, "How can you say we all look alike? Isn't it obvious that the Creator made the Kiowa, His true people, more handsome than all other Indians?"

Little Jonas grinned, his dark shiny face glowing almost orange in the firelight. In the heartbeat of time between The Cheyenne Robber's response and Little Jonas's reply, the fire hissed and popped, sending a shower of brilliant sparks skyward, the sparks fading out against the blackness. The firelight played across all of the faces. In that soft light, Hawwy and Lieutenant Danny both looked so young and trusting—they also looked slightly yellow. Sergeant Hicks seemed more weathered, a weary brown. Dark lines around Sergeant Cullen's eyes and mouth deepened, causing him to look whiter than he was, and very sly. The two Buffalo Soldiers were so dark that their faces could only be seen in orange-gold highlights and their snow-white eyes and teeth. The Cheyenne Robber and Hears The Wolf were the color of the rust-red river of our homeland. Billy, because of his mixed blood, looked somewhere in between the colors of yellow and rust.

Finally Little Jonas answered The Cheyenne Robber's question. "No," he said, as he fell to the side laughing.

In a mock display of warrior aggression, The Cheyenne Robber knelt, a raised fist seemingly poised to strike the cackling Buffalo Soldier.

Pretending to be afraid, Little Jonas yelped, "I give up, I give up! It's true, you are beautiful. It's just too bad there isn't three more of you, then you could love all your selves."

"Just the one is more than enough," Hears The Wolf joked.

Turning on his father-in-law, The Cheyenne Robber

growled like a bear. Unaffected by the threat, Hears The Wolf sloshed the remains of coffee around in his cup as he spoke in a confiding manner to the rest of us. "We once gave him a hand mirror. He was suppose to use it to flash signals in the same way we have known you Blue Jackets to do. That kind of message-sending didn't work so well for us, though."

"Why not?" Lieutenant Danny dared to ask.

The Cheyenne Robber settled back, gave his hand to Little Jonas, helping the Buffalo Soldier to sit up again.

Hears The Wolf shrugged as he continued to stare at the remaining coffee in his cup and drolled on. "We gave the mirror to the wrong man." A smile twitching the corners of his mouth, he looked directly at Lieutenant Danny. "Three times, that one over there signaled for us to advance, then three times he quickly signaled for us to fall back. We were very confused. We found out later he'd been using the mirror while he combed his hair."

The normally timid Lieutenant Danny exploded with laughter. Everyone did—with the exception of Sergeant Cullen. Snorting in disgust, he stood and walked off into the darkness. During the moments he was out of sight, the entire camp became tense, waiting to see if he would come back or if the remaining Blue Jackets would have to be tied up again while Hears The Wolf and The Cheyenne Robber rode him down. Presently he came back into the light and the tension lifted. Immediately Little Jonas and The Cheyenne Robber were playful again, this time comparing the size of their upper-arm muscles. As both had extremely healthy biceps, Skywalker judged the contest to be a tie.

While Skywalker was still in such a good mood, I leaned

in and said, "I would like to speak to you in private."

The only evidence that I had been heard was his setting his cup down, then standing to his feet. When he walked off, I scrambled to stand, and followed after him.

We were still inside the circle of light, but far enough away from the camp to be able to speak freely. We knelt and sat on the backs of our legs, staring at each other over the small distance.

"I want to know what is wrong with you," I said.

"If you mean now," he jeered, "I'm feeling pain behind my eyes." He raised a hand to his forehead, his thumb and middle finger rubbing against the brow bone.

"Why didn't you tell me?"

"Oh, I didn't think you would want to be bothered by my unimportant malady."

Becoming incensed, I rose and left him, going to retrieve my medical bag.

He remained quiet, listening to the laughing voices behind us as I ground up the mixture of herbs in my hand-sized rock bowl. That rock bowl and matching grinding stone have always been my prized possessions. It had taken me a long time to find just the right size rock and then chip out and make smooth the center to form a bowl. My next task was to find just the right size grinding rock to fit the bowl. The grinding rock had to be long, but not too long, and just the right weight. I owned a lot of bowls and grinders, but they were too bulky to take on the trail. The two I'm telling you about were perfect for my travel bag and, knowing how difficult they would be to replace, I guarded them carefully.

Skywalker continued his silence as I placed a dried leaf

inside the bowl and began to reduce it to powder. Even though he was annoyingly interested in the medicines I made for other patients, he never once asked me about the plants I used when preparing his. I believe I understand why. It was because he knew that one of the plants was a poison. He'd sensed this from my careful use of it, the extreme caution I took when measuring it out. And that's true. That plant was highly dangerous but it was also the most beneficial herb in my collection because it has the ability to numb pain. But if the utmost care isn't used when administering it, it will kill. The trouble I had with Skywalker was that, over periods of extended usage, he'd built a tolerance, and the amount I was forced to use was nearing the lethal dosage. He knew that, too, but even so, on that night when he was so angry with me that I felt his anger like a tangible presence between us, he still trusted me not to kill him on purpose.

"Is your pain increasing?"

He wouldn't look at me, instead he studied the blackened space of ground between his knees. "Yes. And that noise you're making isn't helping."

I was forced to make even more noise as I ground the herbs in an effort to be a bit quicker. Feeling more angry, I said, "You know better than to wait this long. How many times have I told you that it's better to attack the pain when it's only beginning?"

He looked up, his eyes catching mine. "I really didn't mind so much about the pain in my head. The pain in my heart bothered me more."

"What's the matter with your heart?"

He scoffed bitterly, then fell silent. The two of us did

not try any further conversation while I reduced the dry herbs to a fine powder. Knowing just what to do, Skywalker opened his mouth and raised his tongue, sat perfectly still while I carefully sprinkled the powder in that watery space between tongue and teeth. Closing his mouth, he took a deep breath through his nostrils.

And then we waited.

This was always the tricky part and I especially hated it that during those times, he was quietly forgiving me for his death. I didn't want his forgiveness because I didn't want him to die. So while he waited and silently prayed, I was holding the antidote, bracing myself for the fight to save the same life he was calmly prepared to lose. When he began to hum his death song, I leaned close and watched him for signs of heavy perspiration, a sudden shortness of breath. When after a span of minutes, these symptoms failed to materialize, I sat back, humbly thanking the Creator yet again, for sparing me the awful guilt of my friend's death. I said this prayer with my eyes closed.

When I opened them, Skywalker was gone.

He hadn't even said, Thank you, Tay-bodal. All he'd done was go off to find his bed. Well, now, that made me really mad. Mad enough to seriously reconsider our friendship. Then I mentally kicked myself for believing that a Kauaun, a commoner, could truly be friends with an Onde, a prince of our Nation, and take such pride in a friendship Skywalker so easily threw away.

Anger gave way to despair, followed rapidly by self-pity. Because of our Nation's class system, I would not be able to look to Hears The Wolf and The Cheyenne Robber for friendly support. You must understand, they, too, were Ondes, and my acceptance in their midst was by Skywalker's sponsorship. He was the sole reason I had ever been welcome in their company. If he ended our friendship, the others would quickly fade away as well. For many years I'd lived in obscurity and loneliness, not minding the one, almost totally unaware of the other. It was on account of Skywalker that I'd found my life filled with love and friendship. Were I suddenly to lose any of it, I wasn't so certain I would have the strength to travel again that bleak and lonely road.

And what of Crying Wind? True, she complained about the duties required of her high status, but if, on account of her marriage to me, those duties were taken away and her sister Ondes shunned her, she would be devastated. I figured that sooner or later she would turn against me, and after that, divorce me.

Every man, no matter how brave or strong he might be, has at least one great fear. The Cheyenne Robber's fear—and one he was eternally teased about—was of spiders. But not just any spiders. He was afraid of tarantulas. Numbering somewhere in the millions, these big hairy spiders live in underground lodges throughout our home country. When it rains hard, those spiders come out of their water-filled hidey-holes and cover the ground in furry masses. And The Cheyenne Robber goes crazy. He won't eat, just in case a spider walked over his food without his knowing, and he definitely won't sleep, terrified spiders will get inside his lodge and walk over his face and body. What he does, is roost on his horse, grimly suffering the downpour, waiting for the rains to stop and the spiders' retreat.

My dread of losing Crying Wind was a thousand times

greater than any silly fear as that. I suppose it was because I understood too well I had done nothing to deserve her. The truth is, if it hadn't been for White Bear and Skywalker, our marriage never would have happened. I would have spent my life loving a woman who was too far above me to even say my name. Suddenly propelled by the fear of losing her, I jumped to my feet and sprinted to where Skywalker lay, giving himself up to medicated sleep, oblivious to the raucous voices of the others. The second I reached him, I solidly kicked his thigh, feeling the force from my toes on up to my upper leg. His eyes flew open and he stared up at me in complete astonishment.

"Did you just kick me?" he cried incredulously.

"I most certainly did," I answered. "And I will again if you go on refusing to talk to me. If you are determined to end our friendship, the very least I deserve is an explanation."

His expression livid, he stared up at me as if I were the most contemptible man he'd ever met. With flourish, he threw back the thin blanket.

Witnessing this exchange, Hears The Wolf and The Cheyenne Robber became very still. Little Jonas fell quiet mid-laugh, when Billy's staying hand clamped his arm. One by one, all eyes became riveted on us as Skywalker stood, stepped in close, his mouth set in a twisted snarl. I did not back down. Admiration for my courage, and determination flitted through his eyes with the speed of a darting minnow. Then he turned away, strode off into the darkness.

That night was as black as pitch. The stars were nothing more than uncountable pinpoints of light and the moon was only about a third full. Skywalker was a dim figure I doggedly followed and although I stepped carefully, each and every contact made between the soles of my feet and solid ground came as a jolting surprise to the rest of my body. But none of that was anywhere as near as jarring as when Skywalker whirled around and yelled in my face.

"Why did you vote against me about coming to Medicine Lodge?"

I had to clear my throat before lamely answering, "I—I had my reason."

"Yes," he fumed, "you most certainly did. And your reason is called Hawwy."

"That's not true!" I shouted. "I didn't even know he would be here."

"That's a lie."

"It is not."

"Yes, it is," he insisted, stepping nearer. The outline of his darkened face came so close that I felt my eyes beginning to cross. "White Bear knew Hawwy would be here, and whatever White Bear knows, you eventually know because White Bear doesn't know how to keep a secret."

"He kept this one," I cried. "I didn't know anything about it until I saw Hawwy for myself."

He was breathing hard, his chest expanding and retracting rapidly. "Maybe that is the truth," he countered, "but I couldn't help but notice that since our first day here you've remained constantly in his company."

Anger ripping through me like fire, I pushed my face close to his. "If you'll recall, White Bear ordered me to stay close to the Blue Jackets. And another reason I stayed close is because Hawwy owns doctoring tools I have been working very hard to convince him to sell to me."

Skywalker retreated a pace, his silhouetted head canted to the side as he considered. I could not see his eyes but I keenly felt his concentrated gaze. The racket made by the chirping insects seemed to increase, their otherwise-cheery clatter beginning to throb against my ears. Working to take some portion of control over my thudding heartbeat, I reminded myself exactly how to breathe—in, out, in, out. Soon I was so fixated with this task that the sound of his low, almost husky voice gave me a start and my heart was charging again.

"And that's the full truth?"

"Can't you hear my mind?"

"No. With this headache I can barely hear myself think."

That statement allowed my brain full rein—a freedom I rarely enjoyed with Skywalker for, when we were together, I consciously loaded my mind with trivialities I wouldn't object to his knowing. Realizing this was one of my infrequent moments of mental freedom, a flurry of thoughts were unleashed—the more dominant . . . jealousy.

Friendships during the days of my early manhood were much more important than they seem to be now. Back then, when each day brought with it a new kind of peril, friends guarded your back, watched out for you, trusted you to do the same for them. Therefore any type of disagreement between friends was a serious matter, but jealousy was the most serious matter of all.

All forms of jealousy have always been frowned on by my people because we know envy to be destructive. More crimes have been committed in the name of jealousy than for any other emotion. Which is why we have tried very hard to stamp it out, most especially the Black Leggings Society, who treat jealousy with such contempt that any warrior accused of it faces a harsh judgment. Of course, jealousy has always been the root cause of the ongoing friction between White Bear and Kicking Bird, even though they try never to allow their squabbles to degenerate to a personal level for it is not considered envious for one chief to call into question another's abilities as a leader. Far from it. Chiefs correcting fellow chiefs is considered prudent, for the lives of young men depended on trustworthy leaders. The only two in the entire Nation who were fooled by their petty bickering were the two most deeply involved— namely, White Bear and Kicking Bird. That these two superior men could fall victim to envy was a lesson for us ordinary folk, reminding us how easily this ugly nature could creep into our hearts and cause trouble.

Just as it was doing now.

Skywalker was angry with me because he was deeply jealous of my friendship with Hawwy. Of course, I couldn't say this to his face.

To spare his dignity and to salvage our shaky friendship, I said, "I apologize. I should have come to you and asked your advice on the matter of Haw-we-sun. That I didn't can be blamed on my anxiousness to please White Bear, and then finally, on my own greed."

He turned, folded his arms across his chest, and stood in profile while he pondered. In a less-strained voice he asked, "What kind of tools does he have that would make you risk so much?"

Instantly I cried, "The most marvelous doctoring tools I've ever seen. He keeps them in black bags. He has four such bags. I was hoping he wouldn't notice if one of the bags got lost. But that's not all. Earlier, when we were burying the dead man, he had a digging tool that folds up. Crying Wind would love that tool. If nothing else, I intend to get that for her."

Skywalker turned his face toward me. "Do you know where he keeps this folding tool?"

"Yes. He put it on the dead man's grave."

"What?" he shouted. "You mean he just threw it away as an offering to a dead man who isn't even his relative?"

"He doesn't think of it like that. He said that the tool is now a marker, that when other whites see it, they will stop to say prayers for the dead man."

Skywalker became angry all over again, for I had said exactly the wrong thing, forgetting entirely that he had taken a blood oath that no more whites would be allowed to enter any territory belonging to us or to our allied Nations. Hawwy's belief that other whites would come, and would do so without fear or regard of the rightful inhabitants, touched a raw nerve. Skywalker's next statement was delivered in a tight voice.

"Take me to the grave."

He first made medicine over the burial site, chanting in a low voice, this form of medicine meant to keep Buug-lah's spirit wherever white spirits went, and to sanctify the ground containing Buug-lah's remains, making the top part fit again for living beings. That done, he tore apart the marker shovels, handing one to me, keeping the other for himself. It took us awhile to figure out how to fold them down, but once we did, they were remarkably easy to conceal as we strode side by side back toward the camp, stopping briefly at our saddles to hide them away. Then, in a display of total innocence, we went to our beds.

But for the sounds of snoring, the camp was quiet. Only Hears The Wolf had remained awake, and as we approached he asked in a whisper, "Are you two all right?"

"Yes," Skywalker answered. "Two old friends had a small disagreement. The disagreement has been settled."

Satisfied, Hears The Wolf flopped down on his bed, snoring almost the instant his head came to rest. Snuggling under my blanket, feeling vastly relieved, every bone in my body felt as if it was melting. My last thought while yawning was, Now all I have to do is save White Bear.

What a conceit!

In the early-morning light—the sky deep shades of pink with a broad stripe of blue just above the horizon—my being the one to save White Bear from anything, struck me as the absurdity it was. Rising from my bed, shaking out the blankets, I very firmly reminded myself that I was simply the tagalong behind Hears The Wolf, Skywalker, and The Cheyenne Robber. That if we could get White Bear out of this current trouble, it would be they, and rightly so, who would receive the credit. But because I loved White Bear, it needn't be said that I wouldn't do whatever I could to clear him of the charge of Buug-lah's brutal death. A death, that I could tell by the slewing of the Blue Jackets' eyes, they were now anxious to report.

There was a problem with that. Hears The Wolf still had possession of their guns and it was still unclear if they were free men or prisoners. This thorny issue changed the mood of the camp. As we all ate our morning meal, gone were

96

the high spirits and camaraderie of the night before. The Blue Jackets, even Hawwy, were wary, on their guard, and sitting clumped together. Billy found himself sitting in the middle, the one link between soldiers and Indians.

Having been born both white and red, Billy was a man torn in half. During the tender years of his life, he had been raised white, but as he grew older and his mother could no longer hide the fact that her son carried Indian blood, she gave him away to an orphan home. He ran away from that place, eventually coming to work for the army. As a scout he learned as much as he could about Kiowas, beginning with the language. Yet fearing he would be rejected again, he ventured no closer than that to his real father's people. During the first days when we were at Medicine Lodge, he continued to believe that because of his white blood, his father's world was closed to him. Troubled on account of this, he counseled privately with Skywalker, their conversations unknown to me until some time later.

But even in the white world, Billy was alone except for his friendship with Hawwy, the only man in that world he had ever known to accept him without question. But that was Hawwy. The man had an immediate and absorbing interest in anyone who crossed his path. In the Territory this was more of a fault than a virtue, and Billy knew right away that his most important responsibility would be to protect Hawwy from himself. He was doing that now, keeping Hawwy firmly in place until he could figure out what was what with The Cheyenne Robber.

Of all of us, The Cheyenne Robber was physically the most formidable. From the outset, the Blue Jackets had been leery of him. Today they had ample reason, for he was in a terrible mood. Being something of a slow thinker, he hated dilemmas, and that morning had presented him with a big one. He really didn't like killing people he'd had fun with, and after the previous night's good time, although regret would not be enough to deter him, he was edgy about maybe having to kill his new friend. Scowling at Little Jonas, his teeth tore at the half-cooked portion of the meat and he glumly chewed, tasting only his own bitterness because of the sorry situation. He was in the midst of another huge bite when Skywalker leaned in, their shoulders touching. Skywalker whispered for a while and then The Cheyenne Robber grunted an agreement.

When they stood, Hears The Wolf and I stood too, the four of us going off to speak privately. We had only gone a pace or two when Skywalker signaled for us to stop. Looking back over our shoulders, The Cheyenne Robber bellowed for Billy. William was already as nervous as a treed bobcat, his eyes so large they looked to be as big as his fists. He was so startled by The Cheyenne Robber's tone that he dropped his portion of cooked meat into the dirt between his crossed legs. As Billy scrambled to his feet, Hawwy moved to stand too. Very quickly Billy placed a hand on Hawwy's shoulder, shoving him back down and muttering to him. Then Billy ran to catch up with us, and without discussion the five of us moved a little farther away.

As Skywalker talked, Hears The Wolf stood to the side, the barrel of his new rifle resting on his shoulder while he watched the Blue Jackets. They in turn watched him, knowing that if any one of them tried to make a dash for the cache of guns, Hears The Wolf would not hesitate to shoot. In this highly charged situation, I concentrated just as hard as I could on everything Skywalker had to say.

"More soldiers will be coming soon."

"Today?" The Cheyenne Robber asked.

"No," Skywalker answered with a shake of his head. "Not today."

"You're certain?"

"Yes." Skywalker lifted his chin in the direction of the soldiers by the fire. "They know it too. At least, that little nervous one does," he said, meaning Lieutenant Danny. "He made this thought in an image. I saw many soldiers riding fast."

"Maybe this is only what he hopes," The Cheyenne Robber offered.

"Maybe," Skywalker conceded. "Then again, maybe it's something he was told would happen after a certain amount of time had passed. The other images in his mind made no sense to me, so I can't be sure."

"What were the other images?" I asked.

Skywalker twisted his mouth to the side as he thought. "One was the very white face of a young woman. She has large front teeth that stick out when she smiles. Then there was a gray ghost like a man. A man still alive to him. They talk."

"How?" Hears The Wolf blurted.

Skywalker pursed his lips. "On flat smooth material treaty makers make marks on."

"Pay-paa [paper]?" I yelped.

Skywalker came out of his near daze, his eyes blinking rapidly. "Yes. That's it. Pay-paa. The dead one is alive on markings on the pay-paa. That young chief over there is afraid."

"I think I'd better find out about that," I said.

"Yes," he agreed. "And there is something else. Something about Little Jonas."

The Cheyenne Robber didn't care to hear that. If there was anything bad about Little Jonas, The Cheyenne Robber didn't want to know. He didn't mind about any of the others, especially Sergeant Cullen. For a mean-natured man, Cullen had given up too easily. Rule of thumb: Never trust an enemy warrior who gives up too easily. All this means is that he's tricky. That he has a plan on how to get even. We were all watchful of Cullen and we despised him because of the way he'd kicked his horse for no reason. With every fiber of my being I longed for Skywalker to discern in Sergeant Cullen the guilt for anything. Irritatingly, he kept coming back to Little Jonas.

"Not understanding their language, I don't know what his secret is. I only know he has one, and it's big. Almost as big as him."

Skywalker began giving instructions to Hears The Wolf and The Cheyenne Robber. "I want you two to go out and look for any signs the storm failed to wash away. Make sure you come back before dark. This is our last night in this place."

"Good," The Cheyenne Robber grunted. "I need a bath and the clothes I'm wearing smell so bad I can't get away from myself."

Hears The Wolf cracked a laugh. "I can't get away from you, either."

Puckering his lips, flinging himself bodily at his father-in-law, The Cheyenne Robber hollered, "Kiss me!"

Laughing harder, Hears The Wolf fought off the mock attack. Glancing back over my shoulder I saw the effect the high-spirited play was having on the soldiers. Tugging the sleeve of Skywalker's shirt, he looked back and noticed too.

SEVEN

The recent rainstorm had been so powerful that none of us truly believed that Hears The Wolf or The Cheyenne Robber would find any lingering signs, but Skywalker felt it was necessary that they try. Before the storm hit, the hoofprints leading out of the murder site indicated continued travel toward the northwest. As I told you before, Fort Larned lay in that direction and beyond that, the Pawnee.

Before our little council disbanded, The Cheyenne Robber let it be known that he was more than satisfied with blaming the Pawnee.

"It only makes sense," he'd said.

He turned his handsome face to each of us, a brisk wind throwing back his long hair, sending it sailing away from broad shoulders. When none of us offered a response, his tone became loud and insistent.

"The Pawnee don't like so many enemy nations this close to their villages. And they take great pride in their friendship with the A-me-cans [Americans]. Pawnees don't want the A-me-cans becoming friendly with us, their enemies."

He looked around again. Not one of us offered a response. I suppose it was because none of us wanted to believe that a man as physically impressive as The Cheyenne Robber could be so dense. But he was, and that has always struck me as a terrible crime against nature, for him to be so beautiful, so wondrously perfect—until he opened his mouth.

"Don't you see?" he cried, becoming exasperated. "Enemy nations making treaties with the Blue Jackets threatened the Pawnee. So they sent spies to Medicine Lodge and those spies mingled among us, looking for a way to make trouble. They caused this trouble by culling out a soldier, then they killed him and left the body to be found."

Reluctant as I was to point out the one or two glaring flaws in this little theory, nevertheless I forced myself to speak up.

"To begin with," I said, "we all know that the Pawnee wear their hair in a highly distinctive style, shaved to skin all over the skull except for a braided topknot. How is it possible for a man looking like that to mingle among hundreds of long-haired warriors?"

Baffled, The Cheyenne Robber quickly looked to his relatives. Skywalker's lips twitched, humor lighting up his eyes. Fighting the need to laugh, Hears The Wolf's expression became so pained that he turned his head away. Turning next to Billy didn't do The Cheyenne Robber any good either, for the frontiersman was intently studying something on the ground. Fuming, The Cheyenne Robber turned on me.

"You know," he said tightly, "sometimes I almost hate you."

Still trying to validate his theory, he cried, "All right. The Pawnees hid themselves until they saw a chance to make trouble." He looked at me and sneered. "Only a real warrior would know this, but that's exactly what Pawnees do." He folded his arms and jutted his strong chin skyward.

Heavily marred though his theory was, it was still a comfort that one of us actually had one. I know I certainly didn't. All I knew of for certain was that Buug-lah had been killed by a single ax wound that cleaved his skull. He had not been scalped but that didn't necessarily prove Indians weren't responsible. Contrary to popular notion, even the army knew during this time that not all Indians took scalps. From what I knew about the life cycle of maggots, I believed that when we found the dead man, he had been dead for about six days. And finally, the valuable horse he'd ridden had been killed by a single shot to the temple. The bullet was lead and its mashed remains rested inside the carry pouch that was tied to my breech-belt.

Now, to me, that dead horse proved beyond any shadow of doubt that no Indian had anything to do with the murder, because no Indian would kill such a valuable animal. Yet, while I knew this to be true, this fact would not be enough to convince the generals, who were more than content to blame White Bear. His turning up in their camp with that stupid bugle was harder proof than anything I might offer on the emotional involvement Indians have with horses. Besides, let us not forget that on account of Major Elliot, the army would have eventually blamed White Bear anyway. I knew this was true because days before he'd ever showed up with that bugle, the generals were already labeling White Bear a troublemaker. They hadn't been able to more than grumble because he was a powerful war chief and he'd committed no crime. But now that Buug-lah had been found so undeniably dead, those generals would happily rush to charge him with murder.

Under ordinary circumstances, neither White Bear nor Lone Wolf would particularly care what the army charged against them. What made this an extraordinary circumstance was the fact that White Bear would stand accused of a violent act when every chief of the Confederacy of Nations had given his solemn word that no violence would be tolerated, and if by some remote chance violence did occur, those same chiefs had guaranteed the army the right to punish any and all offenders.

Now, there was the rub. At the time this promise was made, the only violence anyone considered was perhaps the odd fight resulting from a minor disagreement. Not one chief had considered the remote possibility of a murder or that the army would employ their most favorite means of punishment by hanging. You have no idea how repugnant this form of death is for Indians. Lone Wolf would most certainly go to war before ever handing over one of his own to be hung. And then he would strip White Bear of everything—rank, prestige, Onde privilege—for the crime of pushing him into a war he hadn't been ready to fight. For a man like White Bear, being reduced to nothing and with no hope of future reprieve, would be far worse than being hanged. All of this meant that we needed something to take back to the generals. Something they would not be able to disregard when we claimed White Bear to be innocent. If we could not find that something . . .

In those moments, as we watched Hears The Wolf and The Cheyenne Robber ride out, I wondered if Billy truly sensed the gravity of the situation. His expression, partially hidden by the shade of his broad-brimmed black hat, was totally blank. He also wore a long gray coat, brown cloth trousers, knee-high black boots, and a rust-colored shirt. Billy looked like a white man, but as he fell into step between myself and Skywalker, he carried himself like an Indian.

He never knew the name of his Kiowa father. None of us did. Billy had been born in Texas. As Texas was a favorite raiding ground, his father could have been anyone. It never fails to break my heart when I ponder the others; children with Kiowa blood doomed from birth to walk the knifeblade-thin road drawn between two very different worlds. Billy had come halfway back to us but still he teetered on the verge of the final decision of exactly who he would be. I wanted to pray for him. Filled with anguish, believing our time of friendship was running out, I wanted to pray for Hawwy, even pray for myself.

I didn't know how.

The Blue Jackets had been talking among themselves. Whatever they had discussed left Lieutenant Danny looking not at all well. William sat close to him, keeping one dark eye on us as we approached while talking in soft tones to the lieutenant sitting huddled behind, knees drawn up to his chest, breathing with effort, almost panting through a partially opened mouth. I noticed that his lower lip looked tender, bleeding lightly in the places his teeth had worried chapped tissue. He tensed as we approached, his pale eyes beginning to glisten.

As we lowered ourselves to sit before the soldiers, I forced myself to look away from Lieutenant Danny, looking instead at William. He sat with his legs crossed, arms hugging his midsection as he slowly rocked himself. William looked angry, his mouth tight, expression fixed. Feeling my stare, he looked up at me. Anger faded as his full lips began to quiver with a hopeful smile. When I couldn't bring myself to return the attempt, he hugged himself harder, lowered his head, and went back to rocking.

Little Jonas sat with his spine slightly curled, long legs splayed out. Muscular forearms resting on beefy thighs, his menacing eyes narrowed to slits. I quickly began to wonder what The Cheyenne Robber had done with that strong rope. With dismay I realized that when last seen, it had been hanging from The Cheyenne Robber's saddle. Mentally I cursed him for having gone off, taking our only means of restraining Little Jonas. The big black man growled to Billy.

"Where is The Cheyenne Robber going?"

"He's looking for anything that might help all of us."

"And if he can't find anything?"

Billy's expression became tight.

Little Jonas considered at length, then said, "You tell The Cheyenne Robber that I had a good time. That I didn't know Indians could be fun people. And make sure you tell him that I understand. That I don't hold anything against him because we're both soldiers and this is what soldiers have to do. Tell him I have a good mirror in my pack. He can have it. But the mirror is only for looking at his beautiful self, not for sending attack signals."

Billy and Little Jonas emitted sad little chuckles.

Smoking a cigar, Sergeant Hicks looked off in the direction The Cheyenne Robber and Hears The Wolf had disappeared. Then his eyes slowly slid toward the hobbled and grazing horses. Ever so slightly, he turned his head, his eyes coming to rest on the bundle containing every one of their rifles and pistols. That's when I knew that Hicks was the kind of man who bided his time. I could almost hear him thinking that there were only the two of us now—three, if one counted Billy—while there were six of them. He blew out a plume of smoke as his gaze became locked on the bundled guns beside Skywalker.

Perceptive as ever, Skywalker calmly drew out one of the pistols and just as calmly aimed it at Hicks's heart, cocking back the hammer. Hicks's answer to this was a slow smile, another puff on the cigar, and a nod.

Beside him, Cullen reached inside his jacket, removing a small cloth package. From this package he withdrew a clammy-appearing clump of black tobacco. Hatred for us glittered in his eyes as he bit off some of the tobacco. He chewed slowly as he retied the cloth, replaced it inside his jacket. Then he spit a brown stream to the side, wiped the corner of his mouth with the back of his hand.

I looked at Skywalker and said, "With all my heart I wish we could find something that proved that man guilty."

"We all do," Skywalker said.

Hawwy coughed to pull our attention toward him, then slowly, his hands half raised, he approached the fire, nudged the empty coffeepot with his booted foot. "Choi [coffee]," he said, his question meant to ask if we could make more. For a long time all Skywalker and I could do was stare up at him with open mouths. Didn't he understand just how serious the situation was? Hears The Wolf had already decided that if he and The Cheyenne Robber didn't find anything, not one trace of usable evidence, that we would then have to talk among ourselves about our choices. It would not be a long talk, for it seemed to us that we only had the one choice, and that was to run back to Lone Wolf with the news that while we were very sorry, we'd had no choice but to kill all the Blue Jackets, which now put us at war with the army.

We felt catastrophic failure hovering over the camp that was just a small, packed-down grass circle, a little dot of nothing in the middle of that great sea of prairie. Our failure was as dark as the clouds quickly filling up the sky, crowding out any hint of blue. The air was turning fresh, chilly gusts bowing the surround of grass, rattling seed pods and sending tiny seeds to fly on the wind. I looked at the sky, watching the churning clouds as I waited for Skywalker to say something, say anything. Because I couldn't. I felt ill, my stomach twisting, my throat so tight I could barely breathe.

Skywalker nudged me and I turned brimming eyes in his direction. In a tone so soft it was almost a whisper he said, "It would be a good thing for you and Hawwy to have . . . time, together." He looked quickly away. "And coffee would be nice."

Wordlessly I rose, went to where Hawwy was, and picked up the empty pot.

The two of us didn't talk much as we puttered around, looking for likely fuel to make a fire. I dearly wished Hawwy would chatter in that way of his, but he didn't. I couldn't say anything either, for my heart was busy breaking. Even though he was a Blue Jacket, Hawwy was my friend. I really didn't think I would be able to stand around while he was killed. I knew Billy wouldn't be able to do it either, which meant Billy would probably die too. At last I knew how to pray, and I prayed nonstop that The Cheyenne Robber and Hears The Wolf would find something.

I was still fervently praying as Hawwy and I built up the fire, then used the last of the water from the canteens to fill up the coffeepot. I prayed harder as I measured out coffee grounds and then put the pot on to boil. It was in the middle of this last prayer that Skywalker's voice reached me.

"I am sorry for the things you're feeling."

I looked up at him, the anguish inside me so overwhelming that I was becoming physically ill. "I lied to you," I rasped. "I lied when I said to you that he isn't my friend."

"I know."

I looked away, tears I didn't want him to see, burning my eyes.

"I have decided something very important," he said. "I have decided that it no longer matters to me who you choose to be your friend, for you are my brother. Brothers are closer than friends."

Somehow a laugh spilled out of me. "You would raise me up to be an Onde?"

"No. You've raised up yourself."

I looked at him in disbelief.

111

"It's true," he whispered.

Before I could make any reply to this considerable honor, Hears The Wolf and The Cheyenne Robber came flying in at a gallop.

EIGHT

"Look what we found!" The Cheyenne Robber cried. He threw something to the ground before leaping down from his horse.

Skywalker and I hurried to the spot, to find an army saddle lying at our feet. Skywalker knelt down, his hands exploring the leather saddle which, after being abandoned to the elements, was in a sorry state. There was a leather bag tied to the saddle. Hears The Wolf dismounted hurriedly and stood with his hands on his hips, staring down at the saddle while The Cheyenne Robber went right on talking in a loud, excited tone. Skywalker listened as he worked loose the knot keeping the bag's flap closed.

The Cheyenne Robber said, "The only thing out there are the prints we made. The rain cleared away everything, even rabbit spoor. We were coming back here when I said—"

"No, you didn't," Hears The Wolf yelped. "I said it."

The Cheyenne Robber turned an angry face toward his father-in-law. "Does it really matter who said it?"

"Yes, it does. Especially if you're going to make yourself the hero of this story. And for another thing—"

"Will you two stop it!" I shouted. They both looked at me, their expressions shocked that I had dared to correct them. "It isn't important who said what," I said more evenly. "Just tell us what happened."

They both glanced at Skywalker, expecting him to address my impertinence. Skywalker merely grinned and concentrated on the saddlebag's knot.

Confused, his head turning on his neck as he looked from his brother to a wide-eyed Hears The Wolf, The Cheyenne Robber spoke. "We decided it would be a good idea to turn south, toward the army camp, making our way back here by that means. It was then that I"—he thudded his chest with his fingers, his eyes daring Hears The Wolf to correct him—"spotted bent brushwood. And it was I who thought this might be significant." Folding his arms over his swelling chest, he said smugly, "It was. Whoever threw this saddle away tried to hide it, but the saddle's weight made that patch of scrub bend wrong. That's why I saw it."

Now that I'd heard the report, I was more interested in what had been found. I crouched down beside Skywalker as he finally loosed that hard knot.

"What's in there?"

Tugging at the contents of the bag, he said, "It feels like clothing."

Pulling it out, we saw a soldier's uniform, pants and jacket. The uniform was spattered with dried blood, and stiff in all the places blood had soaked through the wool material. There was one stripe on the jacket's sleeve.

"This is the proof we need," Hears The Wolf crowed. "This proves that soldier killed soldier."

That was most certainly true. Something else equally as important, the nagging worry about what to do with the six Blue Jackets, could be set aside. I was so relived on account of Hawwy and Billy, that for a few seconds I was giddy. Then I glanced at Skywalker, wondering, now that the crisis was past, just how firm the offer of brotherhood would be. Apparently we did not share the same thought for, when we both stood, he turned away from me and called for Billy to bring Hawwy. When they arrived, Skywalker solemnly showed him the jacket.

"I have to have this to show my superiors," Hawwy said.

Skywalker snatched the uniform jacket away. "Not yet." he turned to Billy, speaking rapidly. "Tell Haw-we-sun that while I might trust him, I do not trust anyone else in this place wearing this same type of jacket. This proof of White Bear's innocence will stay with me until we return to the camps. That is my decision." As Billy turned, Skywalker placed a hand on Billy's arm and said meaningfully, "There is no need to tell him anything else."

Dark color came into Billy's cheeks. He spoke crisply to Hawwy, repeated only what Skywalker had said about the uniform. He made no mention of how close all of them had been to death. But Hawwy knew. All I can conclude is that either he was extraordinarily brave, or he had too much faith in my ability to prevent Skywalker from shooting him.

115

I'll never really know for certain. It was the one subject neither of us were anxious to discuss.

Now that we had proof of White Bear's innocence, any interest on the part of Hears The Wolf, The Cheyenne Robber, and Skywalker, as to the identity of Buug-lah's real murderer, fell into a sharp decline. Their only plans for the immediate future was to take in the uniform as proof that White Bear didn't do it, and then allow Lone Wolf the honor of dealing with the generals. All of the Kiowas, even me, were in good moods as we erased the evidence of our camp, saddled up our horses. But there was dissension among the Blue Jackets.

Hawwy was standing off and talking to Billy when an argument took place between Lieutenant Danny and Sergeants Cullen and Hicks. Hawwy didn't notice that part, but he did look up when the two sergeants became physical with the young lieutenant. Hawwy yelled, "Hey!" then took off in a run to the junior officer's aid. The two black soldiers, leading the horses from the grazing field, froze. The Kiowas became very still. Cullen and Hicks were not affected by Hawwy's sudden shout. They were so intent, they reacted not at all. Cullen was livid, his hands on his hips, his upper lip curling back over his teeth, his stare boring into the younger man. Hicks had grabbed on to Lieutenant Danny by the front of his jacket and was still holding him tightly and growling into the younger man's blanching face when Hawwy arrived and made him turn Danny loose.

Hawwy's angry arrival, his yelled threat of "going on report," calmed down the two sergeants. Seeing that Hawwy had the minor situation under control, Skywalker, Hears The Wolf, and The Cheyenne Robber lost interest. Each

116

were leaders of men. For them, it wasn't an unusual thing for a war chief to break up fights occurring among warriors. This was a thing chiefs did. I, on the other hand, was a virtual stranger to the war trail, so of course everything would affect me a tad more profoundly.

While all the others made ready to leave, I watched while Lieutenant Danny earnestly assured Hawwy that the brief disagreement was not important. While he did this, he kept glancing at Hicks and Cullen, who were standing behind Hawwy and sending the lieutenant threatening looks.

Then, too, there was the behavior of William and Little Jonas. They were on the move again, bringing in the soldiers' horses, but while they were doing this, they were hissing at each other like a pair of snakes. Now, their doing that hit me with the force of a jolt. Evidently those two weren't as friendly with each other as I'd supposed. I'd supposed this simply on the basis that they were both black men and both low-ranking soldiers. Well, more the fool, me. I certainly should have known human nature better than that.

But my ignorance can be mildly forgiven. Until the moment I just happened to see William and Little Jonas snarling at each other, they had given absolutely no indication of any animosity existing between them. And here's the really interesting thing. Once they were back in the camp area, they stopped arguing. They were so agreeable with each other that if I hadn't seen them arguing, I would never have guessed their private feelings.

We four Kiowa were so elated about the proof we'd found, that on the way back to Medicine Lodge valley we imagined our triumphant return being greeted by hordes of people, all of them happy to see us and eager to hear what we had to say.

The people did turn out in masses. But not on account of us.

The timing of those thirty wagons filled with gifts, the blatant bribe offerings the government used to lure the Nations to Medicine Lodge, was incredible. For well over a week they had been looked for, and complained about because of their absences, but now—wouldn't you know it?—they'd arrived. I am certain the camp guards spotted the eleven of us the same time they saw those wagons coming in from the east, but they chose to alert the people only to the nearing wagons.

This news immediately revitalized the dull-spirited camps and the great free-for-all race was on. Even before the wearied wagon mules could be unharnessed, the ground on which those wagons stood was swarmed, the dead-still chilly air filled with the cries of hundreds of excited voices. I must say something about the gifts that were sent, for they, more than anything, give enormous insight into the profound confusion of the Eastern white men toward the Plains peoples. Those wagons held not only the promised awls, blankets, and iron cookpots, they also contained things we would look at later and wonder what they were for, shoe-button buttoning hooks being the most perplexing.

The most aggressive in the melee were the women, every one of them squabbling and pushing. Outnumbered soldiers tried to maintain a modicum of order by forming a human barrier between the Indians and the wagons. This pitiful attempt was quickly abandoned as the soldiers quickly saw the wisdom of avoiding being killed in the

118

crush. One soldier lost his hat to a warrior who laughed as he clapped the hat onto his head. Then that warrior was instantly amazed when that same soldier shoved his rifle into the warrior's hands before running off like a scalded hare. The warrior remained baffled a mere second. Then, pleased by the unexpected gift, raised his brand-new rifle to test the sight. Just as the stock touched his shoulder, another warrior put the grab on the rifle. Not surprisingly, a fight broke out between the two and other warriors quickly jumped in, either to back their particular brother or make a separate try for the gun. The fight panicked the few remaining soldiers. They promptly abandoned the field. With them gone, the women became more frenzied.

I spotted my wife just as she came to stand inside one of the wagons. She was happy about this monumental achievement until a Cheyenne woman's hand locked on to her hair and pulled her backward. The last bits I saw of my wife were her legs and feet sailing through the air. But I certainly heard her. Having landed on the far side of the wagon, she let go her fury. It required no leap of the imagination to know that she was now engaged in an all-out brawl with the offending Cheyenne.

I pitied that woman.

Considering the awful days spent (during the time Buug-lah lay above ground) in hot fetid air, defiling us inside and out, being almost done in by a violent rainstorm, then successfully finding the vital evidence that would save White Bear's life, Lone Wolf's prestige, and the peace talks, it came as something of a letdown that we could ride right on through that valley without sparking one bit of interest. But, now that we were on safe ground, Hears The Wolf felt safe in returning to the soldiers their rifles and sidearms.

Leaning forward on his horse, handing Hawwy the saddlebag containing the bloodied uniform, Skywalker said, "We are finished now, you and I."

Hawwy understood the basics of this statement, but I knew Skywalker's true intent. He was telling Hawwy that their truce was over. That it didn't matter that he was about to become a relative by marriage or that he was a friend of mine. As far as Skywalker was concerned, Hawwy would always be the enemy. Evidently, The Cheyenne Robber and Hears The Wolf felt the same way, for when Skywalker rode off, they quickly followed. Feeling ill at ease with their rudeness, I extended my hand. Hawwy gratefully accepted it.

"I am tired, I am filthy," I said, barely loud enough to be heard over the raucous cries of the wagon-looters. "I will come to your camp later on."

Hawwy said he would always be pleased to see me. Turning my horse for home, I fled for the comforts of my lodge.

The creek water was very cold and I hate that, but I took a good long bath, scrubbing myself with vigor. Back inside my home I built up the fire and sat before it, half-frozen and hungry. Despite these afflictions, it was good to be home. I studied each and every corner of my lodge, loving each and every commonplace item.

My wife was a tidy person but she was also a slave to habit. No matter how many times we moved, each and every time she restored our lodge, she placed everything exactly as it had been before. Drying herbs always hung over the kitchen area, the same blanket was used to make the privacy wall that divided our sleeping area from our son's. A rope was always strung between the poles high over the fire for drying clothing, because even on sunny days, it might rain and Crying Wind would have to bring our wet laundry inside. She also insisted on rugs to cover the whole of the interior, and leather boxes, containing everything from cooking utensils to extra sets of clothing, to be placed in the exact same areas, where they acted as small tables for the gourd lamps. No matter where we traveled or how much the scenery changed outside the door, inside our home nothing changed. The effect was a sense of permanence, as if our home hadn't moved an inch. Crying Wind's deliberate routine, a thing at the beginning of our marriage I considered amusing, then—later on—boring, was actually neither of those things. What she did was create a continuing sense of home, a place both my son and I instantly recognized the moment we came through the door.

Now, I thought, if she would just come home and cook me something to eat, life would be beyond bliss. But she didn't. I endured a very long wait, with hunger pangs growing acute.

When I couldn't stand the pangs a moment more, I rummaged through one of her carefully packed cases, found strips of dried meat, and tore into them. Just as I was finishing the last piece she finally turned up, with a blackened right eye, a huge smile on her face, and her arms loaded.

"There you are!" she cried happily. She passed me by and busied around, storing away her newly gained items. "I thought you'd be with the council. Everyone else is there." She rounded on me, showing me a bright blue blanket. "Isn't this beautiful? You wouldn't believe what I went

through to have it. Those greedy women acted like wolves."
She began to refold the blanket. "Not that the men behaved
any better. You would have thought the soldiers would have
done a better job at giving out the gifts. We had to do everything ourselves." Shaking her head, she tisked, "Typical."

She put the new blue blanket on our bed, then came at
me with three little metal boxes. Sitting before me she gin-
gerly pried open one of the boxes. Holding it out to me, her
eyes, even the blackened one, shone with pride. "Look at
these tiny, tiny beads."

I did. They were the glass beads gradually replacing the
carefully cut and dyed porcupine quills that were sewn onto
shoes and clothing for decoration. Porcupine quills are relatively free. All one need do is kill a porcupine, then, as
carefully as possible, skin it. Glass beads, on the other hand,
were very expensive. Somehow Crying Wind now had hundreds of them, and in every color imaginable.

"How did you get these?" I gasped.

"By grabbing," she sniffed. "I'm telling you, it was
madness out there. If I had simply waited to be given something, I would have come home with empty hands."

Carefully she closed the lid and set the box aside. Opening another, she showed off finely made metal needles,
items even more expensive than the beads. Seeing that I
was properly impressed, she moved on to the next box.

"This is for you," she said proudly.

Realizing she had thought of me during the rough-and-
tumble activity, I humbly accepted the box, carefully pried
open the lid. Then I just stared at the contents. "What is
it?"

Impatient with my ignorance, she took the thing out,

unfolding the thin metal strips attached to either side of the pieces of blue glass that were set inside wire frames. To my utter amazement, she stuck the thing on her face, the two pieces of blue glass covering her eyes. I could only stare at her in open-mouthed wonder.

Talking to me while those pieces of glass covered her eyes, she said, "Haw-we-sun and The Cheyenne Robber got into a fight. Again. Sometimes I wonder how those two will ever stand being related." She sighed. "Anyway, the fight was near one of the wagons and when Skywalker intervened—"

"Skywalker?"

Her forehead crinkled. I assumed she was sending me a critical look. It was a bit difficult to tell. Her eyes weren't visible behind those darkened pieces of glass. Crying Wind hated being interrupted. She made no effort to speak another word until she was certain that I would remain respectfully silent. It was very quiet in that lodge for a good amount of time. Finally she continued.

"When Skywalker intervened and demanded they shake hands, he also said that they should exchange gifts. The Cheyenne Robber offered Hawwy a new blanket and Hawwy gave The Cheyenne Robber these things he calls 'Tepne-cals' [spectacles]. Well, after The Cheyenne Robber put them on, the other men wanted Tep-ne-cals too. There were many more boxes of them in that wagon, so Hawwy gave them out. Of course he had to find an extra gift for The Cheyenne Robber, because it isn't proper for a man to give everybody the same gift he just gave the man who will be his brother-in-law. When Hawwy saw me, he made certain I was given a box of Tep-ne-cals to give to you. He said for you to wear them on sunny days, that they would save your eyes." She took them off and looked down at them. "I believe that's true. Everything becomes very dark when looking through these pieces of glass."

She handed them over to me and I put them on. Having the lodge door closed, the only light that of a moderate fire and what little there was from the sun slanting down through the smokehole, the interior of our home was a bit murky. Looking for the first time in my life through sunglasses, everything except for the muted flames in the fire vanished.

"Where did you go?" I laughed.

A shadowy form of my wife leaned to the side, placing herself in front of the firelight. Waving her hand she giggled, "Here I am! Can you see me now?"

I took the glasses off, staring at them in silent wonder. In a husky voice, I said, "This is a magical gift." Then I remembered another magical thing.

The shovel.

Crying Wind was so delighted that I had to tackle her in order to stop her from running out to show it off.

"You can't!" I shouted. "Not now. Not until we're out of this valley."

"Why?"

"Because I stole it."

She tilted her head, her eyes narrowing. I hastened to explain.

She wasn't pleased.

"You mean you gave me something you stole off a dead white man?" she railed.

"No! It was only a marker. Besides, Skywalker blessed

it while he was stealing the other one for his wife."

Crying Wind frowned, threw the shovel at me. I managed to catch it just before it made painful contact with my face. Her fists stuck to her hips, her voice a growl, she said, "I don't care how much he blessed that thing. It was taken off a grave and I won't have it in my home. You just take it right outside and use it to dig a hole and bury it deep. And don't you ever, ever give me another present you stole from a dead white man. Which means you still owe me a present, because I gave you the Tep-ne-cals."

Actually, Hawwy had given me the sunglasses, but Crying Wind was in too dangerous a mood to bring this rather fine point to her attention. While I dug, I prayed mightily that something of worth had been left in one of those wagons. Remembering the mad scrambling scene, mine was a dim hope, but it was all a thoroughly contrite husband had. After burying the shovel, I wandered out to the grazing field to find my horse.

The grasses were being steadily cropped down by the herds. There was still good growth left, but in a few days the pastures would be depleted and the Nations would be impatient to move on. Which made me glad that White Bear's brush with military justice was over. Now the chiefs could get on with the matter that had brought them here and we could leave. No one was more glad than I that our time at Medicine Lodge was ebbing away.

Having just been released for rest in the pasture, my favorite horse wasn't happy to see me again. It shied from my touch, but, unable to run away because of the hobbles, all it could do was snort and bob its head. Taking pity on it, knowing that it had had enough, I chose instead my

125

second-favorite, a buckskin I'd won in a gambling game. It was a good horse but not as good as my dark-red horse. Anyway, once I was mounted, I took myself off to find my wife a better present.

Riding to where the wagons were, I saw with a heavy heart that they were empty. Taking a deep breath, I wondered if it would be possible to steal another shovel. Crying Wind had actually loved the thing. If I hadn't been so truthful about how I'd come to have it, she would still be loving it. An idea dawned. If I could manage to get another one, hopefully she wouldn't make too much of a fuss about having to hide it until we were safely away—but only as long as I was able to swear on my life that I hadn't stolen it from yet another dead man.

Feeling infinitely better, I set off to visit Hawwy. My intent was to nose around for another shovel and thank him for the sunglasses. I must say that I was thoroughly enjoying them on that sunny afternoon, gazing out at a peaceful blue world as my horse trotted along. The world as seen through those glasses was much too beautiful a place to worry about the council meeting Crying Wind had mentioned. It was certainly too peaceful to spare a thought for the evidence Hawwy would present to the generals. Life in that strange blue world was good.

This illusion was blown beyond eternity when a thundering party of warriors came riding up fast behind me. Lone Wolf, riding well out in front, passed me by without a second glance. He was wearing sunglasses too. They sat perched on his beak of a nose. But judging by his severe expression, he wasn't enjoying them all that much.

Just behind him came White Bear and Skywalker, and

behind them, Hears The Wolf, The Cheyenne Robber, and Raven's Wing. Quickly caught up in their number, my buckskin, not appreciating being passed, worked to keep pace. There was nothing I could do to slow that determined horse, and believe me, I tried.

This highborn group did not seem to mind that I was suddenly among their number. White Bear, in an obvious good mood, played a game with me, raising and lowering his pair of sunglasses and laughing loudly.

"You know, you look much better when it's harder to see you!"

I gave up trying to fall back. My horse wouldn't let me and now there was no where to go because Big Tree and Dangerous Eagle were riding too close behind my horse. If I slowed down, there would be an unseemly accident. Still, I did not want to be with this group. For the one thing, I was on a thieving mission and such missions are destined for failure when done as a crowd. For another, I knew Lone Wolf was setting himself on a confrontational course against the army generals. I've never truly cared for confrontation. Oh, on the odd occasion I've forced myself to do it, but in the midst of such showdowns my bowels go watery and my voice has a tendency to crack. Despite the lovely look to the world behind those blue pieces of glass, I knew I was riding straight into a hornets' nest.

Lone Wolf demanded an immediate apology for the army having accused White Bear of stealing from and possibly having done in Buug-lah. It was a reasonable request, but as it was delivered with righteous anger, Lone Wolf merely managed to put the generals' combined back up. The upshot was, they didn't feel obliged to apologize for anything. I thought I knew Lone Wolf when he was angry. I thought wrong. On that day he showed what he was like when he was truly angry.

Feeling the full force of Lone Wolf's wrath, those generals finally had the sense to realize just how dangerous Lone Wolf was. Now, this really put them in a fix, because with the wagons emptied out, they had nothing more to offer in the way of peacemaking bribes. Not that this ploy would have worked. Lone Wolf would not be satisfied with trinkets when what he'd come for was the complete vindication of a Kiowa subchief.

After much conferring, the generals invited all of us to dismount and wait. We did. An hour passed, Lone Wolf growing increasingly impatient. Then, just when he was about to lose his patience altogether, the generals announced that they had the guilty party. When that big black man was brought forward in chains, I'll never know which of us was the more stunned, me or The Cheyenne Robber. To pacify Lone Wolf, the generals were fully prepared to hang Little Jonas right there and then. What stopped them was someone commencing to yell. At first I thought it was me because my rage was boiling over. Even though I was wearing those blue glasses, the only color I could see was red.

But I realized that I was not the one doing the hard yelling. The sound of that voice was well to the front of the assembly whereas I was somewhere in the middle. The shouting was coming from The Cheyenne Robber and, as my vision cleared even more, I saw him fly down off his horse and proceed to wave his arms as he prowled back and forth before the generals.

Little Jonas was the only Blue Jacket I have ever known The Cheyenne Robber to like. While we'd been out on the prairie, they had successfully put aside their glaring differences and realized that they respected each other as men. Now here the generals were expecting The Cheyenne Robber to do nothing while Little Jonas was strung up. Well, his strong sense of a warrior's honor would never allow a worthy man to suffer such an appalling death.

"You are crazy men!" Pointing back to where Little Jonas stood in his chains, he cried, "You have no right to kill him." The Cheyenne Robber raised a fist high over his head, fully intending to strike down the soldier standing close beside Little Jonas.

As that soldier shrank into a cower, Skywalker lunged for his brother, pulling The Cheyenne Robber back, holding on to both of his arms. Without waiting to be asked, Billy joined the fray. With two of them against him now, The Cheyenne Robber commenced to fling himself about like an enraged bull. Skywalker shouted for Hears The Wolf and that one came on the run, only to be knocked down just seconds after entering the skirmish. He jumped back up, hurled himself right back into it, trying to get ahold of the battling The Cheyenne Robber; the latter now yelling even more loudly, mostly about killing all of the worthless, lying bags of coyote offal wearing blue jackets.

Lone Wolf turned away, undone by the spectacle his very own men were creating. I was looking at Lone Wolf, feeling infinitely sorry for the man, when I heard my name being shouted. To my downright mortification, Skywalker was yelling for me. Now, I never told him this, but I tried hard to pretend that I didn't hear him. After he called two

129

more times, Dangerous Eagle shoved me.

"Don't you hear him?" he cried.

"Hear who?"

"Skywalker! He wants you to go help him."

I did not want to do that. I did not want to be involved any further in what I was rapidly coming to consider to be Blue Jacket business.

I am a man whose life was graced with many unwanted things.

NINE

Little Jonas watched all of this high drama with baleful eyes. Clearly he no longer trusted anyone, not even The Cheyenne Robber. He could hardly be blamed. When a man is accused of murder, chained up and threatened with imminent death by hanging, trust is in short supply. Then, too, because of the language difficulty, he had no idea that The Cheyenne Robber's fighting and shouting was his noisy way of coming to Little Jonas's rescue. As he could not understand one word The Cheyenne Robber yelled, and Billy was too busy helping Skywalker in the scuffle to translate, for all Little Jonas knew, his Kiowa friend was demanding his quick death. But before Billy could tell him the truth, comfort him with the knowledge that The Cheyenne Robber was still his friend, we first needed to settle The Cheyenne Robber down. This was not easily done.

I was pretty useless, not knowing where to grab, so I danced about on the fringe as the other three contained The Cheyenne Robber, Skywalker huffing and talking rapidly. As The Cheyenne Robber was becoming more manageable, I heard what Skywalker was saying.

"See? Tay-bodal is here. He can do it. You know he can. He's done it before and for you."

The Cheyenne Robber quit fighting. Cautiously, they began to let him go, and as they gradually released him, The Cheyenne Robber pinned me with his eyes. His eyes were locked with mine as Skywalker patted his brother on the back and said, "Everything is going to be all right for Little Jonas."

We formed a circle and with almost ritual-like reverence, we quietly removed our sunglasses, meticulously placing them inside our carry pouches. It was only good manners that we not be seen using one of their gifts while conspiring against the Blue Jackets. The glasses safely tucked away, Skywalker spoke rapidly to Billy. The entire time this conversation was taking place, my head was twisting on my neck as I searched for a glimpse of Hawwy in the ranks of the officers.

He wasn't there.

Pointing back to Little Jonas, Skywalker said to Billy, "You tell him I know his heart. I know he did not kill that man."

Billy did something I will always think of as uncommonly brave. He talked back to Skywalker. "Yes, and that is what the generals think too. But I know the reason he is accused."

Skywalker's eyes widened, surprised both by Billy's temerity and by what he had to say.

Still in a rage, The Cheyenne Robber stepped in and jutted his face close to Billy's. "Are you going to tell us, or will I have to beat you up?"

Billy chose to speak. "The jacket that was found belongs to Little Jonas. The generals were still discussing this when Lone Wolf came in. Because of Lone Wolf, they decided to go ahead and blame Little Jonas even though they are still convinced that their man was killed by Indians—mainly, White Bear. The thing that will happen now is that they hang one of their own soldiers, but this is what they will say to anyone who listens. That they did what they had to do to hold the peace at Medicine Lodge. That the Kiowa chief Lone Wolf cannot control his subchiefs. That White Bear does whatever he wants. That he is a liar and a murderer."

All the steam went right out of Skywalker.

Unable to control my tongue a second longer, I shouted, "Where is Hawwy? Why isn't he here? How could he allow anyone to be accused without first talking with us? This is not the way he promised it would be." Folding my arms across my chest, I concluded, "If anyone is weak, it is not Lone Wolf, it is Haw-we-sun."

Now, Billy could take a lot of things, but criticism of Hawwy not being one of those things, he came after me with the speed of a striking snake.

"Hawwy did exactly what he was supposed to do. He turned over that uniform just as he said he would. It is not his fault that others have taken charge. You keep forgetting Hawwy is only a little chief. This is the army, not the Kiowa Nation. In the army, a little chief can do nothing once the leader chiefs have taken control. The one making the decisions now is General Gettis. It's on account of him that Little Jonas was arrested."

"Why does Little Jonas look beaten?" The Cheyenne Robber demanded.

"The soldiers had a hard time getting the chains on him. He was beaten to make him hold still."

"Did Hawwy try to stop them?" Skywalker asked softly.

I looked at him askance as Billy answered the question.

"No. The soldiers were acting on orders from General Gettis. There was nothing Hawwy could do." Billy turned, glared directly at me. "He took to his tent. Which is where he is now. He isn't hiding. He's stayed away because he is sick at heart that Little Jonas will give up his life for nothing, because he heard General Gettis say he will always believe White Bear killed their soldier simply to have that shiny horn. He believes the uniform that was found proves nothing."

Actually, I was beginning to feel a trifle ill myself. It would seem that I was no better than the general, who was in such a hurry to close a nettlesome situation, that any victim for the hangman's rope would do. In almost the same type of rush, I had been ready to believe something bad of Hawwy, a man I knew to be kind and gentle. No longer able to look Billy in the eye, I turned my ashamed face away. It was then I noticed the growing impatience among the Blue Jacket generals and Lone Wolf's delegation of chiefs. Clearly, if there was going to be a hanging, they all would prefer we simply get on with it.

"This cannot be allowed to happen," Skywalker said firmly. "The death of an innocent will not restore honor to anyone, most especially White Bear."

He began to confer with Hears The Wolf and The Cheyenne Robber; all of them went into a huddle, turning their
backs on me and Billy. Pushed to the outside of this conference, my attention drifted and I came to notice a crowd
of young men, all of them wearing brown suits and funny
round hats. In the forefront stood a pleasant-looking young
man of modest height, dark complexion, curly hair, and
generous moustache. All of these young men were writing
furiously on small pay-paas, but this one wrote that much
faster.

Suddenly realizing that everyone was walking off without me, I jumped to keep up with the small delegation making its way toward Lone Wolf. Skywalker did all the talking,
carefully explaining what he knew—that the hanging of the
Buffalo Soldier did not free White Bear of supposed guilt
and that Lone Wolf would be no better off than he was as
the generals would still talk about him being too weak to
control his murderous subchiefs. Lone Wolf's already hard
expression turning harder.

Now that Skywalker sufficiently had his attention, he
walked Lone Wolf slightly out of hearing range. I intently
watched them but, as much of our language is spoken in
the back of the throat, reading lips is impossible. Skywalker
normally talked with his hands too, but this time he waved
his hands meaninglessly. Lone Wolf listened, but his set
expression gave nothing away. When Skywalker stopped
speaking, Lone Wolf considered at length. When he was
finished thinking, Billy was summoned. The instant he
joined them, Lone Wolf went striding toward the generals.
Billy was so caught up in the urgency of the moment that

he failed to consider that the most powerful man in the Kiowa Nation, a nation he secretly longed to be part of, was trusting him to faithfully repeat his every word. Actually, it was a good thing Billy didn't pause to reflect, for if he had, that sensitive young man would have become so humbled he would not have been able to utter a word.

To the generals, Lone Wolf said loudly and clearly. "A member of my council has just told me a very disturbing thing. He said that you do not believe this man killed anyone. That you are offering to hang him simply to shut me up. That his death will accomplish nothing. That you will still believe and say bad things about the Kiowa.

"Before coming to this place known as Medicine Lodge, I gave my word no violence would come from any of my own. Now I am given to understand that you do not trust my word. You believe I have no honor, that my chiefs have no honor. You say that one among us was nothing more than a greedy child. That he killed just to have a trinket and that I could do nothing to stop him. You say all of this and still you decide to hang a different man.

"Hear me now, hear the voice of Lone Wolf. I will not stand for your insults against the Kiowa, against the chief known to you as Satanta. Perhaps you have failed to realize that I am a just man, that only the punishment of the truly guilty will satisfy me. Perhaps you need more time to think on all of this."

Lone Wolf pulled himself up to his full height. "Very well. I give you this time. And I will give you something else, and with this something, there is no bargaining, no compromise, for I give you one of the least of us, the man known as Tay-bodal. He will find the truth. I will accept your word that while he lives among you, he will be free to hunt this truth down. Only when this matter is resolved will the chiefs of the Blue Jackets and I speak of peace."

Left completely without option, the generals were forced to agree. His pride only partially satisfied, Lone Wolf turned and called for me. I moved forward, my mind dazed. And then I was looking up into that stern face, hearing that reproving voice.

"You have two days. That is all the time I am able to give."

Unable to breathe or swallow, I could only nod.

Abandoned—that's precisely how I felt as I stood watching the Kiowa ride away. They even took my horse, taking with them my only means for an easy escape. Craning to look back over my shoulder, I saw the Blue Jackets begin to move away, five guards roughly moving along the shackled Little Jonas, directing him toward the prison tent. The generals and the Washington representatives began smoking cigars as they answered questions hurled by the shouting Eastern newspapermen. Only Billy remained beside me, our presence utterly forgotten. Apparently, the generals might be willing to accept my continued company, but this in no way meant that they felt any inclination to be hospitable into the bargain. I quickly understood that food and lodging during my temporary stay was my concern, not theirs. This attitude might have been different had they viewed me as someone relatively important, but by Lone Wolf's own admission, I was insignificant. The Blue Jacket generals were very quick to take his word on this, at least. If I wasn't important to Lone Wolf, then I wasn't important to them, either. They were, after all, surrounded by hundreds of prominent chiefs to whom they were forced to kowtow. One shaky-legged, worry-riddled warrior hardly seemed worth their effort.

Solace came when Billy placed a hand on my shoulder and said, "I'll take you to Hawwy."

Half-clothed, wearing only his trousers and a long-sleeved white undershirt, Haw-we-sun lay facedown on his bed. Dimly he heard the door flap open. Not bothering to raise his curly head he said in a tormented voice, "Is it done?"

Billy answered, for my benefit, in Kiowa. "No. It was not done."

Hawwy bolted upright, blinked several times, trying to believe that I was standing inside his private tent. This was made clear when he put voice to the doubts of his own eyes. "Tay-bodal? Is that you?"

"Yes. I've come to share your lodge for two days."

Hawwy's chin pulled in against his bulky neck. "Why?"

"I was left behind by Lone Wolf to find the real killer of Buug-lah. I find myself dependent on your hospitality and your cooperation."

"You have both," he said earnestly.

I felt both considerably relieved and terribly guilty. I moved quickly to dispel the latter. "I apologize," I said, my voice as dry as sand.

"Apologize for what? I don't understand."

I looked down at my feet. "For being too quick to judge you." It was a struggle, but I forced myself to raise my head, meet his wide-eyed stare. "I believed you were responsible for Little Jonas. I accused you of this publicly.

Billy told me, told everyone, that I was wrong, that you had no part in what was done to Little Jonas. I'm asking you to forgive me."

Haw-we-sun, in that much-too-open way of his, rose from the bed and hurried to embrace me. In the grip of this unseemly hug, I rolled woeful eyes toward Billy. The only help he offered in this thoroughly embarrassing moment was a hearty laugh.

Life in the soldier camp was extremely interesting. I'd lived among soldiers before—but as Hawwy's patient, confined to his doctoring house. I had not lived as a soldier lives. I had been kept separate and my meals were brought to me. In this camp, I was expected to carry a metal plate and coffee cup and stand in a long line with the other soldiers. Right away, this simple task revealed the blinding differences between ordinary soldiers and officers. And the difference, really, between the soldiers and hired frontiersmen and one Kiowa guest.

Hawwy had "dressed for dinner," donning a fine uniform, then going off to a large tent where he sat down at a table, to be served his food by "mess soldiers." As the flaps to that tent were fully open and the mess soldiers were coming and going, the dining officers were clearly visible to those of us of the lower class, shuffling along in the line. I noticed that, the more stripes on the sleeves of the soldiers, the farther ahead in the line they were. Those of us in the frontier class, without a uniform and certainly no stripes, were relegated to the very end of the line.

When eventually it came my turn to receive food, I was glad to have Billy behind me as the men in charge of the enormous pots slopped runny beans and a slab of bread on my plate. The next man filled my cup with coffee then asked if I wanted milk. Billy answered that yes I did, and then that soldier, with a disagreeable grunt, poured the milk from a can into my cup of coffee. When Billy nudged me, I knew it was time to move on.

We sat on the ground to eat our food. We were alone, no one volunteering to eat with us. Feeling this insult, I cried, "How can you stand this? Being shunned, made to eat like a camp dog while your friend goes off to eat in a place of honor?"

Billy tilted his head to the side, lifted his shoulders in a vague shrug, stuffed bread in his mouth. Chewing, he replied, "This is the army. Friendship has nothing to do with order."

"And their order has to do with uniforms?"

"Yes."

Billy knew a lot about the army, the white culture. He shared his knowledge as I ate the beans that were much too salty and the bread that was hard and stale.

The Civil War had changed many things, Billy told me, and during its length, new wonders—meant to make the field soldier's life more bearable, keep him fighting-fit—had come to be. Take cans for instance. Those were designed so that the soldier could cook for himself, independent of camp cooks. Canned meats, beans, bread, milk, and even coffee—known as "coffee essence" and made instantly when this powdery form of coffee was added to hot water—were carried in the soldier's pack. Now, the can opener wasn't thought up until ten years after the can, so prior to this handy gadget, the top of the cans were cut in an X, the four corners pulled back. Heating up the food wasn't much of a problem as all soldiers carried candles. And believe it or not, the candles fit the bayonets much better than the bayonets fit the muzzles of rifles. Stabbing the bayonets into the ground, soldiers put the candles into the muzzle joint and then cans of food were heated up over the small flame. Isn't that ingenious?

Weaponry during the war made tremendous strides, rifles changing from lead ball–and–powder muskets, to single-shot cartridges. Then the weapon makers figured out how to store sixteen cartridges in a chamber, only needing to cock the lever to load a fresh round. Those guns are what we knew to be e-pe-tas (repeaters). Cannons became more mobile when the army realized that the wheels for the small cannon wagons should to be smaller. Smaller wheels moved faster and were able to go through dense brush whereas the larger wheels were awkward, moved slowly, and were habitually "stumped" by dead fall. Since those days, I've heard a lot of people say, "I'm stumped," or "That stumps me." I've often wondered if they realize that this is an old Civil War term that meant a cannon was stuck somewhere and the soldiers couldn't shift it.

When I asked about uniforms, Billy had a lot to say about those, too.

Basically, each soldier was given two uniforms, and as the clothing was only one size, it was each soldier's responsibility to take needle and thread to make his issued uniforms fit him properly. If the uniforms were lost or ruined, the soldier was heavily fined, the money coming out of his pay. To prevent this, soldiers made name marks in their clothing so that if stolen, ownership could be proven.

Officers were not issued uniforms. They went to tailors and paid to have their uniforms made for them. Officers needed at least three uniforms, one for parade, one for field, and one for mess. The only restrictions as to how these uniforms should look was that the color must be dark blue and the material wool. Which explained why so many officers looked different. Some were quite carried away by their own individuality, adorning their jackets with an abundance of brass designs. Other officers, like Hawwy, couldn't be bothered. For them, other than the required shiny brass buttons, their jackets were plain.

The broad hats, which were issued for frontier use, were originally quite stiff, the crown blocked and tall, the right side of the brim forced up and pinned in place by a brass ornament set off with small red-and-white feathers. The pinning-up of the right side of the brim was to accommodate the barrel of a right-shouldered rifle. But in the Territory, rifles were carried in saddle holsters and the soldier's face and neck needed protection from the burning sun. What Territory soldiers and officers began doing was to remove the brass ornament and pin it to the right shoulder of their jackets; then they soaked the hats in water until the hats were soft and floppy. From this was born the slouch hat, a hat which on its own has become a familiar symbol of the high plains calvary soldier. A hat which before the end of the Civil War had not existed.

While all of this was thoroughly fascinating, I could see defects in the common-soldier clothing system. As their uniforms were all made the same way and of one size, items could be easily swapped, even stolen. In that case, it would rest with the offended soldier to prove that someone else was wearing his clothing. Billy said it was true, that petty theft was the cause for each soldier sewing into his clothing an identifying mark. But, I countered, suppose one soldier wanted to incriminate another? What better way than to leave another's uniform near the scene of a crime? Billy and I lapsed into silence, my brain busily remembering that the uniform wasn't found near Buug-lah, but miles away and hidden inside bushes. Then I thought of the reason I'd been caught up in this mess. Crying Wind throwing away my gift to her. The shovel.

Each soldier had a folding shovel. Why those were necessary, I did not know, nor was I particularly interested. It was simply enough to know that each soldier and officer indeed had a shovel. Now, owning such a handy item, if a man truly wanted to do away with incriminating evidence, what better way than to bury it? During the space of time between the murder and our discovery of the body, the murderer had had more than enough time to bury a bison. Therefore I concluded that the finding of that uniform must have been intended.

But why hadn't Little Jonas missed his extra uniform? Why hadn't he complained that someone had stolen his clothing? For those answers, I needed to talk to the accused man himself. Urging Billy on just as forcibly as I knew how, after cleaning and storing our metal plates and cups in the first room of Hawwy's tent—the little room sectioned off from his sleeping room and used as his office—Billy and I went to the prison tent, a tent which, prior to his disappearance, had been Buug-lah's private lodge.

Mrs. Adams' tent had been moved several yards from its original spot, as the lady did not find it comfortable living cheek by jowl with army miscreants—Major Elliot and his cohorts; then, of late, a big black man accused of murder. The twilight sky was painted with slashes of gold and purple colors. Mrs. Adams, wearing a tight-looking bright green dress, the curves of her body pushed into extraordinary angles, sat in a chair under the awning of her tent, rapidly fanning herself as she spoke crisply with two dismal-expressioned white men. As they were wearing brown suits, I rightly supposed that these were treaty men from Washington. Seeing me, Mrs. Adams waved her fan broadly, demanding that I to come her.

As Billy and I neared, I was immediately taken by the fan's flattened blade. It appeared to be made of thin wood, the blade mounted on a handle. The blade was painted with the likeness of a young bearded man wearing a white shirt, a red robe draped over his shoulder. Beautiful liquidy-blue eyes looked up toward a darkened heaven, and an illuminating whiteness surrounded the crown of his head. I would later learn that this man was named Jesus.

"Do you speak Arapaho?" she snapped to me in English.

Transfixed by the fan lying on her lap I answered yes, that I spoke Arapaho reasonably well. She quickly switched to that language.

"I want you to tell your chiefs to behave themselves," she said in commanding tone. "The Kiowa have caused nothing but trouble from the first day. You people are ruining everything, making the rest of us look bad." She lifted the fan, employed it against me the way an angry auntie would shake her finger at a naughty child. "All of this is White Bear's fault. He's a no-good, and I know he killed that young man and somehow placed the blame on the Buffalo Soldier."

"That isn't true," I said calmly.

"Yes, it is!" she yelped. "The chiefs of the other Nations are all saying this is true. They also say that Lone Wolf is only mad because it is clear to everyone that he can't control White Bear."

Canting my head, I asked evenly, "And how do you know this?"

"My uncle told me." Her expression self-satisfied, she sat back, the small chair hidden under her impossible clothing creaking with protest. Then she began to glare at me while rapidly fanning her face, and went on the attack again. "If you intend to prove otherwise, you'd better prove it quick. The other chiefs are also saying that it would be better if the Kiowas weren't allowed to attend the peace talks." She sent me a meaningful look. "And you know what that means."

Indeed I did. The end of Little Bluff's Confederacy of Nations. The end of the existing peace between Kiowas, Cheyennes, and Arapahos. With that gone, the bloody intertribal wars of long ago would resume. Even worse, without the alliance, there would be no united voice to call a stop to the intruders determined to have the prairies.

If the Confederacy of Nations ended at Medicine Lodge, White Bear would be blamed. It wouldn't matter that he had been declared innocent by the army. What mattered was the judgment of chiefs. I reasoned in those passing seconds, that Lone Wolf knew better than Mrs. Adams just what those chiefs were saying. Being a secretive man, he was keeping this vital information close to his chest.

Unknowingly, Mrs. Adams had just explained so very much—explained why Lone Wolf had gone into the Blue

Jackets' camp pushing hard for a public acknowledgment of White Bear's innocence. It was also clear why he'd been too livid to move when his own men had fallen into a public wrangle. One more time, his own subchiefs had made him look bad. If everyone had kept their mouths shut, allowed the army to just go ahead and hang Little Jonas, Lone Wolf's troubles might have been halved. There would still be talk against White Bear, but Lone Wolf would have been able to ask, "If this is what the army believed, why did they hang one of their own men?" A considerable amount of pride could have been saved by this one question but, thanks to his own subchiefs and Skywalker in particular, Little Jonas had not been hanged and Lone Wolf's most difficult problems were still there. But for no longer than two days more. He'd been very clear that that was as far as he was willing to go.

I certainly couldn't blame him. Time was even less on his side than on mine. In two days, Lone Wolf might easily find himself being pitched out of the Confederacy. Lone Wolf was a man with the unenviable challenge of being Little Bluff's successor. He knew, despite his best efforts to prove himself, that he would never come out from behind Little Bluff's too-large shadow. The most he could hope for, now more than ever, was to escape becoming known as the weakest principal chief in the history of the Kiowa Nation.

Realizing I had in fact not one man to save, but three, blood rushed to my head and pounded in my ears. And suddenly I felt so hot I thought I was coming down with a fever. As there was not even a hint of a relieving breeze, I looked at Mrs. Adams and asked in a gravelly voice, "May I please borrow your excellent fan?"

Thrusting the fan into my lifeless hand, she barked, "Keep it. This man"—she said, meaning the painted likeness—"has power. You look to me like a man greatly in need of that power. You also look as if you would do well to have a bit more height and certainly more weight. I can't imagine what Lone Wolf hopes to accomplish by sending the army a skinny little nothing like you. As far as I'm concerned, you are just one more proof that that man doesn't think right."

What a disagreeable woman.

But she gave me a good fan. A few days later I gave it to Big Tree. He liked the picture.

TEN

The two armed guards outside the prison tent were less than delighted that Billy and I had turned up asking to visit with Little Jonas. Billy spoke to them at length. I really can't say about anyone else, but I am very uncomfortable when people speak in a language I can't understand. Feeling excluded, I tend to vacillate between being angry and nervous. I was both of those things, but closing in rapidly on being alarmed when the exchange became heated, Billy shouting at the top of his voice. His anger did him no good. We were being forcibly turned away when Hawwy, still wearing his finest uniform, came sloping along, black doctoring bag in hand.

He did look fine in that fancy uniform and he must have felt equally splendid, for his manner when addressing those guards was haughty. Suitably impressed, the guards stepped aside. As the three of us entered the tent, I glanced at Hawwy, realizing how very like The Cheyenne Robber he could be. That's when I came to believe devoutly that handsome people were born with a little something extra—that something being more than just good looks. I don't know what that something is, I only know I don't have it. No one ever gave way to me simply because I raised my voice or looked down my nose.

Little Jonas was still in chains and he sat on a sagging cot looking forlorn and with blood weeping from a cut just above his left eye. Hawwy immediately set to work, speaking to Little Jonas in a comforting way as he carefully swabbed the cut. While Hawwy concentrated on the physical, I spoke to Little Jonas through Billy.

"Skywalker said to me that he feels you are a man with a big secret. I want you to tell me what it is."

Little Jonas did not want to answer.

Impatiently I cried, "I am here to help but if you will not talk to me, in two days there will be nothing I can do to stop them from hanging you."

Hesitantly Little Jonas spoke. "They're going to hang me anyway, once you tell them what I did."

"What? What did you do?"

Little Jonas looked thoroughly contrite. In a muttering voice he said, "Stole a mule."

I couldn't help it, I blurted out a laugh. This was his secret. The big, big secret that Skywalker had sensed. Watching me, Little Jonas's mouth began to twitch, then a grudging chuckle came out of him.

"It's not funny, Tay," he drawled. That's what he'd heard Billy call me—Tay (Meat). Billy liked to use only the abbreviation of my name. Little Jonas doing that reminded me again of how personal he considered his relationship with the few Kiowa he knew. I appreciated this as he continued. "A black man stealing a mule is serious. If the army found out, they'd hang me for that about as quick as they would for killing that white man."

"Then why did you steal the mule?"

"Had to. Wanted to join up with the army and Texas was a long way to walk from Louisiana. My father was a freeman, farming land his old master, Mr. Marriott, gave him. After the war, Mr. Marriott was dead and his widow wife sold her farm rights to a Mr. Babcock, but she told him that my daddy's little farm was separate. Mr. Babcock acted like that was just fine with him, but after he moved into the big house and got himself all settled, Mr. Babcock took over my daddy's farm, too. Next thing we knew, all the land and the two mules that my daddy knew were his, belonged to Babcock. My daddy made the mistake of complaining to the county sheriff and then the next thing that happened was my daddy got hung.

"My mamma, she said that the paddy-rollers would be coming for me too, that I'd better get out of Louisiana and I better be quick. Couldn't be quick on just two feet, so I sneaked over to Babcock's place and I stole back one of my daddy's mules. Then I went into Texas and joined the army. My mamma sent me a letter to tell me that she was doing all right, that she was going over to live in Georgia, going there as a maid with a fine family. She said I should not ever come back to Louisiana, as Mr. Babcock was having a fit about that mule and she wouldn't be there anyway."

Hawwy stepped back from Little Jonas. He stood there

holding the medicated swabbing cloth, turning it in his hands as he studied the Buffalo Soldier, a perplexed expression on his face.

My attention was drawn back to Little Jonas. He sat there looking up at me, black eyes sunk deep inside swollen sockets, pleading. "I sold that mule in Dallas. I got twenty dollars for it. I was going to save that money and whatever else the army paid me to buy my own place someday. I wrote to my mamma and told her how much I got for the mule, that I would save all my money and that when I got my own farm free and clear, I would send for her. She wouldn't have to be nobody's maid anymore. Everything was going fine for me until I got sent here to the Territory. Next thing I knew, along came Graham Wakefield, the man you Kiowas call Buug-lah."

I was more than a bit disconcerted that the dead man's name had been said out loud, a thing forbidden in our culture. To speak the name of the dead was to summon up ghosts. Sensing my unease, Billy jumped right in, warned Little Jonas not to say Buug-lah's name again. After an indifferent shrug, Little Jonas continued on.

"Anyway, the dead man starts telling me that if I don't give him money, he's gonna tell on me, see me sent back to Louisiana to get hung. I don't know how he knew about me stealing that mule, but he did, so instead of saving my money to buy a farm someday, I was giving him all of what I had, and every penny of my monthly pay. But even that wasn't enough. I had to do work for him too. I guess you could say, I was his slave." Little Jonas's hands, resting against his thighs, became fists. Hot anger flowed out of that man.

Needing to hurry this along, I said, "Now I want to

know about your uniform, why your jacket was found far out on the prairie."

Little Jonas flinched as Hawwy applied stinging medicine to the tender eye area. His teeth clenched as he tried to hold in the pain, and in almost a whisper he said, "It was stolen. I went quick to Captain Mac, told him myself that someone took my best jacket, the one I never wore because I was saving it for good. A soldier's got to have one dress-up jacket for when he wants to feel fine. That jacket was my dress-up clothes, the one I kept real clean and brushed. Made me mad that somebody stole it.

Captain Mac said he'd take care of it and that was the last I heard. Since then, I've been on patrol with all of you and now here I sit in chains. If you want to know what Captain Mac was doing about finding my jacket, you got to ask him. I don't believe the man was doing very much, because he seemed to have had a real serious memory lapse. When the general accused me of killing that no-good, and all account of my jacket, Captain Mac just stood there looking like it was the first time my missing jacket had been mentioned. I tried to jog his memory, but I wasn't making too much sense, what with getting whipped an' all. Little hard to talk an' scream all at the same time. Maybe if you talk to him . . ."

I stopped listening. Actually hadn't been concentrating all that much once that name was mentioned, bringing with the mention an unpleasant memory. Captain Mac did not like me. Hadn't since the day he'd found me near death. He hadn't wanted to save me, but he'd had no choice. The treaty allowing the army to establish a camp in the Wichita Mountains (Fort Sill), had still been a warm handshake on

Little Bluff and Colonel Leavenworth's hand when I had been ambushed and left for dead. If Captain Mac had simply left me to die where he found me and the Kiowas somehow found out, their little camp would have been wiped out. So, feeling there was nothing else he could do, Captain Mac dragged me to the army camp. That was the first time I met Hawwy. That was when he nursed me back to health.

An army scout had been sent to tell White Bear where I was, and he quickly formed a party to ride to my rescue. The army was unprepared for so many Kiowas, and having the upper hand, White Bear had taken delight in bullying the Blue Jackets. I'm told that in that moment, Captain Mac seriously regretted saving me. If he had it all to do over again, I would be nothing more than a few white bones littering the bank of Rainy Mountain Creek. So, hearing that name again, knowing just how he felt about me, how could I not help but anticipate the unbridled joy of our chance reunion?

"Oh, Jesus, Mary, and Joseph!"

Captain Mac, a tall, dark, brooding man, had something of a scooped face. His brow and chin were so prominent that his profile put me in mind of a quarter moon wearing a droopy moustache and muttonchop sideburns. He was afflicted with a noticeable limp, the result of a wound received during the Civil War. According to Hawwy, the bullet had only grazed the lower leg bone, but unfortunately took out a large portion of calf muscle as the lead ball made its exit. The doctors had been able to save the leg (because Captain Mac was an officer and doctors didn't perform amputations on officers quite as readily as they did on ordinary soldiers), but Captain Mac would be forced to favor that leg for the rest of his life. I suppose all this "favoring" was responsible for Captain Mac being such an excellent horseman. He could ride almost as well as an Indian, and when he was in the saddle, there was absolutely nothing wrong with him. But now, seeing me in his private tent, the one place he was free to relax in his long white underwear and socks, Captain Mac was so agitated that he was limping all over the small amount of walking space of the tent's interior while raging at my unwelcome presence.

"That damn Red Stick is nothing but trouble," he yelled to Hawwy, Billy whispering every word in my ear. Captain Mac stopped his hobbling pace, looked wildly about. "Where's my gun?"

"You cannot shoot him," Hawwy said dryly.

Captain Mac's answer was a disagreeable noise in the back of his throat. Eventually relenting to Hawwy's urging, Captain Mac took the only chair. He sat there, bad leg thrust out, glaring at me with snapping dark eyes, elbows propped on narrow armrests, steepled fingers pressed against a tight mouth the whole time he listened to Hawwy.

"Yes," Captain Mac said in answer to Hawwy's question. "Little Jonas did say something to me about his jacket and I filed a report. General Gettis said he never saw the report. But I know I submitted it, for I remember doing it on the same day that Private William Brooks came to me, saying his new trousers were missing. He accused Little Jonas of being the thief."

"Did you file that report?"

"No," Captain Mac snarled. "By then I was a bit too busy to entertain myself with writing up a report about missing trousers. The Kiowas were kicking up rough, as Kiowas are prone to do. The result of the kicking was Major

Elliot and others being placed under guard," he jabbed his chest with the tip of his thumb, "which left Muggins here to take on their responsibilities. As I was otherwise entirely occupied, I left it with the two soldiers to sort out their squabble all by themselves."

"And did they?" Hawwy quizzed.

Hands gripping the armrests he thundered, "Well one would assume so! They certainly didn't plague me further."

It was getting late when we left Captain Mac's tent. As there was no longer a bugler to signal the day's close, a lone rifleman fired off two shots. As the close gunfire was wholly unexpected, I all but leapt into Billy's arms.

"That's lights out," Billy chuckled.

Gathering my dignity I asked, "And that means?"

"Everyone must go to sleep."

"At the same time?"

"Yes."

"But what if not everyone is sleepy?"

"That's too bad."

I mulled this as candles stuck into bayonets stabbed into the ground just outside the small two man tents were quickly extinguished. Ordinary soldiers lived too close to one another and as we walked down a row of these tents, I noticed that they slept too close, too. But the oddest thing was that inside each tent, on one side I could see a pair of feet, while on the other, the top of a head. I pointed this out to Billy.

"The army," he said, "believes it's unhealthy for soldiers to smell each other's breath."

"But it's all right to smell feet?"

Billy nodded and chuckled. I shivered. This was yet another thoroughly unappealing aspect of army life. Then a terrible thought struck.

"I won't have to sleep smelling your feet, will I?"

Billy hurriedly translated this to Hawwy. Both shared a laugh at my expense.

Sleeping in an army cot is horrible. An extra cot was set up for me inside Hawwy's sleeping quarters. Billy already had a cot in there and our three cots formed a three-quarter square. I was given a slip of a pillow that did absolutely nothing for my head and neck and one thin itchy blanket that smelled bad. Yet these were comforts when compared to being trapped alive in that cot. Evidently the canvas body had seen better days for, by the time it came to me, there was no body left in the rough material and it sagged under my weight, leaving me to hang suspended between the frame. I lay there too terrified to move, even more terrified that I would never get out of that thing. I spent a sleepless night worrying my fate while listening to my two tent partners snoring so loudly they rattled the tent walls.

As I was doomed to live through the night fully awake, my busy mind reviewed what little I had learned during my enforced stay, mixing all of that up with what I already knew. Then I remembered the occasion of my meeting William, gradually shifting to the physical differences between William and Little Jonas. Both were good-sized men, but Little Jonas carried solid weight throughout the whole of his body whereas William was slender, most especially in his legs. What if a third party, seeking to fit himself adequately in a uniform different from his own, had intentionally chosen a jacket and trousers to match his body type? Meaning that Little Jonas's jacket would fit but his trousers would be too large. The thief would then need to go for a second man's spare uniform.

William's.

Despite the blurry haze of fatigue, irritation at my tent partners, increasing dread of the cot, in those moments the murderer's temperament became apparent. I lay in that terrible cocoon, indescribable noise rattling the tent walls, seeing this man for what he was. Patient. Determined. Ferociously intelligent. A man who, for his own reasons, was able to destroy another human being without qualm. He was also a man who would have to know—

Trying to turn on my side in that idiot bed caused its noisy collapse, waking Billy and Hawwy with a start. Hawwy lit the lantern and then he and Billy were looking at me lying on the ground tangled in that hideous contraption. I didn't mind that so much anymore as I looked up at them and yelled, "Hawwy! Tell me what was concerning you when Little Jonas was telling us his story."

Hawwy glanced at Billy who stood on the opposite side of my ruined bed. After Billy translated, Hawwy's expression became sheepish. "It struck me wrong."

I managed to get loose of that bed and stand to my feet. Hands on my hips I demanded, "Why!"

Looking embarrassed, he turned his face to the side. "I— I just wondered how it was that ex-slaves had managed to read and write letters."

"I don't understand," I snapped.

Hawwy looked me fully in the face. He spoke, drawing out each word. "In some places, it's against the law to teach slaves to read and write."

158

"Is this Louis-anna one of those places?"

"Yes."

"So being from this Louis-anna, Little Jonas would not have been allowed the knowledge to understand medicine marks on pay-paas?"

Hawwy nodded. "That's right. And neither would his mother. Others would have to read and write for them."

Someone else, I mused, remembering the events of just this morning as well as the things Skywalker had said before The Cheyenne Robber and Hears The Wolf had set out, then coming back with the uniform.

"I would like to speak to Little Jonas again."

"You can't," Billy said. "We are not allowed to move outside this tent until morning."

"Why?"

"Rules."

Throwing my arms wide I shouted, "How can human beings live like this!"

Billy laughed delightedly. "There are no humans in the army. Only soldiers."

I was still awake, this time standing in the tent's smaller first room, looking out through the parted door-flap, watching the sky slowly change from black to gray, then become a smear of pale blue with streaks of pink when three shots were fired, the signal to rouse the camp awake. Taking this as permission to step out of the tent and stand under the awning, I listened to the muffled groans of the soldiers as they stirred inside their little two-man tents. Then I heard Hawwy coughing. After spending so much time with him, I would have known that cough anywhere. He always made that hacking sound whenever he woke up. Why, I never knew. He just did. Returning to the sleeping chamber, I waited impatiently while Billy and Hawwy shuffled around, Hawwy still hacking while he and Billy dressed. As soon as he was clothed and coherent, I sent Hawwy off in one direction while Billy and I made for the prison tent, Billy complaining about having to go at a trot to keep up with me.

We hit a stall when the guards refused us entrance. This time, without Hawwy to persuade them, the guards were churlish and would not be swayed. One guard blithely smoked a pipe while the other relieved himself. Ever resourceful, Billy did the next best thing to a face-to-face interview with the prisoner.

He yelled.

The guards didn't much like it that, one way or another, we would speak to Little Jonas, but as there were no rules concerning visitors yelling their lungs loose, they decided to take a more proper stance. The first soldier put his pipe away while the second, after buttoning up his trousers, retrieved their guns, handing one over to the first guard. Looking official now, they stood there, rifles resting across their chests, while Billy yelled my string of questions.

"How did your mother make a letter for you?"

"She asked Mrs. Mayhew, the new lady she maids for, to do the writing."

"And who read her letter to you?"

"Lieutenant Danny."

"You shared your mother's letter with no one else?"

"No."

I stood there lost in thought, trying to work out how a man like Buug-lah had come to know the information about the stolen mule when the answer came to me in a very unexpected way.

Mrs. Adams stuck her head out of her tent and did some yelling too.

"What is all this noise out here? Don't you understand that a very important woman is still asleep?"

She had more to say, mostly in regard to offensive Kiowa manners, and as she ranted, she rattled pay-paas, using them in a shooing fashion, the way one would shoo off pesky flies. Then it hit me like a bolt. Her shaking those pay-paas reminded me that Skywalker had said that pay-paas were important. Now, he could have meant only letters, but seeing what she had in her hand, I couldn't take the chance these were the only kinds of pay-paas he'd visualized. With Skywalker's cryptic visions, it's always better to be safe. Without pausing for further thought, I irritated Mrs. Adams further by ambling her way.

Well, that certainly put her in a snit. She set to telling me that it wasn't fit for a strange man to see her while she was in her sleeping dress and with her hair tied up. Actually, I thought she looked better than I'd ever seen her, but she kept insisting she, "wasn't decent." I didn't have time to argue. Lone Wolf would be coming back to the Blue Jackets' camp bright and early the next morning to close this situation one way or the other. As what he ultimately decided largely depended on what I could or could not tell him, out of necessity I cut straight through Mrs. Adams' persistent babble.

"I see you have pay-paas there. I would like to know what kind they are."

This direct question set her back, her eyes bulging, mouth open as she gaped at me. Finding at last her well-honed tongue she replied, "They are information pay-paas. Newwwws-pay-paas," she said, drawing out the last words as if speaking to a slow-witted child.

"And you can read the marks on those pay-paas?"

Her mouth snapped shut and held a frown as she looked at me, one brow arched high, as if I had just delivered a terrible insult. "Well, of course I can read them. I am an educated person."

"Could you read them to me?"

Both eyes flared. She studied me as she considered at length, then said, "Only if you fetch me a cup of coffee mixed with milk and sugar."

Billy and I darted off.

Mrs. Adams truly was an educated person. When we returned with the coffee, she was more properly attired, but her hair was still tied up and a pair of clear glasses were perched on the end of her nose as she sat in her chair, reading the newsprint aloud between sips of her coffee.

I listened with rapt attention. In those pay-paas the white people gossiped about one another, and from all over their recognized country. Mrs. Adams could tell me from those pay-paas what was going on in places called, Boston, New York, and Philadelphia.

"Is there any news from a place called, Louis-anna?" I asked.

"What?" she barked. Then seeing that I was perfectly serious, she set her coffee cup down on the side table and began energetically rattling those pay-paas in her search through each and every page.

Finally she found something. "There's only a small

note," she said in a musing tone. Then she read: " 'Mr. T. Babcock, landowner in La Salle Parish, is offering a reward for the return or any information on the whereabouts of a blaze-faced mule. Said mule was taken from his property during the dead of night and made off with. A subsequent search of the surrounding area and share-crop shanties has not proved fruitful. Mr. Babcock has said that this has become a matter of principal far beyond the worth of the missing animal. Mr. Babcock announced that every effort will be used to secure its return. He has put any and all Rebel miscreants known to be loitering with intent anywhere near the region of La Salle Parish, on notice that their thievery will not be tolerated. Sheriff's inquiries remain pending.' "

The pay-paas made a racket as her arms crushed them against her lap and she looked at me in a confused and irritated fashion. "Is that what you needed to know?"

"Yes," I said excitedly.

"Well, I certainly don't understand," she shrieked. "What has a carpetbagger's missing mule to do with Kiowas?"

"Excuse me?"

She leaned forward in the chair. I became captivated by her mouth as her lips seemed to form each sound of the strange word, the way her eyes, when seen through those glasses on the end of her nose seemed as large as an owl's. "Car-pet-bag-ger!"

The more she leaned forward, the farther I sat back, in a feeble attempt to get away from her, my knees drawn up to my chest, arms hugging my legs. Once she'd finished this odd word, she retreated and I was able to sit properly.

"What does this mean?" I asked. "This caa-pet-baa-ga."

She whipped those glasses right off her face as she tore the still air with her cry of frustration. Then she was shouting at me as if I'd suddenly gone deaf. "It means an evil man from the North who steals from the poor of the South."

"And this man stole the land the pay-paa says he owns?"

"That's exactly right." Mrs. Adams regathered her dignity as her well-proportioned bottom wormed in the creaking chair. "It also means that the lawmen of Louisiana are not looking very hard for his stolen mule. Which is why the man is offering a reward."

"One more question."

"What now?" she lamented.

I licked my lips and blundered on. "Everyone reads those pay-paas?"

Once again she spoke in that gratingly sharp tone. "Yes, they do. All educated people read the monthly papers."

I shook my head as if to clear it. "Monthly? I don't understand."

She took a deep breath, expelled it in a heaving sigh. "Papers are . . ." She searched for a suitable Arapaho word. There wasn't one. She was forced to stay with English and hope I wasn't completely thick-headed. "They are printed each time the moon is full." She lifted the pay-paas and rattled them near my face. "This is an old pay-paa. It came to me from the soldier chiefs who have all passed it among themselves."

Her answer caused me to smile.

ELEVEN

Money has always been something of an enigma to Indians. The reason is very simple. When trading, the worth of robes, or horses offered in exchange, is instantly clear. You can judge a good robe by how well it has been tanned, the luster of the fur. A horse by its legs, teeth. But money! How can anyone know the real worth of flat metal coins or strips of pay-paa? These things will not keep you warm, will not take you safely across miles of open country. You can't even eat it. All money can do is lay there in your hand or burn a hole in your pocket.

It's because money looks and feels so worthless that Indians have a habit of throwing it away on useless things. Maybe someday we'll understand it, learn how to use it better, but I don't think so. When you consider how many people have been hurt or destroyed on account of money, it makes me think that something like that isn't worth the effort to understand.

Buug-lah had wanted all of Little Jonas's money. He had made him give up all his money to keep his mouth shut about that mule. This made me wonder—two things. How had Buug-lah connected Little Jonas to a mule that had gone missing in Louis-anna, and why had Buug-lah seemed to need a lot of money so badly? I had to really think about that. And as I thought, I realized again just how much Buug-lah had reminded me of Raven's Wing. Whenever Raven's Wing was with someone important, someone like White Bear, he liked everyone to notice this. That put me to recalling the way Buug-lah had strutted when I watched him walking around with . . .

My pleased smile slowly melted as I realized something else. Mrs. Adams had read of Mr. Babcock's offer of a reward for any information pertaining to his missing mule. I wondered if that reward was worth more money than Little Jonas was able to pay. If so, and Little Jonas realized that Buug-lah was about to report what he knew to Mr. Babcock in order to claim that reward, then Little Jonas would be feeling desperate.

Well, this wasn't going well at all!

I was fuming as Billy and I wended our way through the main body of the camp, searching for Hawwy. With each step I became thoroughly angry, for it seemed that the more I tried to take suspicion away from the one Blue Jacket The Cheyenne Robber liked and respected, the more my findings seemed to lead me straight back to Little Jonas's prison-tent door. Lone Wolf really wouldn't give a toss if I proved Little Jonas guilty, but The Cheyenne Robber would mind very much. I deeply wished Skywalker hadn't gotten me into this, but he had and I was, and somehow I would have to burrow my way out.

I really could have used Skywalker's discerning skills. He might not understand English any better than I did, but he did have a canny knack for singling out guilty hearts. That would have been an invaluable help—but one I would have to function without, as he was in our camp, most probably too caught up in councils with Lone Wolf to spare me a passing thought. I deeply resented his habit of overestimating my abilities. Sometimes he was too trusting in the strengths he believed me to have. And it irritated me half blind when he would casually shrug off my substantial concerns, saying, "If I thought you couldn't do it, I wouldn't have asked."

Fuming now, I mentally fired back, "You didn't ask. You pushed."

I imagined his gloating smile.

We found Hawwy talking to the newspaperman I had noticed during yesterday's disastrous meeting between Lone Wolf and the generals. He was a small man, plain of face, with sad-dog brown eyes and lifeless brown hair. When he spoke, even to my untrained ear, he had an odd accent. Hawwy introduced him to me as Henry Stanley. Smiling broadly, Mr. Stanley extended his hand for me to shake. Accepting it, I found his grip to be surprisingly strong. And he held on to me too long. I had to forceably pull my hand away from his. Fearing he might try to take hold of me again, I clasped my hands behind my back as I regarded Hawwy.

"He talks funny. He sounds like he's singing and talking at the same time."

Hawwy ducked his head to the side, a smile worrying his mouth. When he was able to maintain a more composed state, he spoke to me through Billy. "He comes from far away, from across a big lake. He is from a tribe known as the Welsh. He is very interested in learning about Indians, most especially the Kiowa."

"He came across this lake just to learn about Kiowa?"

"Yes."

I studied Mr. Stanley at length, then said, "Tell him there are already too many wanting to know about Kiowas. These strangers are crowding our homeland, eating up our food. We would prefer they all go home."

Hawwy bayed unseemly laughter. I failed to see that I'd said anything even mildly amusing but evidently I had for when Hawwy translated for Mr. Stanley, he laughed delightedly as he scribbled madly away on a small hand-sized pay-paa.

I glanced from Billy to Hawwy. I was not comfortable with this situation, but neither of them seemed to notice. I was pulled back into the moment when Mr. Stanley addressed me directly, talking in a loud voice and saying his strange words in such a way that left me to realize that the little man thoroughly believed that if he talked loud enough, slow enough, I would understand him. What an idiot. So when Billy translated, saying the newspaperman wanted to know about our religion, particularly our Sun Dance, I talked loud and slow too.

"Our . . . beliefs . . . are none . . . of your . . . business."

Mr. Stanley stood there for a moment, eyes so wide the

168

twin brown orbs swam in white, lower jaw unhinged as he ogled me. Then, as realization hit home, that I had merely done to him what he had so absurdly done to me, he began to laugh. The sound was merely a wheeze at first, then it became a boom. For a little man, he was amazingly loud. Then he clapped Hawwy on the back, saying "By Jove, by Jove." He said other things too but, the Jove is the thing that struck me most. I couldn't understand why he was calling Hawwy, Jove.

I desperately needed a few moments alone with Hawwy, what I got was the annoyingly talkative Henry M. Stanley in tow.

I tried—and just as hard as I knew how—to shut out that man's constantly babbling voice. I learned then that it is the most difficult thing imaginable to shun someone thoroughly immune to this conduct. Even though his questions received nothing more than a stony expression, he went right on asking. Not having any patience for this foolishness, I talked over him, a thing which, by any culture's standards, is rude. Stanley didn't seem to understand "rude" any better than he understood he was being shunned, for the louder I spoke to Hawwy, the louder Stanley spoke to Billy, asking questions of me.

I was literally shouting when I asked Hawwy, "Do you know where the dead man's things were taken?" Unable to outshout Stanley either, Hawwy merely nodded.

And then the four of us set off together.

As it happened, Hawwy knew exactly where Buug-lah's things were, because they were bundled up and stored in his doctoring tent. There were four bundles in all, and as each of us poked through the bundles, I asked who had packed them up.

Hawwy looked at me blankly. Then he turned his head toward Billy and back to me again. "We did."

Now that surprised me. "The two of you? Why?"

Hawwy sat down on a stool, ran a hand through his curly hair. He looked vexed. Then he turned to his trusted friend. Our needing to speak back and forth through Billy in English was a mistake, for the jug-eared Stanley jotted down every word.

"Major Elliott was complaining. He and the others on arrest didn't have enough room inside the prison tent. Billy was helping to move spare cots inside when Elliott began tossing out everything else. Billy picked up the things the major was scattering and brought all of it here. Then he and I packed up the things just the way you see them now."

My relief that the dead man's things had not been gone through or picked over was considerable. But the fact that everything he'd owned was still virtually intact prompted my next question.

"Has anyone else asked about his things?"

Hawwy nodded. "Two. I told each in turn that they would first have to ask Captain Mac's permission, as he was seeing to it that the dead man's things would be sent on to his next of kin."

"Did either of these men receive permission?"

"I wouldn't say so, because neither of them came back."

"Who were they?"

Hawwy's thick eyebrows lifted and his mouth twisted to the side. Following this facial shrug, he answered, "Sergeants Hicks and Cullen."

"No one else?"

Hawwy shook his head.

I didn't ask anything more. I set to digging through the bundle in front of me.

Buug-lah had fine things. His underwear, as Hawwy called the clothing, was made from soft, incredibly light material. I held the long flimsy leggings up, a quizzical expression on my face.

"He wasn't given those by the army!" Billy brayed. "Those johns are silk."

Well, I had no idea what johns or silk were, but I understood, by the chuckles filling the tent, that whatever they were, it was supposed to be amusing that Buug-lah had them. With a shake of my confused head, I tossed the leggings aside. The thing that caught my attention, and surprised me more than the fine-quality underleggings, was that the dead man had an extraordinary wealth of heavy socks. Living in close quarters with Hawwy, I knew he only had four pair. I counted twelve pair belonging to Buug-lah. I lifted them up, one pair at a time, and compared them, noticing that the pairs were of different sizes. In the last pair, one sock seemed especially heavy. Shaking it out, a small, rough-looking leather bag fell to my feet. Scooping it up and opening it, I found two shiny gold watches hanging from gold chains, and a pretty ring.

I had seen watches before, the first being a watch that Hawwy had given Cherish's father, Chasing Horse. When he heard the ticking, then the tinkling music the watch played, Chasing Horse became terrified of the thing, yelling that it was alive. Then he hit the watch with a rock, smashing it into silence. Hawwy never found out that his gift had been ruined, for Skywalker retrieved it, took out all the broken pieces then restuffed the case with magical herbs. The final thing he did was to suspend the watch from a long leather cord. Now that the watch was good medicine, Chasing Horse was happy to wear it hanging from his neck. Whenever he saw Hawwy, he made a grand display of showing the watch but he never allowed Hawwy to get close enough to hear that he'd killed it.

Closely examining one of the watches, I pressed the tiny latch on the side and the case lid sprang open, startling me just as it had once done Chasing Horse. But this watch hadn't been wound for a while so it was quiet. I glanced up at the others, worried that my flash of fear had been noticed. I needn't have been concerned. Each of them was heavily involved with his own discoveries, Billy trying to pry open a small tin box, Hawwy engrossed in looking through a thick picture book, Stanley reading small pieces of creased pay-paas. I returned my interest to the watch.

Neat letters had been cut into the gold metal. I traced each letter with my finger. C-H-I-C-K-S. I had no idea what they meant. Giving up, I placed that watch to the side and picked up the second. Knowing now just what would happen when I pressed the tiny spring, I showed no emotion at all when the case top popped open. I was expecting to find mysterious letters again. What I found instead was a small picture of a young woman with a strange smile. The smile was strange because of slightly bucked teeth, otherwise, she was a pleasant-looking woman, light hair piled high and curly on her head, a long neck accentuated by frothy lace.

I sat there for a long moment, wondering who she was,

and then Stanley started yelping. Hawwy stopped turning the stiff pages of the picture book, Billy stopped digging the tip of his knife at the lock on the tin box. We all stared at Stanley as he rattled on. Completely in the dark, I remained seated as Billy and Hawwy jumped up and went to stand alongside Stanley, the latter reading excitedly and turning one of the pay-paas. The next thing I knew, Billy was kneeling before me, saying something about a "reb."

In order to force him to make sense, I first had to calm Billy down. Which wasn't easy. Stanley and Hawwy were all worked up and their excitement was becoming so huge that it threatened to tear apart the canvas fabric of the tent. Grabbing Billy by the arm, I forced him to follow me outside where we could talk with some degree of peace.

Billy was agitated, pacing back and forth, waving his arms, crying repeatedly, "Don't you know what this means?"

No, as it happened, I didn't.

Billy stopped in front of me, yelled in my face. "It means we've got a Gray Jacket wearing a Blue Jacket. A spy."

"But, isn't that war . . . over?"

"It doesn't matter," Billy scoffed. "A spy's a spy. And maybe he couldn't get out of the Blue Jacket army when the Gray Jackets gave up, which would explain why he's here. And if the dead man found out—"

"He couldn't be allowed to speak."

"That's right!"

I still wasn't convinced. Canting my head to the side, I asked, "How does Stanley know this?"

"He read it from the pay-paas."

Stepping closer to Billy, I said, "I want him to read the pay-paas again. Slowly. And you must repeat every word, exactly as it is spoken."

Billy looked worried. "That will be hard. There are some words that aren't easy to cross over into Kiowa."

I pulled a Skywalker trick. Smiling, I said, "I wouldn't ask if I wasn't sure you could do it."

Back inside the tent, Stanley read slowly and Billy translated with remarkable skill. Evidently the first page was missing. Stanley and Hawwy, during the time Billy and I were outside, had gone through all of the small pieces of pay-paas looking for the first page but couldn't find it. Stanley read from what he had, the second and last page.

> ... things are not improved here, my darling. Yankees own everything now and taxes are exorbitant. We lost the town house as well as the big farmhouse to taxes and have been forced to take up residence in the overseer's house. As there isn't much of a farm left and as Daddy is unable to pay an overseer's wage, that man was obliged to go. I understand the poor soul is quite bitter, what with losing not only his income but the only roof over the heads of his wife and children, but these are grievous times. Daddy did only what he had to do. I am fearful that his protective intentions have run afoul on yet another front. Mama.
>
> She declares those people turned the overseer's house into a sty. She says that's what comes of hiring layabouts. But with the war, Daddy found help where he could, even if that meant taking on

men from the shanties. Even so, she says that they have turned a respectable home into a shanty, that no decent family will ever set foot over the threshold of a falling-to-ruin little shotgun house stuck out in the bottoms. She is distressed that her two daughters will never marry men of their station. Oh, but if she only knew she had only the one daughter to concern herself with, for one is married already, albeit in secret.

Daddy says that Mama should just be quiet and thank God that we're not all living in a tree like savages. They argue like that all the time now, Mama and Daddy, and hearing them just breaks my heart. Before the war they were so loving and considerate to one another, never did I hear them utter a harsh word. Our world has indeed come to a miserable end. None of this do I blame on you, so fear not in this regard. You are a man of strong principles, even though I do sometimes struggle to understand them, and unlike the vicious tongues of our mutual acquaintance, I do not believe you have brought shame to the illustrious Mosbey name.

I know you dearly wish to be home, my love, and my arms ache from want of you, but please do not do anything rash. Daddy still does not allow your name to be spoken and if you came home this very minute and confessed all, why, Daddy would shoot you through the heart and I would die just as surely as you. For a while longer we must forbear and bide in the surety that our hearts were meant to be so lovingly entwined.

Yours forever, loving you,
Opal-Marie

Following a significant pause, I said, "I'm afraid I still don't understand how these words cause all of you to believe this man is a spy."

Hawwy became frustrated. Stanley studied me as if I were a talking bug. Billy sat down next to me, speaking earnestly, trying to help me understand.

"It was the name mentioned in the letter. Mosbey."

I was still at a loss. Billy tried again.

"This man Mosbey—"

"John Singleton Mosbey," Hawwy barked, distaste evident in his tone.

Billy frowned up at him, silently reminding him that interrupting a speaker was terrible manners. Hawwy looked away. Taking a deep breath, releasing it slowly, Billy continued.

"This man Mosbey is a famous Gray Jacket. A big war chief. He did a lot of damage to the Blue Jackets."

"Good for him," I chuckled. No one else was amused.

"In the letter," Billy tried again, "the woman said she did not believe her lover brought shame to this war chief's name, meaning this unknown man and the war chief must be closely related."

I completely understood that part. What continued to confuse me was the almighty rush to the conclusion that the love of Opal-Marie's life was a spy. I couldn't help but wonder if, while Stanley had been reading, Hawwy looking off into a middle distance, and Billy translating for my benefit, any of the three had actually concentrated on what was being said. There is a fine line between listening and hearing. In my heart, I couldn't believe that any of them had ventured to cross it.

I picked up the second watch, gazed sorrowfully at the picture of the young woman. Now, I believed I knew who she was. The only puzzle now was the identity of the man she loved and longed for. The next thing I picked up was the ring. The stone in the center of the ring was something I'd never seen before. It was a pale blue and it seemed to have stars in it. When I turned the ring in the light, those tiny stars seemed to burst. I found that so fascinating that I stared at the stone for a long time. Billy became entranced too, the two of us playing with that ring while Hawwy and Stanley went on the hunt for other incriminating letters. Well, they found more pay-paas, but those were exactly like the ones Mrs. Adams had read to me. Kneeling with his back to me, Hawwy threw those pay-paas aside.

"Wait!" I yelled. Quickly placing the ring and the two watches inside my carry pouch, I rattled to Billy that I would like those pay-paas read to me, too. None of the three were pleased.

And do you know, those pay-paas weren't anything like those Mrs. Adams had read to me. Stanley could not find one thing about a Mr. Babcock offering a reward for his missing mule. The only thing he found of interest was the Dallas search for parties unknown having accosted a Miss Mildred Tuttle, of "nefarious circumstance."

"What does 'knee-fah' mean?" I asked.

Stanley laughed. Hawwy blushed. Billy explained.

"It means a woman who gives herself for money."

"Someone did not pay her?"

Billy chuckled.

"Is this a serious crime?"

Billy stopped chuckling, lapsing into deep thought. "It

would depend," he finally said. "Some of those women, no one would give any attention to. But when I was a child living on the streets of Dallas, I knew some of those kind of women who had become very rich. Those women could be scary. If anyone made them mad, they made a lot of trouble."

"Could they make trouble for men in the army?"

Billy sounded a croaking laugh. "They could make even bigger trouble for someone they didn't like who was in the army."

"How?"

Hawwy didn't know that much conversational Kiowa but he knew enough to convince him that he didn't much care for the current topic. Slapping his thighs, he left the tent. Not understanding our conversation at all, Stanley looked perplexed. Pausing to look from us to the exiting Hawwy, he made a quick decision and chose to follow Hawwy. With them gone, Billy felt more free to talk.

"Listen," he said in a hissing whisper, "those powerful women do favors for the army."

"What kind of favors?" I asked, keeping my voice just as low as his.

"They provide officers with just the kind of women they want. The officers wouldn't like for one of those women to be upset. They would do whatever they had to do to make her happy again."

He looked away, waiting while I grappled to understand what he'd said. After a moment, that light dawned bright and clear. We have women like that, too. Admittedly, those women are captives, but for a nice present they don't seem to mind sharing a stolen moment or two with a needy unmarried man. Those women also have the power to say no. And when they do, those needy men have been known to offer them almost everything they own. Now I was hearing all about how army officers grovel before women.

Astonishing, really, how alike all men are.

Tucking this bit of information deep inside my brain, I went at Billy with another question. "Did you get that box open?"

"Not yet. It's a hard lock."

"Then, quick, while we're alone, let's get it open."

TWELVE

It took awhile, that lock was stubborn and Billy cut his finger on the knife blade during the struggle, but finally the lock gave and he pried the lid open. Seeing the contents of that box, our eyes bulged. That box was stuffed with money, with handfuls of it, Billy grabbing it out as fast as he could. I went for the letter he'd left lying at the bottom of the tin box. While Billy played with the bills, spreading them out on the cot, sorting them into piles, I took the letter. Folding it out, I saw that near the bottom was a shiny seal. Neither Billy nor I could read the letter, which decided me then and there that after I learned to speak English, I would learn to read it. But for now, there was nothing for it but to call back Hawwy . . . and Stanley.

"There are hundreds here!" Hawwy cried, more intent on the money spread out over the cot than on the pay-paas in my hand.

"Is that a lot?"

"It's a fortune."

He began counting it, sifting through that money with such a greedy look in his eyes that he stubbornly refused to look away, pay any heed to the letter I repeatedly shoved under his nose. Then the letter was snatched away from me, my head following in a blurring motion. My vision cleared as Stanley, standing close to where I sat on the cot, began to read silently.

"Out loud," I shouted to Billy. "Tell him to read out loud."

Stanley did.

From the Office of Commissions
To Sergeant Graham Wakefield, Bugler,
Light Division

Sir:

As stated in reply to your initial query, upon receipt of three thousand Federal dollars, the rank of Second Lieutenant will, with haste, be conferred. Commissioning formalities unnecessarily plaguing your mind are once again as follows.

Once the booking of the commission fees is accomplished, orders will be forwarded to the newly commissioned superior officer, as will, of course, an issued statement from this office to the applicant extending our heartiest congratulations. In answer to your final question, all officers are indeed responsible for costs of rank insignia, uniform cloth, and tailoring.

Lieutenant Colonel Piedmont

"My God," Hawwy muttered, sitting down heavily beside me. "He was doing it. He was actually buying himself a commission." Then he looked at me with bare-faced amazement. "But how was he getting the money?"

"By keeping secrets," I answered. I took one of the watches out of my carry pouch, opened the gold case and showed it to Hawwy. "Read this for me, please. Tell me what it means."

He looked at it, his eyes bulging all over again. "Hicks!" he shouted, leaping to his feet as well as to the wrong conclusion. "Hicks is the spy!"

Sometimes Hawwy could be so dense I wanted to hurt him.

Hicks didn't want to talk. Wholly understandable, hemmed in as that rawboned man was by four nosy turkeys. Stanley worsened the situation by firing questions as he stood there, little writing pay-paas in one hand, pen in the other, nib poised to strike. Hicks looked hopefully at the only other army man in this jumble. Hawwy's jaws were locked tight, his eyes blazing. Unable to bare this unproductive tension a moment more, I grabbed hold of the sergeant's arm, pulling at him as I spoke to Billy. Once Hicks understood, I shouted at Hawwy.

"You stay here. And make sure you keep that little man with you."

Billy and I led Hicks off. Away from an angry officer

and a grilling newspaperman, the sergeant proved more forthcoming.

"I did not kill him. I wanted to, but I didn't." He took out a cigar from a worn-looking tin case, bit off the end, spat it an impressive distance. Matches were also in the case. Hicks struck one on the heel of his boot and lit up. He was the kind of man who comfort–smoked, and judging from the reek of his jacket, he needed a lot of comforting.

Fanning blue smoke away from my face, I asked, "Why did you ask to go through the dead man's things?"

"Because he had something of mine."

I pulled the watch out, held it up high by its chain. Hicks's eyes lit up, remained fastened on the dangling watch.

"This?"

Trying to be more considerate now, he blew smoke out of the side of his mouth as he nodded.

"It is worth a lot of money?"

"No. It's only valuable to me."

"Why?"

"My father gave it to me. A year before he died."

"How did Buug-lah come to have it?"

Hicks didn't want to answer. For a space of minutes he battled between the desire to have his property returned to him, and the necessity of giving up the information that would secure the return. To tempt him further, I caused the watch to swing, the sunlight glinting off the gold metal. By the third swing, desire won out.

"He was keeping it until I received my pay packet. According to him, I owed him twenty dollars."

I swung the watch more. "Why?"

"It's all Cullen's fault!" a very frustrated Hicks hollered. "If I hadn't been with him that night in Dallas, Wakefield wouldn't have had anything on me. But because I couldn't prove I hadn't been with Cullen the whole of that night, it was just my word against his. I didn't have enough money so I had to give him my watch until I did."

I took the man's hand, placed his watch in the palm. Tears began to shine in the eyes that looked at me so gratefully. He lowered his head.

"Thank you," he murmured, lovingly caressing the watch case.

He was easy to lead now, and Billy and I led him to the shade of trees, the three of us being quiet for a time. "Tell me," I said, breaking the silence, "what you know of that night in Dallas."

Like a fountain he gushed forth.

"We were ordered to the Territory and given four days' leave in Dallas before the reassignment. Cullen liked to go to the expensive places, but I have a wife and a daughter who live back East. I have to send them money, so I can't afford to spend very much on myself. I went to an ordinary saloon and Cullen went to a better one. I'd promised to wait for him but he was taking a long time. I decided I didn't want to wait anymore so I set off for the stable to get my horse. I was halfway there when I heard shooting. Cullen ran past me, yelling for me to run. I didn't question him, I just ran. We got our horses and rode hard out of Dallas.

"I asked him later what had happened, and he said that a woman had tried to cheat him. That as he was leaving, she hollered for the men working in the saloon to stop him. He wouldn't stop and the shooting started. I didn't think very much of the story until that dead pig everyone is so worried about went after Cullen, demanding money. Cullen said I was involved too, so he came after me. That's all I know."

"Thank you," I said. "You've been very helpful. I will next speak to Sergeant Cullen."

Hicks snorted in disdain, stuck his cigar in his mouth and muttered, barely loud enough for Billy to hear. As Billy and I were walking away I asked him what Hicks had said. Billy grunted, "He said, 'Good luck to you.' "

Cullen has to be the nastiest man I have ever encountered. And not simply because he was noticeably neglectful about bathing. Everything about him was nasty—his demeanor and manner of indolent speech. Yet as awful as he was, if Hawwy hadn't been there, Cullen's insolence would have been much worse.

"Don't know what you're talking about," he answered, languidly shifting the wad of tobacco in his cheek. Sending Hawwy a look of sheer loathing, he spit a brown stream off to the side. Chewing again, he said, "Everybody knows Hicks is a liar and a horse's ass. You can't believe a word he says."

"I believe him," Hawwy fumed.

Cullen's smirk became a mocking half-smile. "Well, Lieutenant, that is your privilege."

The half-smile stretched, indicating that he was not afraid of Hawwy—of anything, really. Nor did he intend to answer any more questions. As he sauntered away, I came to the conclusion that his overconfidence had nothing to do with the recent death of his primary accuser. After all, Hicks and the objectionable Miss Tuttle were still able to testify to his misdeed. This had to mean Cullen had something stronger than two living witnesses.

Stanley was enraged. "That man is a disgrace!"

For once, Henry Stanley and I were in complete agreement.

Having missed breakfast, I was too hungry to think properly. As it was nearing the noontime meal, I started off with Billy to wait for food in the enlisted men's line but Stanley wouldn't hear of that. For some unknown reason, he wanted me to eat with him. As my doing that meant Billy would have to come too, Stanley hesitantly agreed to that as well. Which is how I found myself sitting at a table, dining with all those newspapermen.

Those white men might be there to write stories about Indians, but they were a bit discomfited that one was so near to them in the open-sided tent. Then, suddenly remembering that Mrs. Adams was an Indian too, and not wishing to offend her in any way, aside from the lift of brows, the meaningful exchange of glances, they offered no overt objection. Having never before sat at a cloth-covered table, nor been faced with an array of cutlery, I felt at odds with the situation myself. Following stiff introductions, Billy and I were shunted to the end of the table and promptly disregarded. After hurriedly sitting down when everyone else did, my hands nervously but lightly touched the fork, knife, and spoon lying before me. Mrs. Adams, looking pretty in a bright blue dress with a white collar and white cuffs at the end of long sleeves, rested her elbows on the table, hands clasped together. In this pose she craned around the man seated next to her, speaking Arapaho in a near whisper.

"Have you ever eaten with anything other than your fingers?"

I must have sent her a scathing look, for her expression lost its smugness, became instead startled. Then she turned away, rapidly conversing in English to the man on the other side of her. Instantly I felt sorry at having offended her, for without her, I was at a loss. So was Billy. Our presence was generally ignored, the soft hum of conversation flowing all around us, and Stanley became so caught up in it that he completely forgot his two invited guests.

I was decidedly uncomfortable by the time the food was brought in, carried on big trays by three black soldiers. I didn't look at the soldiers because I was too busy trying to place my napkin across my lap, as I'd observed the others doing. I heard Billy muttering to the soldier placing a plate of food before him and with a pleasant start, recognized William. He beamed me a toothy smile as he placed my plate down, then moved on. I kicked Billy's leg and whispered frantically, "Tell him I would like to speak to him."

"Now?"

"No. After we've escaped these people."

The meal consisted of stewed meat, pan-fried potatoes, and a large slice of bread. From the corners of my eyes, I watched the others, not doing anything until I was sure I knew just what to do. Before anyone ate, a large man at the end of the table stood and everyone bowed their heads. I bowed mine too. Billy didn't. Then that man talked for a while and sat down. Everyone lifted their heads and the meal began and previous conversations resumed.

With the smallest dull-edged knife, people smeared a yellow substance on their bread. When the little crock containing the butter came my way, I, too, slathered my slice of bread, and with the correct knife. The sharper knife was used for cutting the meat, and awkwardly I held that knife in my right hand, the largest fork in the left. Then, before taking a bite, everyone, with the exception of Stanley, switched the fork and knife around. As this seemed to me a waste of effort, I did it the way Stanley did, keeping the fork in my left hand, continuing to hold the knife in my right.

After all that tedious cutting and forking, I was very glad when that meal was over. But after the plates were picked up and taken away, I was confused as to why everyone remained seated. Until William and the other two soldiers came back, once again carrying heavy trays. I had never before seen or tasted apple pie and since then, I must confess, I haven't been able to get enough of it. But when that first wedge was placed before me, I couldn't have been less interested in it if I'd tried. Using the big spoon, I clumsily ate apple pie. It was wonderful, the combination of sharp and sweet tastes pleasantly melting together on my tongue. That dessert was worth every minute of the anxiety I'd suffered through the main meal. I would have gladly gone through it all again for another piece of that pie. Hopefully, I looked up to see if there was anyone who might not be enjoying their portion as keenly as I, might even pass their toyed-over plate in my direction. No such joy. Conversation had become nonexistent; everyone at the table was concentrating on eating this final and most delicious course. Once my pie was gone, I struggled against the temptation of picking up the small plate and licking it clean. Temptation was winning until Mrs. Adams leaned forward and spoke softly.

"You have done very well. These men are saying that you are a credit to the Kiowas."

A pleased smile on her face, she sat back and began to speak across the table to a man who was openly watching me while, forlornly, I only had eyes for the traces of apple-pie filling smearing my plate. I didn't take my longing eyes off of it until that plate was picked up and taken away.

It was easy to get away from the others, even Stanley. The newspapermen might have been impressed with me, but they didn't want to talk to me or be seen standing anywhere near me. Their attitude about Billy was much worse—for, not caring what anyone of them thought, after not bowing his head during that man's talk, he'd eaten the entire meal using just the flat-bladed knife. Their contempt of him was confirmed by Mrs. Adams when she paused before me during her sweeping exit, informing me that Billy was unciv-ilized, that I should choose my friends more wisely. As far as I was concerned, I had. Billy was worth ten of anyone in that tent.

I have yet to alter from this opinion.

We found William washing dishes. He was very friendly, teasing us about our recent ordeal.

"But that last part was good," I said, patting my stom-ach appreciatively. "What was it?"

William said, "Apple pie."

Those were the first English words I ever learned. Billy nudged me and said, "He wants to know if you would like more."

I nodded with my entire body. William laughed as he

stood, flinging sudsy white soap from his dark arms.

He gave me an entire pie, and not one of the busy soldiers working in the large cook tent seemed to care that I ate from the metal plate with my hands. Between gobbling bites, I asked William questions. Savoring each mouthful, I listened to what William had to say.

"I have been in the army for three years. I joined after my old master's place was burned. That was in Georgia. The officer that freed me, gave me a place in the army, was Lieutenant Danny. He is the bravest man I have ever known."

I stopped eating, raised my eyes and fixed on William's. His description of a brave young officer did not fit with the lieutenant I'd known out on the prairie. The even more glaring discrepancy was my memory of the two sergeants roughing up the lieutenant, as well as his appearing to be mortally afraid of them. William seemed to understand my thoughts.

"During the war," he said softly, "the lieutenant wasn't afraid of anything. Men followed him without question." William looked away, the side of his face twitching as he lapsed into deep thought. Taking a deep breath, letting it go with a sad sigh he said, "It's only been lately that he's been . . . nervous." Vexed by this, William stood up from the little three-legged stool he'd been perched on and cried, "He doesn't talk anymore. He used to talk all the time. And laugh—Lord, that man could laugh. He was always with us, his brown boys." William stabbed his chest with his thumb. "That's what he called us, his brown boys. He'd sit right down and eat with us and laugh at all our jokes. He was part of us and he made us feel like we were part of him.

191

We didn't think nothing about following that man right into the mouth of hell because he was Lieutenant Danny, and where he went, we went. No questions asked."

William's expression became indescribably sad. "Since coming to the Territory, he doesn't come around us much. Everything is changed. We hardly ever see him, and when we do, all he says is, 'What do you want, Trooper?' We can't go to him like we used to, we can't count on him like in the old times. Now all we got is Captain Mac, and that man wouldn't care if we all fell off the world tomorrow. This army has become a sad piece of work. I'd quit if I had somewhere else to go."

"You have no family?" I asked.

William barked a laugh. "You don't understand about slave days, do you? Slaves didn't have families. All we had were masters. Now we don't even have that." His eyes locked with mine. "I know you're hunting up a way to help Little Jonas, but if you got time during your hunting to look for the man we once called our friend, we'd appreciate it if you'd tell him that he's missed."

Listening, I heard more "I" than "we" but what I said was that I would do my best to find the Buffalo Soldiers' missing hero.

Rising from the stool, I handed over the emptied pie tin and William took it. I signed that I would like to wash away the stickiness of the apple pie. William pointed back to the big pot with the low fire burning underneath it. I went there and took a good long time about scrubbing my hands, arms, and face in the hot, sudsy water. That kind of bath felt good and that pot held a lot of water. What I liked best was that a fire could be kept going directly under it. I just knew that

Crying Wind would love to have a pot like that. Picking it up and casually carting it off would require the combined strengths of three stout men and one highly enthusiastic boy. That pot was not like the shovels. It wasn't something I could simply fold up and hide under my vest. But still, I knew my wife would want it. She could use it for just about anything—but my mind kept telling me that it would be perfect for winter bathing, that this pot would end forever my turning blue in an icy creek or river. It takes hours to feel warm again after a bath like that. And sometimes the pain is incredible. Yet every bit of this is endured winter after winter because my people have always had a deep-seated need to be clean. The worst insult a Kiowa can give is to say someone is dirty.

Cullen was a dirty person. I thought about Cullen as I finished cleaning myself. When I returned to William, I said, "I have one last question for you. I want to know how you got that wound to your leg."

William was instantly alarmed, then became agitated as he went into a great long tale. According to him, Little Jonas had attacked him for no reason.

"He hit me. Hard enough to knock me down."

"You had no idea what he was talking about?"

"No!"

"When did you discover that your spare trousers were missing?"

"The next day. I went right to Captain Mac but, as usual, that man was about as helpful as a bug bite. I saw him take out the report forms but I wasn't allowed to stay around and make sure he filled them out, so on my own I started asking around and then here comes Little Jonas again, this time saying that everyone in the camp was telling him how I was calling him a thief. Well, that made me mad because I hadn't said a word about him to anybody, except maybe that he'd had no right to hit me the way he had, so I yelled right back, told him I knew he had taken my pants. That's when we really got into it. I was peeling potatoes and had a knife in my hand. In the fight, I ended up sticking myself with it and that's how my leg got cut."

"How long did you take care of the wound before seeking medical aid?"

"Three days." He eyed Billy for a second, then looked away. "I don't trust army doctors. They're the cause for a lot of nubs getting tossed out of the army."

"Nubs?"

William raised his voice. "Men missing an arm or a leg! We call them nubs. I didn't want to be a nubby black man trying to look for work or be begging for handouts, so I took care of myself as long as I could. When it got so bad that it hurt all the time and made me feel sick in my belly, I started thinking that being a live nub was better that being a dead trooper. If you hadn't been where you were the day I got taken into sick call, most likely I wouldn't be walking around like I am, 'cause those army doctors do love to cut off arms and legs. You did me a big favor. I won't ever forget it. As long as I'm on mess duty, when you want pie, you'll get pie."

"Thank you," I smiled. William and I sat down and I asked another question. "When we were all out on the prairie, I did not detect any hard feelings between you and Little Jonas. Not until the final moments when we were preparing to leave. I saw the two of you argue, but then when you came into the camp with the horses, the two of you acted as if there was no argument. Your friendly natures caused me to doubt my own eyes."

William laughed an easy laugh. "That's an old slave trick. No matter what, outside our own kind, we never let on what we're thinking or feeling. We especially don't complain about each other to officers."

"But you complained about your uniform to Captain Mac."

"Well, I had to do that!" he cried. "If I didn't report about my missing pants, next inspection would see my pay packet docked."

As I opened my mouth, preparing to ask Billy what that meant, William raised a silencing hand and spoke to him directly. In turn, the matter was fully explained.

"When there is an inspection, all of our things have to be laid out just so. We have to have one complete uniform on our bodies, another in good repair folded up with our blankets, towels, and socks. If anything is missing, the sergeants get mad. They can't get mad if we have reported anything lost to a senior officer. I tried to talk to Lieutenant Danny but I couldn't find him. That's why I went to Captain Mac."

"Your sergeants are Hicks and Cullen?"

"That's right. We report to them. They're the ones who do the regular inspecting."

"Why didn't you report the loss to either of them?"

William shrugged. "Couldn't find them, either."

I thanked William for both the conversation and the pie, and then Billy and I left. As I walked I noticed with a smile that the hot soapy water had left me smelling almost like

William. Raising my arm, I sniffed at myself and laughed.

"Where are we going now?" Billy wanted to know.

"I want to find Lieutenant Danny. I have something of his."

THIRTEEN

It was a guess, but then everything in life, especially decisions, are nothing more than best guesses. My guess was the watch remaining in my carry pouch belonged to Lieutenant Danny. My second guess was that he would want that watch back even more badly than Sergeant Hicks had wanted his.

Billy and I walked all through the camp without finding Lieutenant Danny, but we did find Hawwy and Stanley. They were seated at a little table that had been set up in the shade of the medical-tent awning, and were playing a game of cards. When I told Hawwy I was looking for the lieutenant he said, "Oh, you just missed him. He was just here telling me that he felt ill. I've confined him to his tent until he feels better."

"He needed permission to be sick?"

"Yes. Otherwise he'd have to stand his duty."

"What's wrong with him?"

Hawwy shrugged, removed a card out of the fan of cards in his right hand, placed that card on the top of the small table. Seeing the marks on the card, Stanley let go a howl. Hawwy laughed. I pushed Hawwy's shoulder to regain his attention.

"It isn't anything serious," he said. "He's just not feeling well. I told him to stay in bed for a while."

"Which tent is his?"

Seemingly anxious for me to go away so they could go on enjoying their game, Hawwy threw his arm in the general direction of the ailing lieutenant.

After some searching and being told to "Get out!" by disgruntled officers not pleased at all by the sudden appearance of my face through their flap doors, I found Lieutenant Danny. He was not in his bed. Dressed in uniform trousers and a very nice white shirt—the nicest I'd ever seen worn by an officer—he sat at his desk, writing a letter, the long black pen pausing as Billy and I entered.

Lieutenant Danny looked frail and shaky, and given this state, it was understandable why Hawwy had mistakenly believed him to be ill. Had his attention not been diverted by the cloying Stanley, he would have seen that the lieutenant was a mental wreck, that what he needed more than bed rest was the relief of talking through his problems with someone he could trust. He had turned to Hawwy, but had been sent away. Hoping to persuade him that I was a man he could trust, I took out the watch, opened it, and held it out to him.

"I believe this is yours."

What little color remained in his face, effectively drained. His gaze intent on the small portrait, his jawline twitched rapidly. After lengthy consideration, he said to Billy in a flat, gravelly tone, "What are your demands."

This was not a question. It was a statement of hopeless resignation. Utter defeat. What a sad miserable thing, for a young man William had described as being fearless, bold, full of laughter.

"Nothing," I said softly.

His hand was unnaturally cold as I lifted it, placed the watch in his palm. Emotions battled across his too-white face as he sat back in the chair, held the watch, and gazed silently at the portrait. Billy and I used this quiet moment to ease ourselves down on the nearby cot. We waited a considerable amount of time, at the end of which, Lieutenant Danny snapped the watch lid closed, set it down on the small desktop.

Turning in the chair, he spoke with a gentle, apologetic tone. "I'm afraid you've caught me during my preparations to leave."

While this was being translated I stared at the revolver resting on the desk, just above the pay-paa, pen, and inkwell, and knew just how Lieutenant Danny had meant to leave.

For a moment, I didn't know what to say, so I simply listened as a playful breeze bumped at the canvas walls of the tent. Then, my tone just as somber as the moment, I managed to say, "Then I'm very glad to have found you before . . . your departure."

His manner became brusque. "Yes, well, if you've come to pick my bones, I'm afraid there's nothing left."

"I am a healer, not a vulture."

His lips turned up in what would have to pass for a smile. In a voice we both had to strain to hear, he said, "Mercy from a savage, none from my own."

"Tell me about your troubles," I urged.

He readjusted himself in the chair. "I don't suppose any of that matters now, does it?" His eyes slid toward the desk, the letter he'd been writing. He took a deep breath, expelled it slowly, then, in carefully measured tones, this is what he said.

"I was born in Connecticut. I have visited the South exactly ten times. When I was a small child, I was first taken there by my mother who was Southern born, and desiring her son to know her side of the family. All I remember of that time is the astonishment I felt, that my mother's people lived so very differently than the world I knew. I did not see any of her relatives again until I was an adolescent, and then only because my mother's father was dying and his last wish was to see all of his children and grandchildren. It was during this sad time that I met my fourth cousin. She was not actually considered to be a member of the family, but as a distant relative she and her parents did attend my grandfather's subsequent funeral.

"She was not a pretty girl, but she had such a shining goodness that I wanted to see her again under happier circumstances. We corresponded, and after a time, I returned to the South and called on her." He looked earnestly at me now, wanting me to understand. "We each were barely fifteen years old, much too young to be thought of as a courting couple. War was spoken of more and more and with each visit I made to my southern grandmother's home, I found myself less graciously received. By this time, my darling girl and I were desperately in love, but because of our age and the times, we only dared meet in secret.

"Each of us now sixteen, we were of a passionate condition and despite the ever-present threat of war, we simply had to have one another. So, as secretly as we courted, we married. Then the war happened and we were torn from each other. She remained in the South and I was in a boarding school in the North. I was nineteen when I finally entered the war, quite glad that it was still going on when I reached majority. I loathed slavery, despised the very idea of it. Then, too, I was determined to battle my way toward my wife."

Tipping back his head, he sounded a humorless laugh. "Oh, I was a capable officer, and I did cut quite a dash, but I got nowhere near my endangered wife. And then I began hearing tales of a scourge by the name of John Singleton Mosbey." He went quiet, allowing me a moment to appreciate this new gravity.

I'm afraid I couldn't.

Little Bluff, our principal chief then, had intentionally kept the Kiowa Nation out of the war between the Blue Jackets and the Gray Jackets. It was the wisest thing that man ever did. Many Nations entered the war on one side or the other, and following that war, those Indians were punished, the degree of punishment dependent on which side the Indians had been on. The Gray Jacket Indians lost everything—homes, even reserved lands—and were made to suffer grinding poverty. The Blue Jacket Indians were hustled back to their reservations and treated like caged prisoners, needing authorization passes simply to travel from their homes to the trade stores. It needn't be said they were no longer allowed to own rifles.

Because the Kiowas were a separate people, had gone their own way (though admittedly there was considerable raiding against both white armies), Washington was now "handling" us differently. All that aside, Lieutenant Danny's mention of a specific war chief belonging to the Gray army, other than to explain Hawwy's angry reaction to that name when Stanley had read the found love letter, meant not one thing to me.

Trying to make me understand, Lieutenant Danny became a bit more lively. "John Singleton Mosbey," he said, measuring each word carefully, "is my mother's brother. He was a general and a great hero to the South, but because of his battle tactics, we from the North called him something else."

"What?"

"The Gray Ghost."

That perked me right up. I instantly remembered that Skywalker had said something about a gray, ghostlike man looming over one of the Blue Jackets. He'd been right. This gray ghost was looming over Lieutenant Danny.

Licking my lips, I said excitedly, "Your being closely related to him was a bad thing."

"Yes," he smiled. "It was a very, very bad thing. I was afraid for anyone to find out."

"Why didn't you leave the Blue Jackets after the war?"

"Because I'm still trying to get to my wife. Where she lives is under military law. No one but the army or the reconstructionists are allowed in. I was promised that, after this duty at Medicine Lodge, I would be reassigned to the place where she is."

"Did the army men making this promise know about your wife?"

"No. No one knew. Not even my mother who forwarded on what few letters I've received from my wife."

"Your mother didn't read the letters?"

Lieutenant Danny's eyebrows lifted, then settled as he said in a sigh, "No, she did not. As far as my mother is concerned, my wife and I are nothing more than childhood friends. And as my mother is still a southern woman in her heart, she felt that her sending on any letters from the South was her patriotic duty. It was her mistaken faith that, if enough entreating letters were read by Union officers, we would cease further destruction of her girlhood homeland."

"And you were careful to hide your wife's letters?"

"Careful enough," he grunted. "Until one day our late and thoroughly unlamented bugler was assigned to mail duty." He looked at me, hatred blazing from his eyes. "I soon discovered that he read any and all letters before passing them on. And before I knew it, there he was, demanding to be paid for his silence. When I ran out of money, he came after anything else I had of worth."

"Your watch."

"Yes. That and a ring my wife had sent to me as a token of her continuing affections."

I fished the ring out of my carry pouch, held it up. Lieutenant Danny's eyes began to shine as brightly as the odd stone. "This is your wife's ring?"

"Yes!" he cried.

I gave it to him and he held it lovingly, turning it so that the strange stone could catch the light filtering in through the seams of the tent. The stone began to glow with its strange tiny lights.

"It's an opal," he said, tears sounding in his raspy voice. "The stone my wife was named for." He looked at me, swallowed hard. "Her name is Opal-Marie."

I stood, went to his desk. He was still gazing at the ring. Not willing to be a witness to this young man's murder of himself I picked up his revolver, turned the cylinder, and removed the cartridges. When he looked up at me I said solemnly, "You cannot go away. That ring must be returned to your good wife." I placed the emptied gun on the desk and tucked the bullets into my carry pouch. Then I said, "You need food."

The one thing William had said he'd wanted was the return of the Lieutenant Danny he'd known. The young man walking slowly beside me was a long way from the officer of William's memory, but he was closer now than he had been during the time spent quietly enduring Buug-lah's tyranny. Even so, when William, seated on that same three-legged stool—this time a white cloth over his lap as he peeled potatoes—looked up and saw our approach and the lieutenant waved to him, William's dark eyes lit up and a broad smile spread across his face.

"Mr. Danny!" William cried, jumping up, spilling curly potato peelings from apron to ground. Then he quickly corrected himself. "Lieutenant Danny, sir." While saying this he brought his hand to his forehead in a salute, then threw it sharply down.

Shyly, Lieutenant Danny's limp hand came up to his own forehead, then dropped. Billy asked if there was any food the lieutenant might have, and this question sent William running for the large cook tent. Knowing he was going for the food, and ever hopeful that there might be more of that delicious apple pie inside the big cook tent, I followed him.

The cook's tent was a sprawling thing, massive in size, the sides rolled halfway up so that the heat from the portable metal ovens and simmering pots on the stoves would not swelter the dozens of men busily preparing the evening meal. Army cooks, I've since learned, worked all day, beginning before dawn, quitting just before dusk. They prepared three meals, going from one directly to the next. As the army was playing host to so many civilian dignitaries—never mind that they were asked to work miracles in the field—the cooks had been challenged to serve up splendid meals, dishes the regular soldiers never saw. Which was why so many soldiers didn't mind working "mess." Pulling this duty, as Billy phrased it, meant that they were able to enjoy better food.

Coming to the edge of the tent's opened doorway, I stood on tiptoe, trying to catch sight of William somewhere among the activity of the cooks and cooks' helpers. The cooks were two white men, the helpers were all Buffalo Soldiers. From where I stood, craning my neck, it was impossible for me to pick William out. There was nothing for it but to venture farther inside.

I was immediately in the way; a hurrying man carrying a heavy pan yelled at me. Trying to dodge him, I backed into a man rushing behind me. That man yelled too, and gave me a shove. I was rapidly making my apologies when I turned and, trying to stay out of anyone else's way, found myself surrounded by bustling men who were much too intent with their own duties to be concerned about an underfoot, lost, and confused Kiowa. It was then, with considerable relief, that I spotted William in the back corner of the tent. Now, like the busy men all around me, I, too, moved with quickness of purpose, but as I drew close to my target, I came to a stop.

William was preparing a plate for Lieutenant Danny, and while he did that, Sergeant Hicks stood over him and yelled. William was looking noticeably upset, his expression becoming tighter and tighter as he continued piling food onto the tin plate. Still yelling at William, Hicks turned and spotted me. I wasn't that hard a thing to miss, as I was the only gawking Indian amid all of that milling activity. Hicks and I locked eyes over the expanse. Neither of us even blinked as heads bobbed between our fixed gaze. A second or two passed, then Hicks forced his mouth into a smile and he proceeded toward me. When he was beside me, he placed his hand very firmly against my bare back. I didn't like that man touching me. I liked even less he's yelling so close to my ear.

I recognized only one word that he said—"pie." The rest was gibberish. His hand pressing at my backbone, he propelled me toward the large table groaning under the weight of prepared foods. I stood as close to William as I possibly could. His profile was sullen as he finished loading the plate.

The pies Hicks seemed so willing to foist off on me, weren't at all like the type I'd come to know. These were shaped like half moons and were about a hand-size in portion. The crusts felt oily and hard. They weren't at all appealing, but I hurriedly took one anyway, then turned and got away from Hicks, fleeing his presence as I tagged after

William, who was carting the filled plate through the busy tent. I felt Hicks's narrow-eyed stare following me during the scant amount of time needed to make a dashing exit.

Lieutenant Danny was looking slightly less strained and he managed a small joke about the amount of food William had brought out. I sat down beside Billy as the lieutenant forced himself to eat, William hovering worriedly behind him. During this lull, I showed Billy the strange pie, wanting to know if it really was a pie, or something else.

"It's a fried pie," he chuckled. "It's what the cooks make when the ovens are too full of bread to bake a regular pie. But it's almost as good. Taste it."

I nibbled at a corner and found the crust disagreeable, but the sweet filling was pleasant. I sucked out the filling and threw the rest away, hoping a starving animal would want it because I certainly didn't. Billy lightly tossed his head to the right, indicating that he would like to speak to me in private. I glanced at the lieutenant and William. The young officer's fork was doing more fiddling than lifting food to his mouth, and William was crouched before him, speaking to him in low tones. Neither noticed when Billy and I stood and walked off.

"That young chief is still in trouble," Billy said flatly. "You do know that, don't you?"

"Yes."

Billy removed his battered black hat, wiped his forehead with the back of his arm. Clamping the hat back on his head, he said, "I think you'd better talk about this to Hawwy. If he agrees to speak for him, maybe he can save him."

"I believe you are right. The best place for that young man's secret is out in the open."

Gobsmacked.

That's an expression Hawwy taught me. It means, when one is so flabbergasted that words fail, one simply sits there staring blindly and with mouth agape.

Which was exactly Hawwy's reaction when Billy and I explained about Lieutenant Danny. After several moments, Hawwy's unhinged jaw closed. Then he found his voice.

"My God!"

Jumping to his feet, standing over me with that superior height of his, he yelled more—but in English, Billy needing to translate at a clip.

"Do you have any idea how serious this is?"

"No," I answered calmly. "I don't understand at all. A man can't help who his relatives are."

Running a hand through his thick hair, Hawwy began to pace the interior of his tent. "Well, of course he can't!" he shouted. "And that was the point of the loyalty oath." He whirled around, dark eyes blazing. "Our recent war was a war of brothers, families literally turning on each other. Which is why all Union officers were required to sign loyalty oaths, list the names of relatives known to be on the other side. And if later other names became known, that officer was required to report them. As our young lieutenant failed to report to his superiors that his maternal uncle was none other than the Gray Ghost, he violated his oath."

"What would have happened to him if he had reported his uncle?"

"He would have been sent down from the field, placed out of the way of sensitive strategies. In other words, he would have been confined."

"Then that's why he didn't," I shrugged. "He needed to remain where he was in order to save his wife."

"His wife?"

"Yes. He was trying to rescue her."

A new suspicion growing, Hawwy bird-eyed me. "Why would his wife need rescuing?"

"Because she lives in the South."

Hawwy's hands flew to his face. "Oh my God."

Staggering now, he bumped his way to his cot, flopped down, lay on his stomach, his head twisting back and forth as he groaned into his pillow.

I knelt down beside the cot and spoke over his noise. "He said he only stayed in the army to get to his wife. That where she is is under Blue Jacket rule and that he can't get to her without his blue jacket."

Hawwy groaned louder.

I shook him. "You have to understand. He is a young man in love, and before the death of that man you and I buried together, that man was forcing him to pay money to buy his silence. But even now he is a young man in great distress. I believe another has taken the dead man's place, threatening the lieutenant as badly as the other one had. But this time, the lieutenant has nothing left to give."

He rolled his head my way, looked at me out of one glazed eye.

"It's true," I said firmly. "When Billy and I found him, he was preparing to kill himself."

Hawwy sucked in a lungful of air, expelled it slowly. "What do you want me to do?" he asked tiredly.

"That young man needs a friend. I believe you should be that friend. If you think about it, the two of you have a great deal in common."

Hawwy did think. He thought about his love for Cherish, a young woman from a people the Blue Jackets considered enemies. He thought about how he would do anything to be with her, keep her safe—exactly the things Lieutenant Danny had done.

"You're right," he finally said. "I am the most logical one to be his friend."

"And you will speak for him when the time is necessary?"

"Of course."

I grabbed on to his arm, pulling him off that cot. "Then this is what he needs to hear. That man needs cheering up."

FOURTEEN

Moving a reluctant Haw-we-sun was like pushing along a big dead tree. He'd agreed to be Lieutenant Danny's friend, saw the sense of it, but none of this meant that he was in any big rush about it. Nonetheless, Billy and I urged him on, and we were halfway through the sprawling camp when we passed by Stanley, who was standing amid a small group of men, all of them chatting in a friendly manner. When that group spotted us, they stopped chatting, their gaze fixing on me, the lone Indian. They were newspapermen and a Kiowa roaming at will through an army camp hinted at being newsworthy. But they were afraid of me so they held back, merely hoping I would do something they could make note of from a distance.

Not Stanley. He wasn't leery of me at all, for he had somehow come to the mistaken conclusion that he and I were great pals. He was the kind of man who hated being idle, and seeing Hawwy, a man he loved associating with the entire time he was at Medicine Lodge, Stanley's teeth clamped down on the little cigar he was smoking, and he came to join us. He had no idea where we were going and he really didn't seem to care about why. He just puffed away on that little cigar and spoke with Hawwy, the latter making no effort to respond. Telling all to an inquiring journalist was the last thing Hawwy felt inclined to do, so he kept his mouth firmly closed. When we came into view of Lieutenant Danny's quarters, we saw the young man himself, preparing to enter his tent.

Catching up with him, I said through Billy, "I've brought someone to help you. To be your friend."

Lieutenant Danny's eyes darted toward a glum-faced Hawwy. Swallowing with difficulty, he replied, "No. Thank you, but no."

Hawwy stepped in close, speaking to the other officer in a commanding voice. The younger officer paled. A heavily resigned look settled on his face as he braced his courage. "Perhaps we should speak of this inside." Lieutenant Danny pushed opened the door flap.

It surprised me not at all that the letter Lieutenant Danny had been writing was missing, that the only items on the desktop were the pen, the inkwell, the unloaded revolver. But when he saw that his farewell address to the world was gone, he had an emotional breakdown. Billy, quite wisely, grabbed hold of the ever-inquisitive Stanley, hustling him out. Hawwy led the distressed lieutenant to the chair, sat him down.

I'm afraid Hawwy's form of comfort merely consisted

of standing over Lieutenant Danny and thundering, "Get hold of yourself, man!" while the young man in question sat forward in the chair, holding his shaking head, weeping more forcibly. As my presence had been totally forgotten, I was free to slip inside Lieutenant Danny's bedchamber.

Now, from my limited knowledge of a common soldier's life, the enlisted man's lot was very strict. At all times a soldier was required to be neat, what little he had was subject to the inspections William told me about. But this rule for soldiers did not seem to apply to the officers. In the few officers' tents I'd had a look in, it appeared to me that these privileged men had a way of making themselves thoroughly comfortable. Hawwy's bedchamber, because he was an unrepentant sloven, at times could be too comfortable. Which is why he paid a soldier five dollars a month to keep his living area straight, his life somewhat orderly. Even so, once Hawwy had finished his duties for the day and retired to his tent, he would thoughtlessly slob up that soldier's efforts. I'd been fully expecting to find the identical disorder in Lieutenant Danny's bedchamber, but there wasn't any. His sleeping area was pristine, the cot tightly made-up, the canvas flooring swept, two small cases and one trunk aligned in a row.

Curious about everything pertaining to the Blue Jackets, I went to the cases and the trunk. Easing open the trunk lid, I was assailed with the gentle odor of flowers. I lifted up a white shirt, sniffed at it. The flowery perfume was thoroughly pleasant. After carefully placing the shirt to the side, I examined all of the clothing. There wasn't very much. One pair of socks, just one extra uniform, and one set of the leggings Billy called "johns." They were white and of the same light material as those belonging to Buug-lah. Knowing now just how Buug-lah had gotten his, I closed the trunk lid.

The first case contained blank white pay-paas. There was only one which was lined with a flowing scrawl. Again I cursed my inability to understand the medicine marks inked on pay-paas, but I studied it intently as I flogged my brain unmercifully, trying to remember exactly what the missing letter had looked like. After a few seconds, I gave up, folding that lined page into a small square, placing it inside my carry pouch. Then I snapped that case closed and opened the remaining bag. Turning an ear to the voices in the other canvased-off room, hearing a level of calm coming into Hawwy's tone, I knew my time in the bedchamber was running out—which I felt was a shame because I have always loved to meddle in other people's personal possessions.

Examining what a person owns, holds as valuable, tells me much about that person's character. But here I was met with disappointment. This bag, with its sectioned-off compartments, was nearly empty. But I believed I knew what it had once contained. Hawwy had a bag just like this one and in it he kept a shaving mug made of thick pottery (of an exceptionally ugly brown color), a bone-handled shaving brush, a dark-wood-framed mirror that was badly cracked right down the middle, and a straight razor. Lieutenant Danny had only a razor and a small bottle with a silver-topped cork. Unstoppering the cork, I knew why his person and his clothing smelled of flowers when there wasn't a single bloom anywhere in that vast prairie. It was because of the little bottle of clear liquid. Loving the scent of it, I again inhaled that lovely fragrance.

All right, I wanted to steal the bottle. Prior to being caught up with Lone Wolf's mob headed for the Blue Jackets' camp, my original intent had been to find a new present for my wife because of the shovel. Well, even though I knew she would have loved to have had it, that big black iron pot William used for washing plates and cups was too big and too heavy for me to cart off. But the bottle of sweet water was just right. And it fit perfectly inside my carry pouch. But it just wasn't right to steal from a man who had next to nothing left. I couldn't be just another vulture in Lieutenant Danny's life. Hating myself for it, I put the bottle back where I'd found it and closed the bag quick, before I could change my mind.

When the voices beyond the canvas wall became muted, I hastened myself and slipped back into the small front room of the tent. I wasn't noticed until I asked of Hawwy, "Does the young chief have a soldier-servant?"

Hawwy and Lieutenant Danny blinked at me. Because Hawwy hadn't understood the whole of my question, he went to the door and called Billy back inside. Seconds later, Billy repeated my question.

"No," Lieutenant Danny answered. "For some time now, I haven't been able to afford a steward."

Well, that made sense, as Buug-lah had been steadily draining him of his finances, reducing him to the necessity of handing over his personal as well as cherished items. A young man like that wouldn't have the spare money to pay for an attendant. Still, as neat as he appeared to be, I couldn't see that he actually had need of one. I looked back over my shoulder to the bedchamber. Until my meddling, nothing in there appeared to have been touched. Which meant that whoever had come in, had meant to take only the letter left lying in plain view on the small desk.

I looked back to Billy. "Ask him what he'd been writing. Tell him to explain as thoroughly as possible."

Lieutenant Danny was given to dizzy spells when overly distraught. His hands on the sides of his face, he reeled around almost drunkenly as he blathered on about his total ruin. Hawwy guided him back to the chair and sat him down.

"I'd been confessing all," he lamented. "I'd felt that there was no point in holding back once I'd settled on my final course."

Stanley came back inside just as the lieutenant was slumping farther in the chair, moaning his doomed fate. Really, for a young man with his entire life stretching before him, a loving wife anxiously awaiting the day they would be reunited, Lieutenant Danny seemed almost anxious to give up without a struggle. And for once Hawwy and I were on opposing sides of this issue. The more Lieutenant Danny wallowed in self-pity, the more impatient I became, whereas Hawwy had become the very spirit of sympathy. Billy and I rolled our eyes, and Stanley, standing close to Billy, madly scratched at his notepad. In low tones, Stanley asked questions and Billy—that thickhead—answered! When Stanley again said something under his breath then let go a tiny whistle between pursed lips and scratched even faster, I kicked Billy's leg.

"What are you telling him?"

"He asked how the young chief was related to the Gray Ghost. I told him the Ghost was his mother's brother."

"And what did he say just before he whistled?"

Billy was trying to tell me, when a shot rang out.

I looked questioningly at Hawwy, then at Billy. "Was that another type of signal for the soldiers?"

Hawwy jumped to his feet and ran out of the tent with the rest of us—even Lieutenant Danny—hard on his heels.

Hicks was dead, shot down and left lying just outside the camp near the grazing area for the army's horses and mules. Brigadier General Augustus Gettis had a pinched-looking face, made even more so by a murder committed completely in the open, in full view of two companies of soldiers and herd guards, and still not one eyewitness to the deed. Hicks had been shot neatly through the heart, powder burns on his jacket indicating that the shot was delivered at close range. Because I was with Hawwy, General Gettis allowed me access to the victim's body. As a doctor, Hawwy's duty was to pronounce Hicks officially dead. While he checked his watch, seeming to time the length of inactivity of the man's heartbeat, I busily looked for signs of a struggle, any bruising on arms or wrists. There were none. To my mind, this meant that Hicks had voluntarily met with his killer, thoroughly unaware of any danger until the fatal shot was fired. Examining the outside of the dead man's jacket, I found a telltale brown stain.

"Where is Cullen?" I asked.

Hawwy looked confused by the question until I pointed to the dried tobacco spittle on the jacket sleeve. "By God!" he boomed.

General Gettis, hands clasped firmly behind his back, paced. His face was a berry red color, his expression livid. The soldiers surrounding him were given the odd task of standing at attention yet remaining out of the way of the briskly striding general. When Hawwy stood to his full height, and me right behind him, the general stopped, executing a remarkably sharp turn by placing the ball of one booted foot close against the heel of the other. Then he stood there, his full-on wrath challenging Hawwy.

"Do you have any idea just what the hell happened here?"

"This man was shot, sir."

"I am well aware of that, Doctor!" Gettis raged. "My question is, do you have any idea as to the culprit?"

Hawwy hesitated, his eyes glancing away from the general to the man lying dead at his feet. "We have two, actually. The first being that this murder could not have been committed by the trooper currently in custody. The second, that the killer, a tobacco chewer, is most probably the same man responsible for the death of Bugler Wakefield. One such man springs instantly to mind."

"And that man would be?"

"Sergeant Cullen."

The general stubbornly refused to spare Hawwy's opinion a second's thought. "I find this deduction to be totally without merit. I am quite certain of the guilt of the actual party in Wakefield's case. And so would you were you not so . . ." his words faded as a hand toyed with his chin. The hand fell away and the strong chin lifted as he stared at Hawwy over the few yards separating them. "How to put this . . . so emotionally embroiled with the Kiowa. For all any of us know, this same miscreant sneaked in under our very noses and committed yet another act of barbarism against the United States. 'Counting coup' I believe its called. Yet one more sin that poor darky will be made to die for."

I was lost during this exchange. All I knew was that Hawwy was getting mad. I watched as his spine stiffened, his color changed, and his jawline tightened. Wanting to know what was going on, I chanced a furtive glance toward Billy. Keeping his face blank, and without acknowledging my questioning gaze, he subtly hand-signed, White Bear. He accuses White Bear.

Hawwy and I were put on the hunt again, but this time we were armed with a vital clue. With a legion of soldiers and officers coming with us, Hawwy explained, just in case Cullen got rough, we went looking for the sergeant. As we all trooped along, I tried not to think too much about the fact that I was walking in front of a host of soldiers, all of them pointing guns directly at my back.

When this parade of armed men caught up with Cullen, he was no longer arrogant. He was scared—so scared that he swallowed that big lump of tobacco in his jaw. Alarmed by what he'd unintentionally done, his eyes flashed. Feeling the scalding burn as the tobacco slid down his throat, he placed a hand against his chest, his face beginning to glow a bright red. Then he proceeded to gag.

A brisk wind had come up. Even though we were all standing in fiercely bright sunlight, that steady breeze crisp, I shivered, envying the Blue Jackets' their thick coats and hats. I even envied Billy with his long, dull gray coat and battered black hat. Just that morning I'd felt quite comfortable in light clothing but now as late afternoon rapidly approached, I was clenching my teeth against the cold. The prairie during the autumn season is unpredictable, mild one minute, biting cold the next, making a constant change of dress necessary. As a stronger wind whipped by—sharper, able to penetrate to the bone—it vigorously ruffled the flattened grasses of the camp.

As Cullen continued to make disgusting noises and act as if he were choking to death, and Captain Mac yelled to his fullest capability, I shook my head and turned away, contenting myself to watch the dark tangle of our shadows moving across the wind-fluttered grasses as if in a type of dance. Captain Mac collided with me, bringing me roughly back into the moment as he and several soldiers grappled with Cullen, trying to fix heavy chains on his wrists.

"I didn't do it," he wheezed as he struggled.

"Then just stand still, soldier, while we sort this out! If you stand still, you won't be chained."

Cullen quickly stopped fighting and did what he was told. The soldiers stepped back from him. A second or two later, Captain Mac was relieving Cullen of his side pistol.

The sergeant stood with his head down as two troopers came forward to stand on either side of him while the captain sniffed at the muzzle of Cullen's gun. Then, with quick, expert movements, Captain Mac opened and checked the cartridge chamber. Looking from the gun to us, his eyes were a tight squint; his mouth was such a pucker that it looked little more than a pink dot set just above an exceptionally strong chin. Anger flitted across his face as he waved the pistol, snapping the cartridge chamber closed.

"This gun has not been fired!"

Pointing an accusing hand toward me, he launched himself into a tirade. What he yelled, Billy assured me, did not bear repeating, for every word coming from Captain Mac's mouth was unabashedly obscene—a slur not only against my parent's union, but also their subsequent begetting of me. Somewhere in the middle of all that, Hawwy interrupted him, reminding the captain about the stain on Hicks's jacket. That's when Cullen began to laugh.

"Well, he chewed himself, didn't he?" Cullen brayed. "Used to eat what was left of those cigars of his. The man was too cheap to buy cigars and chewing tobacco. Said he didn't need to. That using cigars for both kinds of tobaccy suited him just fine." He turned his head, looked me directly in the eye and laughed louder. Then he turned toward Captain Mac.

"Is that all you got? Just some scrawny Injun's say-so an' a little Hicks spit?"

Realizing that yes, he had jumped to making an arrest based on a scrawny Injun's say-so and a dash of spittle, Captain Mac's heavy jaws bunched. As there seemed to be only one way out of this humiliating circumstance, Captain Mac took it. Ordering the soldiers to stand down, he let it be known that he would personally vouch for Cullen's innocence to General Gettis. He would also express concern that a "bad-boy" Kiowa felt free to roam the temporary military installation spreading lies and causing mayhem among the troops. That said, Captain Mac led the gloating sergeant and the others away.

I really can't say how Hawwy, Billy, or Stanley felt in those moments of defeat, but I felt as if we were starting all over again, looking for a killer among too many men who looked virtually the same. And that uniform sameness was beginning to drive me crazy. Hawwy touched me on

221

my trembling shoulder, asked if I was cold. After I said yes, he led me off in the direction of his tent, and there found a spare coat.

Its simplicity made it beautiful, a dark blue with a single line of black buttons. Hawwy explained that it was his going-to-town coat. One he wore when he didn't want to be seen wearing his uniform. Officers, he said, always had to be in uniform but in some towns where the Rebel faction outnumbered occupying Union soldiers, a man alone and wearing an officer's blue-jacket uniform was viewed as a walking target. I thought about the coat Lieutenant Danny was wearing. I had not seen another coat in his tent. To my knowledge the one he was wearing was the only one he had. It was not a nice coat. It looked old and worn-through in places. Maybe the condition of his coat was on account of his wearing it all the time during the war. Then again, maybe not.

"Towns like . . . Dallas?" I asked.

Hawwy laughed as he buttoned me up inside the warm coat. "Especially towns like Dallas."

As he was working on the last buttons, I lifted my arm, breathed in the aroma of rich wool tinged with the subtle redolence of Ha-we-sun. My arm was in the process of falling to my side when Hawwy stood and admired the sight of me in his coat.

"I would like to visit Little Jonas," I said.

Stanley and Billy were lolling just outside the tent, sharing back and forth a small white-colored cigar. A cigar-ette, Stanley called it. As Billy and Hawwy were fascinated by this latest smoking fashion, recently begun in the East, Stanley began to roll up shreds of tobacco in tiny, whisper-thin pay-paas. As I didn't care to share, I stood enjoying the warmth of the coat while they rolled up and smoked, Stanley blowing smoke rings at the sky. Now, in my culture, offering smoke to the Four Corners of the earth, then the sky, is a religious practice, so I reverently bowed my head. The next thing I knew, Stanley was trying to put that cigar-ette between my lips. In self-defense I smoked as he wanted me to do, and while I did, I noticed something about Stanley. Puffing eagerly now on that cigar-ette, I stood just as close to him as I possibly could. After a second or two of this familiar contact, I more anxious than ever to get to Little Jonas.

The guards at the prison tent buckled over, *haw-haw*ing at the sight of me in Hawwy's long coat. I looked so comical that they granted almost instant permission for the four of us to visit their prisoner. Once inside, I sat down on the cot next to Little Jonas, with Billy, Hawwy, and Stanley standing before us.

"Hicks is dead," I said solemnly.

Little Jonas said nothing.

I tried again. "I suspected Cullen."

The huge black man grinned, said that I must be one smart Injun.

"I once thought that Hicks and Cullen were friends."

"Cullen doesn't have friends," he snorted. "Neither did Hicks."

I mulled this for a second, then said something offhand, the remark meant only to keep the conversation going, about how even good friends can often have strong arguments—these arguments even leading to fights where one man accidentally hurts another. I told him that such things were normal and that he did have friends, and on and on I went, his big head turning between Billy and me while I droned on and Billy dutifully translated. I continued to blather and as I did, Little Jonas's hands became huge fists. When his voice became a roar, I jumped off· the cot and stood just out of his reach, looking expectantly at Billy.

"He said . . ." And Billy went on to explain. He was still interpreting as I grabbed Little Jonas's hand and shook it so vigorously that I rattled his chains. Confusion shone from his black eyes but he kept his mouth firmly closed. The instant I let go of his hand, he turned his face away and pretended I was no longer there. But that was all right. I understood why he was angry and besides, I already had what I'd come for. Walking the few steps necessary, I went to Hawwy, indicated my desire to leave. As we walked out of the tent, I informed him that I needed to reexamine the uniform found out on the prairie, as well as Hicks's corpse.

Hawwy stammered that I had better begin with the latter as the army wasn't known to lollygag when it came to burying dead soldiers. Then he led us straightaway to where the short-shrift funeral would soon be taking place.

Hicks's final home was located in a good place. The grave being dug would face east, each day offering the dead man a glorious sunrise. What I liked best was that his grave would always be sheltered by the long, hanging branches of a tall cottonwood. Turning away from the grave, I saw that this site, high on a gentle slope, afforded a splendid view of the wide valley. When he'd been alive, Hicks hadn't inspired the impression that marveling at the downright splendor of the frontier was something he bothered with, even on a perfunctory basis. Dead, he was bound to be considerably less appreciative. Looking now at the wrapped-up remains of Sergeant Hicks, I thought about what he'd said, that he had remained in the army because he had a wife and child to support. I pondered that, while Hawwy spoke with the two soldiers digging the grave. When he had finished talking, Hawwy spun on his heels and sprinted back to where I stood waiting with Billy and Stanley.

"They said we can look," Hawwy told us, "but that we'd better be quick. The chaplain and a team of officers will be coming soon to begin the burial."

Billy was still in the midst of translating this when I hurriedly went for the body.

The first thing I noticed as we untied the ropes lashing the blanket to the cadaver and pulled the blanket away, was the strong smell of cigars. That odor, having been trapped inside the thick blanket, wafted for freedom. After a few seconds of exposure to cool air, the initial pungency subsided and was reduced to a strong hint rather than an outright reek. Hicks had been stripped down to coarse-textured, long white underclothing. Surprised by this, I looked across the body to Hawwy. Billy clearly wasn't happy about having to be so close to the dead man, but because Hawwy needed him to talk fast for us, he stood as near as he could without having to shout. Stanley, on the other hand, was hovering just behind Hawwy, his expression eager.

"His uniform will be cleaned, mended, then reissued."

"His boots too?"

"Yes."

"What about his gun? His side pistol?"

"Guns do not belong to soldiers," Hawwy said flatly. "Guns are army property."

"Are soldiers permitted to make warriors' medicine marks on their weapons?"

"No," he said, his tone final, "they are not."

I puzzled that one. The warriors I knew would not think of going on the war road without having their weapons . . . well . . . "blessed," if you must. Then those weapons were marked not only with the signs of ownership but with the signs of whatever spirit power was with that warrior. If the army did not allow soldiers any personalization of pistols and rifles, how did anyone know which gun belonged to which soldier?

Throwing that question aside I next looked for any personal items inside the shroud. "Where is his watch?" I cried.

"Oh," Hawwy said in an impassive tone, "they must have taken his watch to send back to his family."

This most certainly was not a respectful way to treat the dead. A man's most prized possessions needed to be buried with him. Shaking my head at the barbarity of the whites, I went on to the examination of the corpse. The dead man wasn't warm anymore, but he wasn't completely stiff. As easily as if he were still alive I could push his lips around, raise them up and pull them out, even open the mouth while I inspected teeth, gums, and the area under the tongue. And while I did this, Stanley hung over Hawwy, asking, "What is he doing? What is he doing?" I know because Billy chuckled, said that our enthusiastic newspaperman seemed to know only one question when it came to all things concerning me, that question being, "What is he doing?"

Which is yet another reason why I didn't like Stanley. He made me feel as if I were an oddity, an interesting spe-

226

cies to study while scribbling down his observations. When he did this, he made me mad enough to want to jump up and down, make outrageous noises, convince him that I was indeed the fearsome, mindless savage he so longed for me to be. I couldn't help but remember as I raised Hicks's tongue and scraped the underside with my fingernail, how Stanley had invited—no *pushed* me into sharing the noonday meal with him, foisting my very unwelcome presence on the other newspapermen and the Washington dignitaries. I realized now that he had most probably done this in the hope that I would behave in some far-fetched manner. Seething as I concluded the examination of Hicks's mouth, I took small comfort in imagining his disappointment that I'd managed to bluff my way through that uncomfortable meal, never mind that I'd been so self-conscious that, until the pie was served, I hadn't appreciated any of the food. The more I thought about Stanley thrusting me into that kind of fiery test, the more determined I became to pay him back. Just when and how, I couldn't think, as I had more on my mind at the moment than petty revenge.

I looked up at Hawwy. "I've found what I came for."

"Good," he sighed, looking relieved.

He tensed up again when I said, "Now I need to inspect this man's uniform."

This need took us straight back to the bombastic Captain Mac.

"God's eyes!" he roared. "Will he never leave?"

Captain Mac was waving his arms while his quarter moon–shaped face was shoved incredibly close to Hawwy's, the latter standing with his chin so tight against his neck that his profile, growing red with anger, blended in almost perfectly with his Adam's apple. Suspecting that any second the confrontation would turn physical, Stanley sidestepped several paces away. Evidently, if fists were about to fly, he wasn't fond of the idea of being caught by a stray. Billy must have had the same exact thought for he huddled close to me, whispering madly against my ear, repeating the clash word for word.

"That Red Stick is a nuisance—a menace. I've said it once, I'll say it again. He has no right to be poking his nose into army business and he most certainly does not have the right to go around accusing innocent troopers of murder."

Hawwy came strongly to my defense. "May I remind you, sir, the commanding staff have issued him the right to do just that—to find whatever information is possible to be found, either confirming or repudiating the charge of murder currently leveled against the trooper who, at this very moment, is locked in chains and confined to quarters; this Indian you profess to despise is our best hope of averting a war that we most certainly will not win."

"We have Gattling guns," Captain Mac fumed.

"But not enough bullets to feed those guns in order to defend ourselves from the tide of warriors surrounding this valley."

Captain Mac stepped back, his face beet red. In a try for composure, his hands tugged at the hem of his jacket as his straightened his spine.

Hawwy opened his mouth to say something more, but I cut him off.

"Tell the captain there is one way to settle the matter. That if he will indulge me, I will be as quick as I can."

Hawwy only partially understood me. I turned to Billy but he stood there like a mute, looking mortally afraid of Captain Mac. Roughly pushing him, I yelled, "Tell him what I said."

Hesitantly, he did. Which sent Captain Mac on a new tear. No longer caring that he was defaming me as well as every one of my grandfathers, I stood my ground, shouting over his bellowing to Billy. Once he stammered through this translation, Captain Mac, seeming eager to prove me a complete fool, escorted us to the supply tent where the uniforms—one belonging to Sergeant Hicks, and the jacket and trousers belonging to Little Jonas and William—were being kept.

I went to the mismatched uniform first. Lifting up only the jacket, I sniffed at it. My actions seemed so ridiculous to Captain Mac that he raised his arms to the ceiling of the storage tent, tipped back his quarter-moon face and let go a belly laugh. As my opinion of the man was that he was little better than an idiot, I was not offended. He continued laughing, whacking Hawwy so hard on the shoulder, that he bucked forward as I set that jacket down and picked up the one belonging to Hicks. Hawwy sent me pleading looks, hoping against hope that I would not let him down, make him look the fool to a superior officer.

Working toward that end, Captain Mac immediately stopped laughing when I took Hicks's pistol out of the holster, brought it up to my chin, allowed it to rest there for a second, then leveled it at him. My holding a gun that was aimed at his heart shocked the very breath out of him. Ever the combative warrior, he was desperately trying to draw out his own sidepiece when I casually cocked back the hammer.

FIFTEEN

Hearing that warning sound, Captain Mac gave up the tussle of trying to get his gun out of the holster, his hands charging higher than his shoulders, the sign of surrender. A very nervous Hawwy followed suit. Seeing a friend with his hands in the air reminded me of Hears The Wolf seizing the moment and my instinctive reaction to it, surrendering right along with the Blue Jackets. Now I understood why Skywalker had gotten so mad, because looking at Hawwy behaving in the same stupid way had me fuming too. Captain Mac was shocked again when I eased the hammer gently home, then approached, offering him the pistol. Captain Mac looked to Hawwy, and on his nod, both cautiously lowered their hands. The captain took the offered gun and then held it in his two hands as if at a loss as to what to do next. Finding his courage, Billy leapt to my side when I called for him, translating as I spoke to Captain Mac.

"I apologize for my former stupidity. For a time I believed that Cullen had lied. That the dead sergeant did not chew his cigars. That's why I needed to look inside the dead man's mouth. Hawwy took me to the body and I had a real good look, and to my surprise, I did find traces of tobacco wedged between his teeth and lying under his tongue, so it's as Cullen said—the tobacco stain on the jacket could easily have been made by the dead sergeant. But then I thought, What if Cullen had shot him after all, and once the man was dead on the ground, he simply switched pistols? This could very easily been done, as by Hawwy's account, all of your guns are exactly the same."

His eyes flaring as he stared at the weapon he held, Captain Mac roared, "The rotten little swine!"

My feelings exactly, but for a different reason.

Before I could say anything more, Captain Mac turned the animosity he had held against me, onto Henry Stanley, yelling for the reporter to get the hell out of the supply tent, not to show his face again if he knew what was good for him. Stanley made the mistake of pointing out some particular freedom which he and his brother newspapermen shared, and that was enough for Captain Mac. After sticking the pistol in his belt, he picked the smaller man up and heaved him out of the tent.

Stanley landed inelegantly on his backside. Picking himself up and dusting himself off, Stanley had a lot to say concerning physical abuse. Captain Mac's answer was to close the tent flap in Stanley's face. When he came back to me I handed him the pay-paas I'd taken from Lieutenant Danny's case.

The new foursome—Hawwy, Billy, Captain Mac, and I—formed a tight circle as Captain Mac read the pay-paas.

"Are these marks things he is saying to his wife?" I asked.

"No," he said, his expression utterly confused. He looked quickly up at me. "I wasn't aware that he had a wife." He went back to reading. "These are just copies of reports." He looked from the pay-paas to Hawwy, and they went into a discussion. Feeling on edge, I turned to Billy.

"What are they saying!"

Billy looked bewildered. Then, with a shake of his head he said, "It's not that important, Tay. They're only talking about how old the reports are, that they should have been filed months ago."

That really hit a nerve. "What are the reports about?"

"About the dead sergeant Hicks, and Cullen. The lieutenant was recommending both be . . . punished."

"But they never were?"

"No. The reports were not given to Captain Mac."

"Why did he want them punished?"

Billy asked Hawwy, then turned back to me. "It doesn't say. The lieutenant did not finish writing."

As the last of this began to fade from Billy's mouth, I exclaimed, "Tell Hawwy that I would like to look through the first dead man's things again."

Captain Mac went with us as we hastened back to Hawwy's doctoring tent. This time, knowing just what I was looking for, I concentrated on Buug-lah's personal effects and all of his clothing. Captain Mac was overawed by the expensive items belonging to Buug-lah.

"Well, it's no damn wonder he said he couldn't live in

a regular soldier's tent!" he bayed. "And there he had old Gettis convinced that his living like a regular soldier placed him in jeopardy!"

"Why?"

Captain Mac explained angrily. "It was some drivel about the troops threatening him simply because he was the bugler. All right, it's true that in the army the bugler is something of a pariah because it's the bugler's duty to wake up the troops when they'd rather sleep and he is the one who sends them charging into battle, which is why Gettis probably swallowed that twaddle about his being threatened and gave him private quarters, allowed him to live above his station. But this!"—he shouted, throwing down a fine white shirt in disgust—"is beyond the limit. No ordinary soldier should have had any of this!"

Carefully handling the silver-framed mirror and the silver-handled shaving brush, I quite readily agreed. These were the things of a young soldier chief who, because of love, had been reduced to a pauper. I began to set aside all of things I knew belonged to Lieutenant Danny. It wasn't right that those things would be sent to Buug-lah's family. While I sorted through the items, Hawwy incited Captain Mac further by informing him that their dead bugler had been in the process of buying a commission. Captain Mac exploded, demanded to see the proof of that with his own eyes. Hawwy complied, showing him the letter and the tin box full of money. Those two were working each other up about the duplicity of the dead man as I instructed Billy on the return of Lieutenant Danny's property. That done, I announced that I wanted to go home.

* * *

Neither Captain Mac nor Hawwy wanted me to leave. In fact, they insisted I stay. Captain Mac even went so far as to offer to put me up for the night in his tent if I was feeling too crowded in Hawwy's. But that wasn't why I was anxious to leave, and through Billy I made them understand that the meticulous examination of the dead man had defiled my person, that I needed to purify myself through an exhaustive ritual which would take the whole of the night.

Actually, that was a lie, a little cedar smoke and a good scrub with soap and water would have done the trick, but I was tired of white people and I missed my wife. Then, too, I did need to talk to Skywalker. Amazingly, the instant I mentioned the mysterious ritual, both Hawwy and Captain Mac began to blather on about how they fully understood, that of course it was right I should go. I have noticed that, whenever anything bordering on mystic beliefs is voiced, white men, and women, get nervous. They begin saying they fully understand when they so obviously don't, and seem mortally terrified I might actually commence to demonstrate dark and peculiar rites right then and there.

Captain Mac took charge of the money box and went off, and Hawwy sent a trooper to fetch me a horse. Even though the sun was going down and the air was definitely colder, I returned Hawwy's fine coat. He wanted me to keep it, bring it back the next day, but that wasn't wise. A stronger, more aggressive warrior might put the claim on it and then I wouldn't have it to return to him. So I took it off and gave it back, along with my thanks for its use. When the saddled horse was brought forth, I eagerly mounted up and rode for my home camp.

My wife was the only one pleased to see me. My unexpected appearance produced a crowd of men, every one of them arriving just in time to witness Crying Wind hugging my neck and raining kisses on my face. When I, too, ignored their presence, began kissing her back with a building passion, White Bear stepped in, pulling us apart.

"What are you doing here?" he bellowed. "You were told to stay with those Blue Jackets until Lone Wolf fetched you out."

"There was no need for me to stay," I said, holding my wife's warm body tight against mine.

"You know who killed that soldier?"

"Yes."

The Cheyenne Robber shouldered his way forward. "It wasn't Little Jonas, was it?"

"No."

"Then tell us who it was," White Bear shouted, stepping in closer to me.

"I think you should know," I said evenly, "that I've recently touched another dead white man."

Clearly repulsed, everyone stepped well back, and with a cry, Crying Wind wriggled out of my arms. Then her fist collided with my shoulder.

"How could you touch me and kiss me when you knew you were unclean?"

Loving even the sight of her scrunched-up, angry face, I said humbly, "Because during the whole way here I had thought of nothing else but the two of us bathing."

A sparkle came into her eyes. "Oh! Well, that's all right, then." A smile on her face, she instructed her cousin White Bear to take our son to her sister.

* * *

Sitting in that stream, the water so cold that my body became numb, I missed that big black pot with the fire under it and its hot soapy water. One way or another, I was going to steal that pot. I no longer cared if taking it required a team of us to carry it away, I would have it and that was that. As the coldness of the water penetrated our very bones, Crying Wind and I did not linger with our bath. Bundled up in thick blankets, we made a headlong dash for home and, sitting side by side before a good fire, I added a good supply of cedar chips to the flames. When we felt a little warmer we knelt and, using our arms to call up the pungent smoke, washed it over our naked bodies. Completely clean now, like a pair of frolicking otters, we began to tussle beneath the covers of our bed.

"Come up for air!"

We did, both bobbing up at the same time, the blanket settling around our hips. The voice shouted again.

"You're not newlyweds you know."

I scowled at my wife. "He can be the worst nuisance I have ever known."

"I know you want to talk to me," the voice outside laughed.

"True," I hollered, "but not just now!"

"Now is all we have," came the reply. "Lone Wolf is expecting company."

Wrapping a small blanket around my waist, I scrambled across the space between our bed and the door. Opening the flap, poking my head out, I saw that familiar lanky form, that mocking half-smile.

"Who?" I quizzed. "Who is he expecting?"

"Ten Bears," Skywalker replied.

My reunion with Crying Wind had to be put off. Ten Bears, chief of the Comanches, was Lone Wolf's most staunch ally. If he was coming to council with Lone Wolf, odds were high he was bringing bad news.

Skywalker waited outside. Leaning against a pine, contenting himself with the brilliance of a glorious sunset while my wife and I bustled around inside our lodge and she helped me dress. As I was to take part in an important council, she wanted me to look my best, insisting I wear my new shirt, best leggings. Somehow I was to put these things on, holding completely still while she combed knots out of my hair. The end result was that I felt grandly thrown together as I made my escape from my wife's tender clutches.

"You look nice," Skywalker said, as I passed him by.

I came to a jerky stop, turned at the waist. When he made no attempt to move from his spot, I yelled, "Why are you just standing there? You said we had to hurry!"

Skywalker, the very essence of aloof, pulled his weight away from the trunk of the pine. "True, but a dignified walk makes a better impression than a worried scurry."

The image of dignity, we wended our way through the heart of the camp, eventually arriving at Lone Wolf's lodge. Before it stood dozens of tripods, each bearing a war shield. I instantly recognized Ten Bears' shield, then one by one, the shields of every other important chief in the five Nations. This was impressive company we were about to keep and my heart banged nervously inside my chest as Skywalker bent low and entered the lodge. Summoning my nerve, I followed.

Skywalker took his rightful place in the seated circle while I stood at the back. Now and then some of these great chiefs looked over their shoulders at me, wondered who I was. I tried to look important. The trouble was, I didn't know what to do with my hands. Waiting for those moments when no one was looking, I tried three different poses, finding each of them too awkward and too uncomfortable to maintain for any length of time. So I settled with just clasping my jittery hands behind my back. Then there was nothing left to do but listen.

In council meetings, when outsider chiefs are in attendance, while passing the pipe each man is required to relate, as briefly as possible, his family history. This can be especially trying as the names of the dead cannot be mentioned. Therefore, the dead relative must be described either by appearance or by a remembered deed, just as a Cheyenne chief was in the process of doing while I was searching for a dignified stance.

"I am the son of the man who once found a roan horse. That was a good horse and because my father could find no owner's mark on it, he kept it. Well, that horse belonged to a Crow chief and he wanted it back. My father wouldn't give it because he never did trust the word of a Crow, so they had a war which became known as the Roan Horse Fight. My father's father was . . ."

Now, while all of this was very interesting, there were simply too many stories to tell, and I was standing whereas everyone else was comfortably seated. By the time a third chief began to speak, except for a burning sensation in my locked knees, I had no feeling in my legs, and my hands, tired of being locked behind me, were hanging limply at my sides. Still I suffered through another hour of individual genesis, until finally the pipe was handed back to Lone Wolf and the cause of this council was stated.

"I well know," Lone Wolf began in a gravelly tone, "that because of certain blunders"—he glanced at White Bear—"the need for a Kiowa presence at the treaty talks has been called to question. I have also heard it said that I am timid. That if the other one [meaning Little Bluff] were still alive, none of this would have happened."

Avoiding any direct eye contact with Lone Wolf, the other chiefs nodded their heads, muttered, "Ho"—that this was so.

Lone Wolf considered at length, then said, "I am a man who speaks the truth and that truth is this. I was only recently elected to my high office and the two who would have preferred themselves over me, have not had sufficient time to settle down, to understand that neither of them were chosen by the people."

The two in question responded in very different ways. White Bear squirmed. Kicking Bird lifted the corner of his upper lip in a sneer. Lone Wolf dryly continued.

"On advice from my most trusted council member, I selected one to stay in the Blue Jackets' camp. He was to stay until I came for him," he twisted his head on his neck, looked directly back at me. "But I see that he has come back." He sat forward again. "He disobeyed. I am told that he did this because he can prove that no Kiowa was the cause of the death of one of the Blue Jackets. They also tell me that the sacrifice of the Buffalo Soldier is unnecessary."

Lone Wolf took a deep cleansing breath and released it. "This last thing makes me glad. I do not know this Buffalo

Soldier, but others do. They have vouched for him. It is good that a worthy person will not be thrown away." He nodded as the others let go a chorus of agreement. When they gradually became quiet, Lone Wolf spoke again.

"Because I agreed with the ones who spoke for that Buffalo man—that he should not die unnecessarily—I delayed all further decisions concerning the Blue Jackets. Doing this caused me to look weak, uncertain, a bad leader of a great nation. I know that all of you have come here to pass this judgment. I ask only that you listen to the one I mentioned, and if whatever he says fails to convince or dissuade you, there will be no need for you to vote on what to say about me. Without argument, I will stand aside, give up being chief. It is better for one like me to lose office, lose honor, than to cry against what my fellow chiefs say and know that my Nation will no longer have a place at the Council Fire of Nations—a fire, I do not have to remind any of you, that was sparked into life by the one before me, the man responsible for ending the generations of wars that once divided us."

His mouth thinning until it was little more than a shadow of a line, Lone Wolf bowed his head.

And there it was, Lone Wolf's long-awaited decision. A pronouncement that left me holding his chieftainship in my trembling hands. So dazed I couldn't move, my throat so tight I could barely breathe, all heads turned in my direction.

The lodge was so crammed that there was nowhere for me to go, so I did not, as has been later testified, move to the center of that important assembly with any type of dramatic sweep. All I did was stand exactly where I was and

241

squeak out the things I knew to be true. And I did this just as quickly as I could—not because I was too afraid to dazzle and impress the great minds present but simply because, just as I was readying myself, I'd heard The Cheyenne Robber mutter to Hears The Wolf, "I hope he doesn't need to talk for a long time. I have to pee."

Thus inspired, I got right down to it.

"It has been my privilege to do this small favor for a man I know to be a wise chief," I said. Hearing this, Lone Wolf turned his bowed head, his eyes peering at me. Well, I had voted for the man to be our new principal chief. If he was about to lose everything, common decency demanded he know that someone in the lodge still thought highly of him. Then, swallowing nervously, I rambled on.

"The Blue Jacket world is a strange place. Their rules are not the same for everyone, their leaders have no love for their men. As you all know, if a chief has no love or concern for his warriors, then they cannot trust in him. But this is the way Blue Jackets live, in a state of arrogance and restrictive laws. Which makes them dangerous, not only to themselves but to others."

"Ho!" shouted the assembly.

"In the short time I was with them," I began, "I learned many dark secrets. . . ."

I spoke for no more than five minutes, and at the end of my statement, a Cheyenne chief, his eyebrows crunched together, asked, "You can prove this, can you?"

"Oh, yes," I answered confidently.

All of them turned away from me, the chiefs talking in whispers among themselves. When they came to a mutual agreement, Ten Bears spoke, lauding Lone Wolf's daring stratagem, praising his steadfast wisdom in the midst of political turmoil.

"Your guiding hand stayed true, you did not flinch or turn your face away. Even when others talked against you, you walked the hard road. This is the way of chiefs. I say now, this is the way of Lone Wolf."

Looking back at me once again, Lone Wolf nodded.

The following morning was slated as the first day of the peace talks. Even though Lone Wolf had said that the Kiowa would not talk peace, would not say anything until the issue of his honor was settled with the Blue Jackets, the Kiowa attended but remained silent. As I would have to speak again, this time to General Gettis, I went to the conference too, riding at the back of the hundreds of warriors being led to the Blue Jackets' camp by all of the chiefs of the five Nations. Everyone looked splendid, the chiefs wearing their bonnets of eagle feathers, every warrior dressed in his best clothing, each horse painted to display its owner's accredited deeds of valor. I had taken extra care of my appearance and my horse was painted too, but not with the usual signs: the vivid colored press of a hand above the symbol of a horse with small stick marks under it to indicate how many horses had been stolen; or a drawing of a man with stick marks under that to indicate how many enemies had been killed. On its left flank my horse displayed two men, one looking ill, the other offering a bowl. There were dozens of little stick marks under that to indicate just how many patients I had successfully brought back to good health. I felt just as splendid as the others looked, for I was wearing the new winter clothing my wife had made for me. Her love for me was in each and every stitch, and I felt so confident because of her that not one man in that cantering horde of hundreds sat taller in his saddle than I.

Mrs. Adams turned up for the proceedings wearing a bloodred dress. I saw Stanley standing off to the side in the shade of trees and in the forefront of the other newspapermen. The resplendent generals came out of a large tent and sat down behind a long table. Coming to sit next to them were the darker-suited Washington men. As these men— more than the generals they shared the long table with— held the true power, all officers of the three companies of the calvary took a defensive stance behind them. Gatling guns had been set up in four strategic corners and were manned. Squads of armed soldiers were everywhere, dog-trotting in perfect cadence while holding rifles across their chests. This display was meant to show us that soldiers could go anywhere and go quickly. All it showed us was the needless tiring-out of valuable men.

But because the army had taken such measures of distrust, tensions were rife as the horses belonging to all of the Indians were hobbled, then left to be attended by young boys of the Herder Society. Then, by rank, the swarm of Indians moved forward, each man knowing his place in the formation. All of us spread out small blankets and sat down on the ground. Then the officers standing stiffly behind the table were given permission to sit, which they did in impressive unison.

My attention was diverted by the troopers helping Mrs. Adams, placing her chair in between the table and the row of seated chiefs. Behind her chair came to stand the primary interpreter, Philip McCusker. A man, I must remind you,

244

able to speak only passable Comanche. What good this primary interpreter would be to the Kiowas, Kiowa-Apaches, and Cheyennes, didn't appear to have been thought through all that well, but the Arapahos had a fighting chance at understanding the proceedings, on account of Mrs. Adams.

Actually, I believed that we Kiowa had a valuable weapon too. But exactly where Billy had gotten to, I didn't know, because I couldn't spot him. Seated as I was on the very last row of warriors, and being the listening sort, I listened to the soft buzz of conversation all around me. One of these conversations captured my complete attention. Leaning forward, I glanced down the row. Two of White Bear's younger sons having just reached warrior status and consigned to the back with the likes of me, were quite lively in their exchange with a warrior I knew very well.

I'd removed a bullet from his backside, and by last account, he still owed me a fee for this highly personal service. But what a warrior of Three Elks' merit was doing on the last row, I couldn't understand. So I listened to those three with considerable interest.

Last night, once I had finally been free to leave, to enjoy my wife, that's what I had done. Therefore, hearing those three saying that, following the council—when I'd taken myself on home—the chiefs, except for Lone Wolf, had gone to the Blue Jackets' camp, came to me as a huge surprise. Next the three young men talked about someone called Returned To Us, a person I'd never heard of.

My attention was diverted when a chief stood, began to speak. Straightening my spine and craning my neck my eyes went for Lone Wolf. I saw him sitting there just as still as a statue. Evidently his subchiefs visiting the Blue Jackets did not affect his promise that he would not talk until the issue of his and White Bear's honor was effectively settled. Still craning my head up in order to see around the many heads in front of me, I saw that the chief who was speaking was Ten Bears of the Comanche. He first extended to the Blue Jackets and the Washington men the traditional welcome. Then he began to list Indian grievances.

"There has been much trouble on the line between us, and my young men have danced the war dance. But it was not begun by us. It was you who sent out the first soldiers and we who sent out the second. . . . The blue-dressed soldiers and the Utes came for us out of the night, when it was dark and still, and for campfires they lit up our lodges. . . ."

As Ten Bears had set the tone, the day wore on, with more and more chiefs speaking for their people, listing crimes against their Nations, their families. Mrs. Adams and Philip McCusker did their best, but their weak attempts really didn't matter. The Washington men weren't listening. I know this is true because I watched their faces. After a few hours, the first day of the Medicine Lodge Council was over.

I was going for my horse when a hand clasped my shoulder. Turning, I found myself staring Three Elks in the face.

"Skywalker said I was to stay close to you, to bring you forward on his signal. He just gave it." He pointed off to General Gettis's tent. "I am to take you there."

I looked around as he escorted me. A great mass of the warriors were leaving, but the chiefly honor guards were loitering with intent very near General Gettis's canvas doorway. These notable warriors watched me as Three Elks walked me past them, stopped, then indicated that I was to enter without him. As I pushed open the flap, Three Elks went to stand with the others. I noticed that he wasn't limping anymore and he wore a long vest that hid his backside. I dismissed the amusing incident of his wound as I bolstered my courage and entered the tent.

Inside, none of the Washington men or newspaper reporters were present, but making themselves comfortable were the representative chiefs of the five Nations, General Gettis, Captain Mac, and Hawwy. Skywalker was deeply involved in a whispery discussion with a Kiowa warrior I'd never seen before. Skywalker turned at the waist as I entered. Waving his arm, he beckoned me to him. Before I could get a good look at the stranger, Skywalker turned, inadvertently positioning himself between us as he spoke quickly to me.

"Good. You're here. I want you to sit down and wait until I indicate you are to speak."

When he turned away, I felt well and truly dismissed. And confused. I looked around for one of the interpreters. Mrs. Adams in one of her strange costumes would have been a welcome sight, but she wasn't there. Neither was McCusker. How was I supposed to speak to that forbidding-looking general with any hope of being understood? Wondering yet again what Skywalker had managed to get me into, I looked for an available chair.

The back row was already filled with chiefs. The front row, a place I did not want to go, had two available chairs, one of them being next to Lone Wolf. Deciding that standing off alone would be the wiser course, I was about to head off for a corner when Lone Wolf looked at me and slapped his hand down on the seat of the wooden chair beside him.

This being an outright command, I hesitantly walked there and sat down.

White Bear, on the other side of Lone Wolf, was having a whispery argument with Kicking Bird, who was seated directly beside him. Lone Wolf, ignoring the hissing debate, turned to me and asked softly, "Did you see them?"

I knew he was asking about the Washington men—had I seen their indifference when the list of grievances had been given by each chief?

"Yes," I answered, my voice—even to my own ears—thick and sorrowful.

"I did too," he said. Then he lapsed into an impenetrable silence.

Beginning to mull other worries, my gaze traveled back to the warrior with short hair, the one standing with Skywalker. When Skywalker moved a little to the side, I got a clear look at the stranger. The young man noticed me and threw me a wave.

I sat back in the chair, my eyes wide with disbelief, my heart thumping. Lifting my eyes, I found Hawwy. He was sitting with General Gettis on the other side of the tent. Hawwy looked pale, sad, despondent. The very things one would expect from a man who'd just lost his best friend.

The Kiowa warrior with Skywalker—the one I was hearing being referred to as Returned To Us—was Billy.

SIXTEEN

The change in his appearance was incredible. Amazing, what a simple change of clothing will do for a person. Billy was dressed completely Kiowa: chest plate, choker, vest, breechcloth, leggings, and moccasins. His shoulder-length hair was brushed straight back from his forehead, revealing to me his entire face. He was light in coloring, especially his bare arms where the sun couldn't touch him because of long-sleeved shirts and his coat. He was standing in profile, and I could see—now that there was no longer that black hat to obscure his features—that the shape of his eyes, nose, forehead, and cheekbones, were just as Indian as Sky-walker's. I glanced again at Hawwy. His head was down, he looked to be intently studying the tips of his shiny boots. General Gettis, however, was staring hard at Billy, hatred blazing from narrowed eyes. I leaned across Lone Wolf and whispered to White Bear.

"When did he . . . come to us?"

"Last night," he whispered back. "I offered him my hand and he took it. Skywalker said that that one has walked a long, lonely road. That he doesn't realize his value. He said we are all to be very kind to him until he settles in, knows who he is, and is comfortable with that knowledge." White Bear sat back, his broad face becoming a large question mark as something occurred to him. "You know," he said, his voice too loud now to be a whisper, "those are almost the same things he once said about you!"

A smile tugged the corners of my lips. "Skywalker is a collector of lost persons."

"Yes," he agreed. "And some of them would have been better off if he'd let them stay lost. But you've worked out pretty well, so we feel willing to trust him about this one, too."

Sitting back, I realized I was very glad about Billy. Glad because we had gained a valuable person and glad because Billy had finally decided who he wanted to be. But Hawwy . . .

I had to let that thought go. It was just too sad.

We had to wait until everyone was present. The Blue Jackets seemed to be dragging their heels. After a few more minutes, Philip McCusker, Captain Mac, and Lieutenant Danny entered, the lieutenant smiling shyly at me, Captain Mac conversing with the general. Then the two officers sat down alongside Hawwy while McCusker took up a standing position just behind the general's chair. I was waiting for them to bring in Little Jonas, but they didn't.

A soldier guard closed the tent door flap, then stood before it. Evidently the few gathered Blue Jackets were all we
were to have, for General Gettis was irritably letting it be
known that he was ready for the conference to begin.

I was expecting Lone Wolf to stand and speak, but he
didn't move a hair, refused to open his mouth. Skywalker
spoke for him and through Billy. I listened attentively for
Skywalker, when he chose to be, was a good talker, and on
that day he was really outdoing himself.

"I was not in favor of the Kiowa chiefs coming to this
place," Skywalker said. "I spoke against it, saying this council was no good for our people. Now, too late, many of my
fellow chiefs agree. Particularly the chief known to you as
Satanta.

"From the first day all of you have talked against him.
But on the day he put a stop to the senseless killing of
valuable buffaloes, a crime committed by your own little
chiefs, your mutterings became shouts. And then the next
thing happened, his finding something belonging to the
army. If finding a lost thing makes him a murderer, then I
too must stand accused."

Skywalker removed a small item from his carry pouch.
A shiny army button. He tossed it. Captain Mac instinctively raised a hand, catching the object. In the next seconds
he looked grimly at the army button lying in the palm of
his hand. He passed it along to Hawwy who studied it with
open interest, then tried to pass it to General Gettis. The
man was not receptive, refusing to give the button so much
as a glance. With a lift of his near single brow, Hawwy
pocketed the button as Skywalker continued.

"I found that thing not far from where this lodge stands.

I assure you, I killed no one to have it. It was simply there on the ground. So too was the horn White Bear found when riding the distance between the camps. And why was it there?" Skywalker lifted his shoulders in a dramatic shrug. "Maybe it was there because it had been thrown away on purpose, or, maybe it had been dropped by accident. None of us will ever really know, for the man it once belonged to can no longer speak. But White Bear could speak, and he did. He promised he had harmed no one when he found that horn. You wouldn't listen." Pointing an accusing hand, he concluded, "Today you will." Turning at the waist, he looked meaningfully back to me.

I had been sitting there, one leg crossed over the other, both arms resting on my knee, totally enthralled. The Blue Jackets weren't quite as captivated. Captain Mac and General Gettis were becoming so angry that they were steadily gaining color in their faces.

Which was precisely Skywalker's intent. And now that he had them sufficiently riled, had their full and undivided attention, he summoned me forward. Evidently we were to trade places, for, as I walked toward him, he turned and aimed himself for my vacated chair. Passing me, he murmured, "Don't be nervous." The next thing I knew, I was standing beside Billy, looking straight at that row of tight-faced Blue Jackets.

When I began to speak, there was a quiver in my voice. There was no such tremor in Billy's as he translated. Billy's presence, his strong voice, gave me courage. And so I told everything I knew.

"There are two killers among you, and neither of them is Kiowa or the Buffalo Soldier known as Little Jonas. The two are your Lieutenant Danny and the Buffalo Soldier known as William."

The blood left Lieutenant Danny's face in a rush, leaving him with no color other than his big, red-rimmed blue eyes. Hawwy's head swiveled on his neck as he glared at the younger man who was now so terrified he couldn't move. Captain Mac leaned forward, braced his upper-body weight on the arms resting on his thighs. General Gettis was leaning back in his chair, listening more to McCusker, talking rapidly against his ear, than to Billy.

"Prove it," Captain Mac dared.

Oh, I do love a challenge, and as Captain Mac and I seemed forever destined to be both foe and associate, it was to him that I directed my entire focus.

"You didn't see the first dead man," I said evenly. "The violence done to him. His face was cleaved in half. This told me two things, first the killer's rage. Secondly, that only someone the dead man hadn't been afraid of, could get him so far out of your camp, get that physically close to him in order to kill him in such a manner. This would not have been as easy as you might suppose. The dead man had many enemies. He made these enemies because of his burning ambition to become a little chief. To be a little chief in your army, he needed money. At first I did not understand this. To be a chief in my Nation, a man must be brave and generous, most profoundly generous. But in your nation, only money would earn him a place at your council of chiefs. This man had no money, but he had a sneaky mind. He made it his business to find out secrets of his fellow soldiers, then he forced them to give him money to keep his tongue still. He knew so many secrets and so many were buying

253

his silence that he could no longer trust that he would awaken each dawn if he slept among his own kind. So, he begged for, and was given, a separate tent."

I paused both for breath and for Billy to finish translating. While he was doing that, my eyes locked with General Gettis's. The man was leaning forward, listening to Billy but staring unblinkingly at me. Seconds after Billy finished, I began again, this time speaking directly to the general.

"A man so terrified for his life, and with good cause, does not meet anyone alone. Unless he considers he is meeting a friend. And therein lies the fatal flaw of the dead man. His skewed perception of friendship. His liking, even admiring someone, did not mean that he was above using or controlling that person. He liked, admired, and controlled Lieutenant Danny."

His face draining of color, the general sat back, glanced at the lieutenant. The young man avoided his eye, raised a trembling hand to his brow.

"He knew all about the lieutenant's marriage, his family ties to a southern hero. The lieutenant didn't want any of this known, so he had to give up valuable things to keep this man quiet. He was a young man filled with rage that this person had not only taken all of his money but had begun taking away his most precious possessions. But, the thing which sparked his killing anger was that this man—who had almost enough to buy what he wanted and had begun using him to manipulate his way into the company of bigger chiefs, earning their gradual acceptance of his hovering presence—soon would not need him anymore. Lieutenant Danny had to have been plagued by the worry that once this man had bought his chieftainship, he could not be counted on to keep his secrets. In fact, exposing Lieutenant Danny would most certainly make him a hero in the eyes of his brother chiefs. This worry became a murderous fear and the dead man, morally devoid as he was, did not expect his victim to turn. Did not understand that the man he tormented would eventually cry enough. Not until it was too late."

Captain Mac chewed the corner of his mouth as he bird-eyed me. "But the uniform—"

"Oh, that," I chuckled. "That was my best proof of all. Little Jonas never wore his missing jacket. He was saving it, 'keeping it for good,' as he phrased it. William knew just where he kept it, stole it, and passed it along to Lieutenant Danny."

"Why?"

"Because Lieutenant Danny said he needed a soldier's uniform. William hero-worships Lieutenant Danny. He will do whatever that man says, and without question. So he gave him Little Jonas's jacket and, knowing that the trousers would be too big for the lieutenant, he gave him his best pants. He did not know until we found the dead man just why the lieutenant had needed these things, but before that, Little Jonas had been making noise about his jacket. To cover his theft, William made noise about his trousers. Then when he saw with his own eyes the horror that had been committed while the lieutenant had been wearing this clothing, he was physically ill. Recovering from that, he stayed near the lieutenant, the two of them talking in low, earnest tones. I imagine that Lieutenant Danny was explaining why he had no choice, and William, eager to believe him, finally accepted this. Then he saw the dead sergeant and Cullen threaten the lieutenant."

255

Captain Mac sat back, his creased brows meeting at the bridge of his nose. His tone came at me in a bellow. "Well, now you've lost me! Why would two sergeants threaten a superior officer?"

"Because of a thing that happened in Dallas."

Captain Mac tossed his hands in the air and shook his befuddled head.

A hint of a smile toying his mouth, Hawwy touched the man's arm and said, "Bear with him. I'm sure he really does know what he's talking about."

But even Hawwy became hesitant when I made my next statement.

"It's all to do with smell. The different odors of men. The dead man had a fine long coat, but it held the faint trace of flowers. Little Jonas's jacket had that same faint odor, the odor of Lieutenant Danny. I knew by this that Lieutenant Danny had worn Little Jonas's jacket, and that the coat in the dead soldier's possession really belonged to the lieutenant. From this I knew that it had been the soldier, not the lieutenant, who had been wearing the coat in Dallas when the soldiers were given permission to go there before coming into the Territory. So it was that man dressed like an officer, not the lieutenant, who witnessed the two sergeants running away while being shot at on account of Sergeant Cullen stirring up trouble with a lady named Tuttle. But the dead man was given money by both sergeants, who believed that their money was being passed on to the lieutenant. It was after that man was dead that the two sergeants turned on the lieutenant, because they knew who the killer was, and knowing this, Cullen felt safe. He could not be accused by the lady in Dallas because he now had an obliging officer to protect him.

"The reason they figured out the lieutenant was the killer was that The Cheyenne Robber found the uniform. None of the Blue Jackets got a clear look at it, but the sergeants knew a uniform was missing, on account of Little Jonas. Days before his jacket was stolen and he made a fuss about it. He went to you," I said, meaning Captain Mac. "And by your own account, he was upset, and knowing the volume of his voice myself, I can well imagine that everyone within the general vicinity of your tent heard him too. Which meant the thief, William, heard him and knew he had to act in order to avert suspicion. He did this by quickly reporting that his trousers were missing. He also told me that he and Little Jonas had had a fight, the result of the fight causing him to be wounded in the leg.

"Now, all of that was true, up to a point. I treated the wound, so I know that it was real. What wasn't real was William's contention that Little Jonas attacked him. He didn't. It was the other way around. I know this because when I talked to Little Jonas, explained William's version, Little Jonas became quite irate. Then the true purpose of the fight became clear. William had picked the fight to draw any notice away from the lieutenant. Another point which became clear during Little Jonas's fury was how supremely stupid I had been.

"First I had been concerned about the lieutenant, because when I went to talk to him I found him writing a letter and about to commit suicide. He was not doing this for anyone's benefit. This had indeed been his real intent and I allowed his defeated emotion to sway me. But my suspicions were aroused again when I came back to him, bringing with me Lieutenant Haw-we-sun as a way of offering him hope, and the letter he had been writing was missing. He tried to make us think that the letter had been stolen, but it wasn't. He had gotten rid of it and he had been too obviously coming out, not going into his tent when we arrived.

"Second, when William had been telling me about his missing trousers, I had been so involved with eating a pie that I had been listening without hearing when he revealed something completely unintended: that he knows how to read."

Eyes flared, mouths dropped.

"William is from Georgia. I know that Little Jonas is from Louis-anna and, being from that place, he wasn't allowed to learn how to read. Hawwy said that the rules about slaves learning this craft are different in various places. Evidently, in Georgia, it was all right for slaves to be taught to read because William had learned. He let this be known when he said that he saw Captain Mac take out the report forms but did not stay to watch him fill them out. Now, the important thing here are the report forms. Lieutenant Danny had two such forms in his case and they were old. Captain Mac said himself, that those reports stating that the two sergeants needed to be punished on account of the lady in Dallas, should have been given to him a long time ago. But they hadn't been. They had been kept in Lieutenant Danny's case.

"When I found the reports, I noticed something strange about Lieutenant Danny's tent. It was too neat. The other officers are not neat at all. I asked if the lieutenant had a servant and he said no, that he could not afford to pay one.

But I had seen the way William took care of him, the way he rushed to get him food, the way he hovered. Then I knew why the lieutenant was so neat. William took care of him there, too. So, having access to the lieutenant's quarters meant that William saw his hero being steadily reduced to poverty, and reading the hidden reports, he naturally assumed that the two sergeants were responsible.

"Out on the prairie, when he learned about the dead man and the lieutenant told him why he'd had to kill him, William also saw that the lieutenant was still in danger when the two sergeants became physically abusive. Knowing how protective he was toward the lieutenant, the dead sergeant came after William. I imagine he warned him off, told him to say clear of the lieutenant. I can only imagine this because I didn't understand what was being said, but I did witness the sergeant's threatening posture, watched William's close-to-the-surface anger. In order to protect the man he admired, the man he believed he owed so much, William felt he no longer had a choice. He killed one of his hero's tormentors, and he did this with the dispassion of an executioner, not the intense rage that was evidenced against the first man. So, aside from the fact that the lieutenant was with me and several others when the sergeant was killed, I knew immediately that there were two killers. It just took a bit longer to understand that both had killed for the same purpose: the protection of the young man known as Lieutenant Danny, the Blue Jacket war hero who, as it happens, is also the nephew of the Gray Jacket hero known as the Gray Ghost."

I really wasn't allowed to say anything after that, for the furor that erupted would have drowned me out even if

I'd tried. The sobbing lieutenant was quickly arrested and soldiers were sent to hunt down William. While all of this heated activity was taking place, Lone Wolf stood, walked out, the rest of us following him.

I did not witness the hangings. There are some things that are simply beyond me. But I did ask if the lieutenant's things were being sent to his wife, and Hawwy said yes.

I know the young woman had tears on her face when she received them. Skywalker had already seen her tears; I had just mistaken them for the tears of loneliness, not understood that they were instead, tears of grief, for receiving her husband's things meant she would never see him again. To help her be proud of the husband she lost, her family was sent a letter telling them that the lieutenant had been excecuted for being a Gray Jacket spy. As far as I know, no mention was made of him being a murderer.

The next day, the council at Medicine Lodge resumed. The gathering was just like it had been on the day before, except this time Three Elks went to sit in his proper place and when he did, he and The Cheyenne Robber began to bicker. I watched them, knowing in my heart that big trouble would sooner or later erupt between those two and when it did, Three Elks would have more to worry about than a silly wound to his backside.

Yet again the generals were dressed in their most splendid uniforms. Looking ill at ease, they stood off waiting for the late arriving Washington men. It was with a superior air that these men finally meandered on to the scene, talking among themselves as they resumed their places at the long table. After they were seated, the generals sat. I have since learned the names of those Washington men. I made it my business to do so, for it was those men—beginning at Medicine Lodge—who brought into play the resulting destruction of a world, an entire way of life, a freedom that will never be known again to any race. Of course it took the United States ten long years of hard fighting to accomplish this goal and I've never seen any of the original men since, but they were present on day one of an ancient civilization's destruction, and for no other reason than this, they should be named.

The commissioner of Indian affairs was Nathaniel Taylor. Next to him was Senator John B. Henderson. Then down the line were William S. Harney, Alfred H. Terry, S. F. Tappan, J. B. Sanborn, and C. C. Augur. Across from the long table these men shared, a separation of only a few yards of open space, and seated on blankets spread over the ground, sat the chiefs of the assembled Nations. Those chiefs, hoping for so much, could have been for all intents and purposes, sitting cross-legged somewhere far away, say, on the face of the moon.

Lone Wolf maintained his silence all through the following days of the council. Having seen the indifference of the Washington men, he didn't waste words on them. Nor did he sign any treaty agreement. Only White Bear spoke for the Kiowa, and to this day, I remember every eloquent word, the fullness of his voice. And when I look out over our changed world, those words and that voice come back to me.

"I love the land and the buffalo and will not part with any of it. I have heard that you intend to

261

settle us on a reservation near the mountains. I don't want to settle. I love to roam over the prairies. There I feel free and happy, but when we settle down we grow pale and die. . . . A long time ago this land belonged to our fathers; but when I go up to the river I see camps of soldiers. . . . These soldiers cut down my timber, they kill my buffalo; when I see that, my heart feels like bursting; I feel sorry."